JOHN PLAYER

GW00501324

AMONG THE

LESSER GODS

LIES, DECEPTION, COVER-UPS
LEAVE US TRAPPED BETWEEN FACT AND FICTION

Other books by this author

This Troubled Earth (radical philosophy)
The Boomerang Pommies (a £10 Pom's story)
You Can't See the Wind (a novel)
Knutt in Oil (a seafaring romp)
Knutt in Khaki (an extremely reluctant soldier)

The events depicted in this book are fictitious. The eponymous hero however is very real and spins a very good tale after a few drinks.

Published by Pomegranate Press
Dolphin House, 51 St Nicholas Lane, Lewes, Sussex, BN7 2JZ

ISBN 978-1-907242-37-3

British Library Cataloguing-in-Publication Data
A catalogue record for this book is available from the British Library

Printed by 4edge Ltd Hockley Essex. www.4edge.co.uk

Introduction

My name is David Kent. In view of what I am about to relate, you may be excused for thinking it is not my real name. You may also consider that none of it can possibly be true. Truth has many faces of course, depending on who claims to be delivering it. Truth could in fact be considered as an individual belief. That being so I believe that what I witnessed, and actually became part of in 1962, and the years following, is truth.

In the late autumn of that year I was posted to an army camp in a remote part of Wiltshire. I was 32 years old and nearing the end of a 12 + 2 year stint in the Royal Signals. During that time I had reached the dizzy heights of Sergeant Major, and with approximately three months to go I was looking forward to a pensionable semi-retirement.

Up to that time I had always been prepared to accept what went on in the world as the norm. I grew up in WW2 and had followed the conflicts that gave the lie to WW1 being the one to end all wars, so I knew that the world could be a very unsafe place. I accepted the inevitability of wars generally. The Korean War, which had added six months to my National Service, had ended officially 7 years previously, but the truce was still an uneasy one. The conflict in Vietnam had been going for a couple of years and seemed destined to become a very long and bloody war or attrition. There too had been 14 years of cold war with our former allies of WW2, the Russians.

'Peace in our time' was an ongoing myth, first proclaimed in September 1938 by Neville Chamberlain, fluttering a piece of paper signed by Adolf Hitler; a man with his own individual version of truth.

I must admit to a high degree of scepticism when I was first introduced to the Complex, and at times almost believing that it was all a dream or a product of an unsound mind. But for the fact that all those I met there appeared to be quite ordinary, normal people, albeit working at extraordinary things, I think I would have left in a hurry and might still be running. The Complex was eventually to become untenable during my absence on a little hush, hush business in America.

**

It was in the remote, desert wilds of Nevada while engaged in this business that I found myself in a position of some danger and was advised to quit the area in a hurry. Encouraged by a

3

close associate I undertook to exit in a rather bizarre way; well a way certainly, that defied convention. At the time it was an experiment being conducted by certain individuals who must on pain of death; mine – by accident -- remain anonymous. It concerned time travel, but I was to find out that interdimensional doorways are often much more than that.

Okay, that's incomprehensible to those of us who have spent most of our lives clockwatching and busting a gut to keep appointments, but I, among others, am living proof that H.G. Wells wasn't exactly a complete nut case, he just wasn't up to speed on future technology; he was still in clockwork mode. The result of instant teleportation is not unlike that portrayed in a current TV entertainment; Star Trek, but I doubt that the methodology is anywhere near the same.

`Chapter 1
Adelaide, South Australia 1980

The date on the Adelaide Advertiser, this morning is December 30th 1980. It contains an article by a Professor Paul Davies in which he offers considerable scepticism with regard to UFO's and extraterrestrial beings. The professor has more letters after his name than a Khmer alphabet, and had he accompanied me on my travels during the 6o's and early 70's he would now, like me and others of my acquaintance, be a firm believer in a peopled universe.

My wife Genna and I have been spending quality time with old friends who are over from England to visit their daughter and son-in-law. In the two weeks we've been here we have finally , run out of reminisces and feel it is time to head back to our home in Melbourne. It is while Genna is completing our packing that I'm taking time out for a browse through the local rag.

In the last two weeks I have had reports by phone and teleprints of a wave of UFO sightings in and around Todmorton West Yorkshire, including an alleged encounter by a police officer with a bearded extraterrestrial. There is also a short column report in the Adelaide Advertiser of a Cessna 182L piloted by an Australian, Frederick Valentich, that went missing over the Bass Strait a few years back. It appears that incidents like this are again coming under scrutiny, by people who are not prepared to accept them being brushed aside and very often officially denied as ever having occurred. Just prior to his disappearance Valentich reported to Air Traffic Control that he was being repeatedly buzzed by a UFO. He confirmed at the time that its behaviour was unlike any conventional aircraft. A search failed to locate the missing plane or its pilot and a verdict of unknown cause was recorded.

This month alone, in the three days over Christmas, repeated sightings and actual landings of strange aerial vehicles have plagued two RAF stations shared by the USAAF in the vicinity of Rendlesham Forest, Suffolk UK. Multiple witnesses of the sightings, included officers and other ranks of both services, and some that experienced almost hands on contact are convinced that the intruders are not of this world.

There is also a report of a commercial airliner being forced to make an emergency landing in Spain during harassment by several UFO's. The whole circus of confusion, aided and abetted by government denials and misinformation, goes on.

My arrival in this country at the opposite end of the world some years ago also beggars belief.

Proof as they say is in the pudding, but there is little chance that any reader of this will walk into a room in a restricted area of America and walk out of a room in a restricted area in South Australia a few moments later. I know -- it was some time before the feeling of disembodiment wore off. I have never wished to repeat the experience, or to continue in the kind of work I was then involved in. I wasn't to know how quickly that kind of work was about catch up with me again.

Living now in an age where high tech gadgetry in the shape of sophisticated computers and mobile phones are commonplace, I am amazed that they have taken so long to get here.

Most remarkable inventions of course have been around for a lot longer than they are credited for, the inspiration for them a lot longer than that. Many to my knowledge have been kept secret or suppressed either in the interests of national security or to keep giant industrial conglomerates in business. Even today I carry the indelible mark of an ID, inserted by laser in 1962, several years before it came into the public awareness, by the woman with whom I was destined to share much of my life. My lasered implant allowed me the freedom of the Complex and perhaps more importantly, access to many highly classified projects.

Let me take you back to those times.

I arrived at the Wiltshire camp on a cold mid-morning in November 1962...........

Chapter 2

Ganymede Wenban-Smith is a rather unusual name, but the man thus christened in a parish church in the wilds of the Hampshire countryside thirty eight years earlier was a rather unusual child who grew to be a rather unusual man.

His birth in 1924, I was to learn later, evoked more in the way of doubt than surprise; the surprise being that he was born seven months after his father's return from the 'troubles' in Northern Ireland instead of the customary nine. The doubt in everyone's mind was of course more than justified. The elder Wenban-Smith had spent over a year in the hands of the IRA prior to being returned to the bosom of his family.

Ironically his presence in Ireland had no military or political implications. As a gentleman farmer he was there solely to spend a day or two touring agricultural shows. His rescue by Free State forces also resulted in a bullet crease on one side of his skull. He spent a while convalescing until the buzzing in his head stopped, and then once more took up residence and control of his farm property on the borders of Hampshire's New Forest. His disenchantment with Ireland continued right up until his premature death in 1942 when a crashing, German Heinkel 111 exploded on the roof of his home, and he and his wife perished along with the four-man German crew.

Assurances that his son was just one of the many premature births brought on by the austerity of the war years mollified his father's suspicions. It was a time too when smoking by women had reached new heights and the wartime diet may have lacked certain essentials necessary for healthy, full term babies.

Not that Ganymede was in anyway puny, on the contrary he was a robust child from the word go. It was a matter of discomfort to his mother that he didn't favour his father in the looks department, leaving her with her own guilty secret.

Her brief fling with US army lieutenant Arthur C White, spending a goodwill term as a guest of the British army, had proved that one should never delay the interruptus in coitus interruptus for more than a few split seconds. It was also bad luck that army lieutenant White was a full blood Navajo Indian whose tribal name was White Eagle, hence the adoption of White as a surname.

Ganymede's birth had one other unusual aspect; he had two black eyes and a twin brother. Apparently, even at that early age there had been a struggle to be first past the post. Ganymede's twin lost, but not before leaving his mark on Ganymede. As a precaution, in case they should lose both boys, Ganymede was christened on the same day as his sibling's funeral.

His jet black hair and swarthy, hawk-like features contrasted sharply with his mother's red hair and freckled looks. His father stoically refused to compare his own mousey locks and fair skin with that of his son.

Ganymede's looks as he reached puberty guaranteed that he would never be devoid of attention; not least from the fair sex. By the time he was fifteen he had already discovered the major differences between boys and girls, and had taken full advantage of that knowledge.

His broad shoulders and slim hips already indicated the emergence of the alpha male. At one stage though he did catch the attention of a school sports master whose too friendly arm found its way around his shoulders. It was summarily shrugged off and the master's unwanted attentions were met with an icy stare. The master retreated shame-faced, never again to repeat the exercise.

He enlisted in the army in 1944 and was commissioned into the 11th Hussars, with whom he fought from the beaches of Normandy to the gates of Berlin. Field promotions on the way resulted in a rapid rise through the ranks to captain. He transferred to the Intelligence Corps soon after the German surrender and spent time with the Allied Control Commission. His activities after the start of the Korean War became increasingly obscure as a consequence of whatever work he was engaged in. He finally retired from the army with the rank of Lieutenant Colonel in 1958.

All this emerged not long after I met him in 1962, which I did soon after I finished a week's leave. I received the news of my new posting only days before in the mail, plus a travel warrant to this odd camp in Wiltshire, but odd hardly describes it. It further directed that any of my kit remaining in my previous camp would be forwarded on. Well virtually all of it was, as having been on leave I was in civvies. At that time I did think it all a bit strange, but then I had long learned to live with things that the army did.

I assumed, quite wrongly of course, that I was due to spend my remaining few months of service in this cushy backwater of the Wiltshire countryside.

8

I did say odd, didn't I? Well except for the sole occupant of the guardroom, a pale-faced corporal who directed me to my new billet, the place appeared to be deserted. Most camps in my experience were a hive of activity, occasionally rising to manic, and this one didn't even have a guard mounted or a sentry on the gate. I had yet to learn just how strange this place would eventually turn out to be.

Up until then I had spent most of my time initially as an op spec, (Army speak for special operator) monitoring the military movements of unfriendly countries; namely the East Germans and the Russians. Latterly as I rose through the ranks I went on to instruct others in the art of intercepting the coded messages flashing across the air waves. All the camps I had been posted to both at home and overseas had, although easy going, been of a high military standard. This one would have given the legendary RSM Brittain, apoplexy.

As I trudged across the postage stamp-size parade ground with my suitcase there was no denying the air of dereliction and dilapidation of the buildings surrounding it, or the unkempt and overgrown grass and shrubbery.

It was a cold November morning. There were smudges of hoar frost on the tarmac pathways, and it sparkled in the weak sunshine on the hut roofs and a solitary, leafless tree. Warm air welcomed me as I pushed open the door of the hut that I'd been directed to.

**

He lay on his bunk with his hands behind his head regarding me coolly; he was in civvy shirt and slacks. At first, taking in his tan and because it was winter, I thought he was an old sweat back from somewhere in the Middle East. It was when he grinned and swung his legs around until he was sitting up with his hands on his knees that I realised it was his natural colouring. I judged him to be a little older than me.

I dumped my case on the next bed, I was already feeling the warmth from the tortoise stove, so I took off my jacket, draped it over my case and sat down beside it. I leaned forward and held out my hand.

'Kent,' I said, 'Dave Kent.'

'Of course.' The grin became a wide smile as he gripped my hand in his.

'Wenban-Smith, Ganymede Wenban-Smith'. There was no hint of embarrassment as he relayed that information; I hoped

9

my face didn't betray amusement. 'It would seem that we're in this shit together, major.' The smile faded slightly as he regarded me.

'Sorry?' I took another look at him, wondering what he was on about. I wasn't a major; I was a WO2; a squadron sergeant major, but my being in civvies he would hardly know that. I eventually acquired the rank of sergeant major a good many years after signing on at the end of my national service. That signing had been a mistake, after being rudely awakened from a romantic dream; I'd been dumped by a girl I had hoped to marry. But I'd nearly seen it through, all 12 years of it. Perhaps this guy was confusing me with someone else, Kent wasn't an uncommon name. I wondered what this shit was he spoke of?

'Major Kent, yeah, it suits you.' It appeared to amuse him, he was grinning again; like the proverbial cat. I hovered between annoyance and curiosity.

'Look mate. I'm not a major and I won't be around long enough to be one.' I was wondering what he was. Being also in civvies, there was no indication of rank, although he did carry an aura of authority. He must have read my look, but he obviously wasn't going to enlighten me. He shook his head, and then, as if a sudden thought had struck him he seemed to retreat behind a fading smile again.

'Of course not, silly of me -- sorry.' He swung his legs back onto his bunk and resumed his former position. He studied me for a moment longer, and then said. 'Do you know why you are here, David?' It was my turn to shake my head.

'Orders for this posting came on the tail end of my leave. I was sent a travel warrant and told to report here without returning to my unit. It's all a bit weird; all my army kit is still with my own unit. In answer to the question, no I don't know why I'm here. You appear to, so why?' I was beginning to find this man of mystery a bit irritating; it seemed that he was going to continue to be so.

'I think tomorrow might hold some surprises for you, not unpleasant though.' He closed his eyes in some sort of dismissal; it was obvious he wasn't going to enlarge on what he had intimated. I left him to it and started to unpack my bag. The world was full of odd balls; I'd met a few. It looked as though I could add one more to the list.

It was a four bed hut with only our two beds made up, the others just bare iron frames; it was far from homely. By the time

10

I'd sorted my gear he was snoring lightly. It was 10 am by my watch; time for a cuppa and a wad. My six o'clock breakfast had departed southward hours before, leaving a gaping void; I was starving. I figured the cookhouse, if there was one actually still functioning in this dump, would be shut. I was also beginning to wonder again why the whole place was so quiet. I considered looking for the sergeant's mess but any optimism as I made for the door was shot down in mid-flight.

'You won't find one.'

I froze with my hand on the door handle, I looked back. He was awake and smiling again. He sat up and swung his legs to the floor once more.

'There is no longer a sergeant's mess or a Naafi on this camp.'

This was spooky. I turned and walked back towards him.

'How ...?'

'Did I know where you were off to?' He shrugged and stood up. I was surprised; he barely reached my shoulder, and I need to strain upward to reach six feet.

'I guess you just had that hungry look David, and when the cookhouse is shut there are only two alternatives.'

'And here there is neither?'

'Nope. But there is a nice little pub just down the road. I'm hungry too, and I'll join you if you don't mind?' I didn't mind, his irritating quality was less evident, and I was hungry. 'Yeah, fine. For a moment there I thought ...'

'What?' His smile faded slightly once again.

'Oh nothing'. But for a moment there I thought he was some sort of mind reader; I can't even imagine why I should think that.

**

The guardroom was empty when I looked in, and still no sentry on the gate. It was peacetime, but an unguarded army camp ...? Well, most unusual.

Everything about the place was decidedly odd, the silence, and no sign of another soul apart from me and Ganymede and the pale-faced corporal who had booked me in, and even he seemed to have vanished into thin air.

I checked my watch with the guardroom clock; it was two hours slow, or stopped. I looked at Ganymede.

'Probably had its day like the rest of the place,' he said.

'Why's that?' We passed through the unmanned gates.

'Ours is not to reason why ...' the sagely saying petered out. 'Didn't they tell you what kind of place they were posting you to?'

'No. I just accepted that it would be somewhere where they said they could make good use of what they called, my special abilities, although what the hell they are beats me. They must have realised that I've only a few months left to do.'

'What did you have in mind for the future; important plans?'

'Not really. Just loaf around a bit until something interesting turns up.'

Ganymede stopped and looked at me; his brown eyes sparkled with amusement.

'Perhaps it already has.'

'What has; what is this place all about?'

He studied my face for a moment, then he laughed and took my arm and we were walking again.

'I guess it won't be long before you find out, David. Come on, let's go eat.' He let go my arm and patted his jacket pocket. 'It's my treat, major.'

'Well thanks, but let's get one thing straight, I'm not a bloody major.'

'It could be just a matter of time, David. If you go along with what I have to say you could be wearing the crowns on your shoulders in a matter of hours.'

I remained puzzled and silent as we covered the short walk to the pub. Not until we were seated with a couple of pints did I dare to ask the question.

'Just who are you Ganymede, and what is it you are going to tell me?'

He sipped his drink and gazed at me for a moment before he spoke.

'For the time being David Kent, I'm your boss.' He raised his hand at my look of surprise. 'I say for the time being because after I have had my say and you have enjoyed the hospitality of this pub, you are quite at liberty to leave here and rejoin your unit and forget that you ever met me.' He paused and took another sip of his beer. 'The steak and ale pie here is rather good, by the way.'

I sought refuge in my own beer as I tried to get my thoughts into some sort of order. Then Ganymede was speaking again and my thoughts just went out of control.

'We have had our eye on you for some months David, and we had no hesitation in deciding you were the man who would best serve our interests, and of course your own,' he added with certainty. 'You do have obvious abilities and it is no surprise to us that you also have abilities of which you are currently unaware.'

I had been around army types for quite a few years and references to 'we' and 'our' indicated that he was not just a common or garden soldier, in fact was far from being one. His whole demeanour reminded me of those who had interviewed me at Bletchley Park where I had sought ongoing employment towards the end of my National Service. It was prior to my decision to sign on as a regular soldier.

There had been three of them in smart but casual dress. In the centre, the youthful hanging judge was flanked on one side by an equally youthful member of the inquisition with the half-moon moustache favoured by members of the SAS, and on the other an older man who gave the impression of a slightly demented boffin from the currently popular sci-fi films. I was given no reason for failing to meet their criteria for the Diplomatic Wireless Service. It was that and the failed relationship that had thrown me back into the arms of the army for a further 12 years.

This man before me was giving the impression that I had been head hunted for some reason and I wasn't sure that I liked the idea, or the fact that he appeared to know things about me of which I had no knowledge.

'Look... Ganymede... I'm finding this all a bit difficult to follow. Just who are you really, and what's with this deserted camp that I have been sent to because I have abilities that I'm not aware of? Until I walked into the hut today I thought I was just a normal, sane individual, but having met you and all this weird talk I'm beginning to wonder.'

Ganymede raised his hand again and gave a nod of understanding.

'Okay David, I'll try and give you as much of the picture as I can. There are things that you do not need to know at this stage, and unless you agree to be co-opted you'll never have a need to know. By the time I've filled you in with what is necessary for now you may decide that you want no part of it. Should that be the case you will be free to leave and forget that you were ever here.'

13

I was studying him more intently now as he spoke. He spoke with a certain authority.

'The thing is David; you were chosen to accompany me on various projects that are very highly classified.'

'Chosen! Who chose me?' I found the fact that something had been going on behind my back becoming increasingly annoying. 'The next thing you'll be telling me is that you are some sort of an officer.' I took a long swig at my beer and glared at him. He looked back at me soberly for a moment, and then said.

'Not some sort of an officer, David, an ex Lieutenant Colonel actually.' I stiffened. He went on with a tolerant smile. 'At ease, David. I opted out some time ago, I'm a just another civil servant nowadays.'

'So where do I fit in with all my unknown abilities?' I found it difficult to avoid the sarcasm. It appeared to go over his head anyway.

'That is something that, all being well, we will go into at a later date. Right now I need a 'man friday' David, and you appear to fit the bill. You are obviously not a man to take shit, even from people like me.' He was grinning again now. 'Anyway here comes the grub.' The food was set down by an attractive brunette. I noted his thoughtful look as he watched her retreating back. He waited until she'd gone before continuing, 'You don't have to decide right away. You could be a fully paid major by this time tomorrow and who knows what the future might hold.'

'Why the sudden promotion?'

'I need a man who has a bit of authority when dealing with little, know nothing, gobshite officials and junior officers, David. You are also a very fit man.' He chuckled. 'How are you at climbing drainpipes, and breaking and entering; that sort of thing?'

I was lost for words. He lifted a forkful of pie towards his mouth. The odour of the food was already turning on my juices. 'Get stuck in David. Talk some more later eh?' I could only nod and begin to tackle my pie.

We ate in silence for a while then he paused with a forkful halfway to his lips.

'Join with me David for … how can I say … a walk into the future?'

'How come … sir?' Was this how it was going to be; a bloody Times crossword. I didn't find such cryptic comments particularly amusing.

'That's for me to know, and if you join me, for you to know in the fullness of time. You can cut the sir too. If you must call me something, make it plain guv.' Having said his piece, which I would obviously have to be content with, he continued to enjoy his meal.

**

I couldn't help wondering how I reached the decision to land myself with a diminutive boss, who didn't appear to be more than a few years older than me, and one seemingly as odd as the whole set up here. He was right about one thing; the steak and ale pie was excellent.

Chapter 3

Ganymede was as good as his word. As Major David Kent I emerged the next morning from the hut and went in search of the officer's mess. At 32 years of age I was walking taller than John Wayne the cowboy actor. I had awakened to find an officer's uniform at my bedside that could have been tailored for me. Furthermore the shining crowns were already in place on both shoulders.

It took me all of ten minutes to discover that there wasn't an officer's mess or any mess exclusive to rank, such amenities were, according to Ganymede, now behind anonymous boarded-up buildings; surplus to requirements. There remained, for a while anyway, a cookhouse with limited function. He had left the hut earlier to, as he said, check on something. He intercepted me on my way to the cookhouse; it was 9 a.m. and I was starving.

Bacon, eggs and fried bread was served up by a lone catering corporal and we sat as the sole occupants of the dining hall.

'Where is everybody?' I said as I poured tea into two pint mugs. Ganymede stirred sugar into his before levelling his spoon at me; his dark eyes glinted.

'We are just about everybody, David.'

'You what?' I slopped tea on the table.

'Apart from the cook corporal, you and I David are the only ones on this camp at present.' I slopped more tea and I watched as he cut himself a forkful of bacon and stuffed it into his mouth; mine just hung open. He studied me with amusement as he chewed and swallowed and added more bacon to his fork; it paused on the way to his mouth once again.

'I think I'd better fill you in a bit more now David as you've already agreed to join the club.'

'That wouldn't be a bad idea...guv.' He acknowledged that with a wry smile. I sat back and waited, my meal and hunger temporarily forgotten.

'It's all a blind,' his gesture took in our surroundings and beyond; a deserted, almost derelict army camp without even a caretaker staff. 'Even the locals don't know what we really have here.'

'We?'

'The powers that be, David.'

'I'm still not with it.'

'There's no reason why you should be at this stage.' He smiled and I had to wait while he continued to feed the inner man, then he tilted his fork towards me once more.

'In a few days this camp will be closed and officially cease to exist and we will move into the Complex.'

'The Complex?' He was going into mysterious mode again. 'And what's that when it's about?'

'Difficult to explain really David, and if I did you would still find it difficult to envisage; much better to see and experience it for yourself. Eat up David; we've got a long and busy day ahead. When we've done here I'll take you to see some of what really goes on here, better than giving you just a lot of words right now.'

I could see there was nothing further forthcoming and my hunger had reappeared. I settled down to enjoy my breakfast. His idea of words was more like cryptic clues, I thought.

**

We moved quickly in the chilly air, and a watery sun was already smudging the rambling concrete building as we approached. It reminded me of a wartime control tower. Paint had peeled from its walls showing patches of algae, and November chill and gloom hung overall. Perhaps it hadn't always been an army camp, an airbase maybe. It was not difficult to imagine the ghosts of those who never returned.

A dilapidated, wooden door with a small peephole opened as we approached and warm air enveloped us as we passed through. The door closed behind us. I looked back; there was no one there, we appeared to be alone. Ganymede took the lead and I followed him along a short passageway lit by a single naked light bulb; it was the last thing I was to see that day that even remotely resembled the familiar world outside.

He stopped beside a steel door. To one side was an illuminated plate set with numerical buttons. He pressed four of them in quick succession and the door slid silently open.

'You've just witnessed tomorrow's front door key, David' he said, anticipating my question. I followed him through and we stood for a moment at the top of an escalator that disappeared into the bowels of the earth.

'You mean…?'

'We are in the world of the push button, David, and I mean with a vengeance, and we are on the point of moving on beyond that. Some of what you will see here will hit the world in the

17

very near future. Some of it will remain highly classified, perhaps forever. There's a war on you know.'

'A Cold War, yeah I know that.' I didn't mean to sound smug.

'It's hotter than you think David, a hell of a lot hotter. Those atom bombs on Japan set off a chain reaction that was never envisioned, a reaction that will reverberate around the world for hundreds, even thousands of years into the future.'

I remained silent. What he was saying was a bit over my head, I hoped it would make sense as I discovered more about this technological time shift I seem to have blundered into. Looking back now it all seems a bit old hat, but at that point in time I experienced something approaching awe.

I surveyed our surroundings as we descended. Nothing much unusual about the escalator, I had ridden on them as a child out shopping with my parents, but this one appeared to be what they called state of the art; it flowed silently downward. It was like moving down an eerily lit glass tunnel, opaque and flawless, but how could that be? When you tunnelled below ground you had to build retaining and support walls and roofs, any fool knew that. The whole effect here was one of an opaque, glass tube, smooth as a baby's bum. Ganymede noted my interest in the surroundings.

'Remarkable stuff chalk, you can tunnel through it like a maggot through cheese. This whole Complex exists thanks to chalk.'

'What is it, a bunker, like Winnie and Adolf had during the war?'

'About the same size; our living and working area, that is. We do have an experimental workshop, but that is further afield. Their bunkers of course, were more sumptuous, especially their quarters; this is a purely functional one, nothing five star. Like theirs this has two levels. The lower level houses the air-conditioning and electrical generators. Down there too is our fresh water storage, in fact all the below stairs stuff you'd find in a hotel.'

The escalator terminated at another steel door where Ganymede again played his little numbers game. I felt I might somehow be losing the plot again here because a few steps later we were moving again but no longer under our own steam; the floor below our feet was on the move. I looked at Ganymede, he shrugged.

'Call it what you like David; the idea has been around for over a hundred years. It was first introduced in the 1890's; this is a version that was developed around 1946. They've improved a lot since then but some of the old gear is still useful you know. I think it was named the travolator, this was installed soon after this place was commissioned in 1947.'

'This place has been going for a while then?' I could do my sums. Over the last few years I had found it difficult enough getting to grips with the idea of nuclear power and something called an electronic brain, and even more recently something called a mainframe computer. Being a Sigs wallah I obviously knew a bit about how messages could be transmitted over the airwaves, and how pictures could fly through the air and end up on a television set my parents had acquired back in the mid 50's; and now all this. It was all a bit unreal. Only moments ago I was in a common or garden army camp; well not all that common. Now I was plunged into a world of seemingly effortless, labour-saving devices. Bewildered was a good word, even an understatement.

In many ways my life in the army had been a sheltered one and I hadn't been exposed to some of the more advanced systems of communication. Probably the most advanced technology that I had heard of apart from the rocketry for space travel were planes capable of travelling faster than the speed of sound.

'You okay, David? As he spoke I could see we were approaching a short, flat panel set flush in the side wall.

'I'm not sure, guv. Some of this could have come out of the world of Dan Dare.'

He laughed at my reference to a kids' comic book where the hero was always in conflict with little green men from outer space. In the diffused light there was no mistaking his look of merriment.

'You really ain't seen nothing yet David. The truth is, you even left 1962 behind what will seem like 20 or 30 years ago.' He ran his hand along the wall panel and nodded for me to do the same. It was the last thing I remembered doing as I came round on what appeared to be a hospital trolley; my arm ached.

**

If there is one thing I'm genuinely attracted to as far as women are concerned it is shoulder-length, golden-blonde hair. If that is accompanied by eyes like a summer blue sky and a friendly smile, I'm hooked. It was a wonderful vision to wake up

19

to. It momentarily took my mind off what the bloody hell I was doing there anyway.

'How do you feel, sir?' I found the lilting Welsh voice more than complimented her other assets; I felt cheeky.

'David, please. I don't like the formality of sir, and I've yet to be knighted.' She ignored it, but the smile remained. 'What happened...?' She was wearing a form-fitting sort of jumpsuit of silvery fabric so it didn't seem she would answer to, nurse. She looked apologetic.

'You got knocked out I'm afraid sir.' I must have looked puzzled. 'The sentry is programmed to disable illegal entrants.' Things were still not making a lot of sense.

'But I was with Ganymede.' I lifted my head and looked around; there was no sign of him.

'Who?'

'Ganymede, he brought me here.'

'I'm not sure who that is. I'm fairly new here. You were already on the cot when I came in to attend to you. I'm sure this Ganymede will be around here somewhere,' She placed her hand on my arm, it seemed to ease the ache; it was probably psychological. I like a bit of fuss made of me, especially in the shape it now came. I went to sit up but she shook her head.

'Better not for a while. I have to ask you something, well, two things really.' She held her head closer and her hand remained on my arm; I liked it being there.

'Okay, fire away.' I'm single and over twenty-one, I thought, and if one of the questions is 'do I fancy you', the answer is yes. She didn't appear able to read my mind perhaps that was just as well.

'First I've been asked by a Mr Wenban-Smith if you intend to officially take up his offer.'

So that was it, she did know him, it was just the Ganymede that had thrown her; it would throw anyone. I knew from my schooldays that Ganymede was a satellite of Jupiter. The fact that he was also a beautiful young boy who took the fancy of the Greek god Zeus should have deterred any parent from inflicting their offspring with a name like that.

'Okay, what's the second one?'

'It's a bit more personal.'

Ah! Now that sounded more like it. How would you like us to get better acquainted? Wait for it, Davey boy. It wasn't to be. She continued.

'You were of course knocked out as you passed the sentry because your ID wasn't in order.'

'ID?' I must have looked as puzzled as I felt. 'What sentry?'

'I'm sorry. I realise that this is all very strange to you.'

'You can say that again.'

She was smiling again, and it added a whole new dimension to the word beauty.

'This place is of the highest top security and unless you carry a proper ID, and you can be identified, you'll be zapped every time you pass a control point.'

'So how do I get this ID?'

'I'll explain. If you intend to officially accept Mr Wenban-Smith's offer we can go ahead and process you. If not then you will be at liberty to leave and return to your unit.'

Ganymede had already explained that to me. My mind was working again and it was deciding that having come this far my curiosity was getting the better of me. I'd never be happy not knowing what this whole business was all about, and if presenting me with this vision of loveliness was a ploy on Ganymede's part to reel me in he had certainly chosen the right bait.

'I'm taking up his offer; it would be a shame to have to remove these crowns.' Fools rush in, I thought. 'So what's the process?'

'There's nothing to it really. We just implant a little chip in your arm.' She patted it.

'Chip?' I felt my mouth drop open.

'Silicon chip, you won't feel a thing.' She sounded reassuring. I didn't feel particularly assured.

'How big is this chip thing?'

'This one is about the size of half a grain of rice. It is a necessary procedure, David.' At last she'd dropped the, sir. I liked the way she said my name.

'It is the only way you'll be able to move around the Complex. My instructions are that you are to be a given a high security clearance, but first I need your signature on this.' She held a clipboard with a typewritten sheet of paper attached. I propped up on one elbow to read it. It was a consent form with the usual waiver of rights if anything goes amiss with whatever process was about to be performed. I had a little ping of nerves.

Implant sounded new and ominous, and what was this Complex thing so far underground, and what in the name of hell was a silicon chip; I really didn't want to show my ignorance by asking. She was waiting for an answer.

'Oh well, in for a penny.' I reached for the pen she offered. 'I'm ready for processing,' I said lightly. I didn't feel particularly light, more like a chicken on the conveyer belt waiting to be plucked, gutted, trussed, and made oven ready.

'It won't take long.' She went away and returned almost immediately pulling an apparatus on a small trolley. She removed what looked like a probe connected to it by wires.

'What is that thing?'

'I can't tell you exactly but I've heard it referred to as a laser. It's ......'

'Highly classified... Yeah I should know by now.' I looked at the probe, it didn't look particularly dangerous. It had a blunt rounded end with a recessed opening. 'What does it do, shoot this implant thing into me?' She nodded

'Sort of. It also provides an entry point for the chip. All you'll feel is a slight sting.'

'It won't dig a hole and plant this ID thing then?'

She smiled, this time tolerantly. 'I can assure you, David, that you left much of the world of conventional surgery behind when you entered the Complex. For what it's worth, it will provide you with a permanent ID, one that you can't lose or misplace or have stolen.'

'I'm stuck with it, forever?' She appeared to consider that.

'I can't answer that. I'm only trained in the implant procedure David, but I suppose that is a possibility.'

Her words raised the frequency of the nervous ping, but I felt it would be a bad time to back down.

'Do you have a name by the way?'

'I am Genna Rees.'

I had already made the decision. I wanted to know what went on in this place so far removed from the outside world I was familiar with. I also wanted to get better acquainted with Genna Rees; if it took a bit of pain, so be it.

I looked at my hand when she had finished and trundled off with her trolley. The tiny red spot tingled, not unlike an insect sting.

Footsteps approached and I looked up; it wasn't her. I wondered if and when I would catch up with her again. Ganymede grinned down at me like a satisfied hawk. I pushed myself up into a sitting position; it made me feel a bit less like prey.

'Welcome to the club, David.' He held out his hand and I shook it; I winced, despite a supreme effort not too. He grinned 'A bit sore I guess. Those sentries do pack a bit of a wallop.' No apology for not warning me; I decided not to challenge him, perhaps it was all part of my initiation into this weird world.

'You are already a signatory to the Official Secrets Act David so I'll now be able to introduce you to things that may well astound you.' He chuckled. 'In fact at times, they might even blow your mind a bit. You'll think you've slipped off the planet,' He was openly laughing now. 'In fact you might well just do that occasionally.' I could hardly, at this stage, be expected to know what he meant by that. 'Your ID will give you access to all the areas and facilities of the Complex except the data banks at the moment, but information from those will be provided if and when that becomes necessary. In the meantime a computer course is being arranged for you. Once you have qualified you will be able to do your own data processing.'

'What data guv?'

'Your main area of research will be analysing and collating all incoming UFO reports.'

'I've heard a lot about those things recently, are they for real? There's so much controversy I'm not sure what I'm prepared to believe.' He gave an understanding nod.

'At the moment David, the powers that be, and that includes us in a smaller way, see no reason not to fuel that controversy. Now that you are part of the team I can assure you yes, that despite the high percentage that prove to be natural atmospheric anomalies, hoaxes and phoney photography the visitations are very real indeed.'

'Is collating the data the main purpose of this place?'

'Secondary really. Primarily, in conjunction with the Americans we will actively investigate all sightings, close encounters and abductions etc, but I'll explain all that to you at a later date. Now if you're feeling up to it after your zapping and implanting we'll take a grand tour of what we have here. You'll very soon be able to find your way about, everything is laid out in a grid pattern, just think of avenues in parallel intersected by roads at right angles; a Yank city in miniature.'

'All cut out of chalk?'

'All cut out of chalk David. Tiny dead sea creatures that are providing safe and secret underground havens that may one day mean the difference between the survival, or the end of the human race.'

'Things will never be that bad surely?'

'We sincerely hope they won't, but ever since Hiroshima and Nagasaki and the proliferation of nuclear weapons between the East and West, it remains a possibility.'

'An irresponsible nutter pressing a button?'

'Exactly.'

The Grand Tour took just over an hour and covered an area of roughly 5 acres on two levels, an overwhelming combination of offices, lecture rooms and others not yet designated for any function. The accommodation suites alone could have graced any 3 star hotel. Any similarity between the bunkers of WW2 leaders was surely a reflection of Ganymede's humour. There were locked doors with observation panels that revealed empty rooms of immense proportions.

'Hangars,' was Ganymede's simple comment, as we moved on.

'You mean that you have aircraft here as well?'

'We are working on it.' We were at the door of what appeared to be a well appointed dining area equipped with a self-service area. It was empty of diners and the grills were down over the service counters. Two men in spotless, white overalls sat smoking at the only occupied table. Once again Ganymede fielded my query before I gave it a voice. 'It's a funny thing you know David. Here we are with probably the ultimate in current technology at our fingertips and we wake up one day to find that we can't cook a simple thing like an egg.'

'Sorry guv, you've lost me.'

'Electronics David. Everything here is driven by it.'

'So?'

'It takes just one fractured soldered joint in that mass of connected gizmos to bring things to a standstill.'

'And that means no coffee and donuts until it's sorted.' He saw that I'd got the picture.

'That's what those two, who look as though they couldn't give a fuck how long it takes, are there for; to locate and repair. I am sometimes tempted to requisition for a good old-fashioned gas range and cooks that could work without pushing buttons.' He turned away and checked his watch.

'I think that will do for today though. It's time for a pint and what looks like some pub grub out there in what passes for the real world. What do you say?'
I could only agree. A pint in a pub, in a familiar world, I could get my head round that.

Chapter 4

I awoke with a head. It's a funny thing about body parts; you are barely aware they exist until they cause a problem. I should have stuck with the ale, but a single malt whisky can be very persuasive, enough so to lead to several more. Ganymede was emerging from the shower cubicle at the far end of the hut. He was wearing a bathrobe and he indicated behind him.

'I've left it running,' he said as he headed for his bed space. It was an obvious cue for me to start the day. By the time I'd showered he was dressed and at the door. 'Catch up with me at the cookhouse,' he said and left.

For a change there were people in the dining room; three of them apart from Ganymede. The man sat beside him was an older and heavier built version of my new guv'nor. Ganymede introduced us. He was in a US army uniform sporting 2 stars on the shoulder tabs and a liberal helping of what we were inclined to refer to as fruit salad (medal ribbons) on his left breast

Arthur C White's handshake was exaggerated, crushing, leaving me as always, when there seemed a need for a macho display, with a feeling of mistrust. The young woman opposite him was slim, dark-haired and decidedly oriental, she smiled and took my hand gently; she said something I didn't quite catch. Arthur C White filled the gap.

'Quan Ling is my secretary Dave and a damn fine one at that.' He had a hearty, self-assured manner and his middle-aged bulk made it difficult for me to equate him with a Red Indian brave riding bare-back and shooting arrows into a stampeding buffalo. The other person present leaned over and tapped the palm of my hand lightly with his. There was no mistaking his northern Mediterranean origins. Dark, slightly kinked hair framed a deeply tanned face that sported a full moustache. Brown eyes looked, rather coldly, I thought, directly into mine.

'Philo Makris.' There was no accompanying smile.

'Philo looks after us.' Arthur C gave a short laugh. 'He keeps the wolves at bay.' I looked at Ganymede, he went wide-eyed and shrugged. I put down my plate alongside Quan Ling and sat down, perhaps someone would explain later.

My new acquaintances had already finished eating. The clock on the wall showed 8.32 am. Arthur C pushed his plate away and rose. I judged him at just over six feet; was that a bit tall for a Red Indian? I thought. His age, which was probably 50 plus, and

26

a fair bit of good living since he had fathered Ganymede, had given him a generous waistline.

'I hope you'll excuse us, we've got rather a busy schedule today.' He looked down over his belly at me. 'It's a project I hope you'll be joining us on one day Dave.' With that he strode purposefully from the hall. It occurred to me that for all the sightseeing and tuition in the ways of this new world of mine that I still didn't know what my real function here was. Building a database with the aid of one of these new-fangled computers didn't sound as if it was intended to bring out my so-called hidden abilities.

Philo also stood up. He looked slight, almost delicate. He nodded in my direction and moved with athletic grace towards the door; Quan Ling remained seated nursing her coffee cup. She had removed some papers from a briefcase and was studying them. Philo paused at the door and pointed towards her.

'Quan Ling will take you down to the lecture room; she has things to say that will interest you.' He looked towards Ganymede. 'You will find us in the usual place, sir,' Ganymede nodded, wiped his plate with a wad of bread, and popped it into his mouth before turning to me.

'I'll leave you in this good lady's care then David, and I'll catch up with you this evening.' With that he rose and followed the others out.

I hurried through my meal not wanting to feel I was holding up the day's proceedings. Quan Ling was replacing the papers in her case. When I made as if to move she raised a restraining hand.

'Finish your coffee major.' She took a sip from her cup. 'It is half an hour yet before my talk begins.'

'David, please.'

She nodded acceptance, and smiled. 'Okay David, there is no hurry.'

'You are doing the lecture?'

'Of course, you seem surprised.'

I shouldn't have. Women did lots of things during and since the war that were not normally associated with them.

'Sorry. I've never been lectured by a woman before.' It was a feeble attempt to lighten the moment. I could see she was aware of my discomfort. 'What will you talk about?' She studied me intently for a moment before answering. 'Things that are not of

27

this world David.' Her voice had a low and soft caressing quality.

'Oh, right.' I couldn't restrain a laugh. 'There seems to be a lot of that around here.' Her smile was tolerant; she appeared to change the subject.

'Do you believe in ghosts David?'

'I…well…how can I say… How about, I don't disbelieve in them?'

Her smile reminded me of the Mona Lisa; almost self-satisfied.

'What's your perspective on UFO's?'

'I can't say that I have one.' I wondered where she was going with this. 'I remember there was some sort of a flap about UFO's in the early 50's just after I'd finished my National Service but it didn't seem to come to anything. I don't think anyone really took it seriously. There were rumours going around at the time too of people meeting men from space and having rides in flying saucers.'

'Did it ever occur to you that there might be some truth in some of those reports?' I wondered if she was picking up where Ganymede had left off.

'I thought it was quite fascinating at the time, people from other planets visiting us, but it never seemed convincing somehow. So much of it could be explained away. I think if I could have witnessed an event …I suppose like ghosts I can't discount the possibility of UFO's, space beings and the like.'

'I like that; you are open-minded, eh? You'll certainly need that here…David.'

I wondered why. I was beginning to get impatient with all these hints regarding the function of this place.

'I try to be, it's not always easy.'

'Good.' She finished her coffee; it was a signal for me to do the same. You will see much here that will keep it open, even if at times it makes you question your sanity.' She rose to go and waited until I was on my feet. 'We can go together if you like.'

I liked. She came up to my shoulder; I felt strangely protective.

At the silent sentry I waved my magic hand and passed through unchallenged.

We passed through a small room occupied by two women operatives who sat with their backs towards us. They were looking into screens of some sort. 'What are those things?'

'They are computers.'

I had heard the word in association with an electronic brain that was being developed at some university or other, but I was given to understand it was as big as a fair sized room. There were also the rumours circulating in Sigs that the breaking of the German Enigma Code by those at Bletchley Park was only one of their mind-boggling achievements. I must have once again looked suitably astounded as I grappled with the way at which technology had left me limping along so far behind. She tried to help me out. 'It's the nearest thing to a human brain, but it can make calculations at phenomenal speeds.'

'You mean they can actually think?' She laughed and patted my arm.

'Not yet David.' Her look indicated that might simply be a matter of time. Here was me still fascinated by pictures flying through the air and showing up on a television screen. Once again I was cowed into momentary silence.

I noticed a metal strip that ran the length of the room between us and them. Quan Ling caught my look.

'Your ID won't get you past the strip David. Those data banks are classified, mostly on a 'need to know' level. There is a coded entry key for those who have a need to know what goes on there. Need to know is the highest classification here.'

'I see.' I didn't of course; what could be so top secret that only a few would have access? It was after all peacetime, and War 2 had been over for 17 years. Alas by the end of the day I was to realise that there were many things the general public knew nothing of and were never likely to.

The Cold War was still swinging between calm and tension and there was nothing to indicate an end in sight. The Russians of course, ever since the ending their year-long blockade of Berlin, had kept up their campaign of engineering international trouble- spots. Nobody was really sure what they would get up to next. They seemed determined to support anything and everyone that could in any way be detrimental to the Western Alliance. Most of my time in Sigs had been spent in monitoring their military and naval movements, especially around the Eastern Bloc and the Baltic. The past few months had been spent closely watching the escalating friction between Kruschev and Kennedy over missile sites in Cuba. UFO's and the like were now largely overshadowed by the threat of a nuclear war. I asked Quan Ling if she had a perspective on that.

'I don't think we need to worry too much over that David. Sabre rattling is a negative response that is standard procedure when neither side is prepared to initiate an actual conflict. I think you'll find when the dust settles over this Cuban thing that it was already settled and agreements made before the world's media pressed the alarm bells.' I must have looked as incredulous as I felt.

'You mean...agreements...with Reds? ... We've been at loggerheads ever since...' She was smiling, indulgently, and shaking her head.

'Only in public David, there is so much that goes on behind the scenes. We are in the process of discovering how false the public face of events really is. So much is engineered by people in high places; even wars between nations are planned, even orchestrated, solely for the benefit of those who sit back and profit from them.'

I could understand some of what she was saying. I didn't doubt for one minute that arms dealers of neutral countries sold weaponry to both sides. But I was one day to discover that was only small beer compared with the real issues involved. It was there that our conversation ended and I took my seat in the lecture room. I hoped that perhaps the good Quan Ling would now shed some light on some of the mystery surrounding this place.

I looked around. There were about a dozen other guys in the room, all male and about my own age. They were scattered among the four rows as if they were avoiding contact with each other. I did wonder how they got here as I'd seen none of them in the camp outside.

Only one looked vaguely familiar. He was seated in the front row. I was seated a couple of rows back directly behind him and I could only see the back of his head. I shuffled along a couple of seats to the end of the row and was able to see slightly more of his profile; it was definitely familiar. I had to settle for that, but I was now in a better position to observe Quan Ling as she took to the stage. She looked up from her notes and began.

If I was expecting her to be talking about current affairs which was usually the gist in army lectures, and the occurrences in this year, 1962, I couldn't have been more wrong. It was some moments before I could get a grasp of what she was on about. Atom and hydrogen bomb tests and the McCarthy witch hunts for reds under the beds were definitely not on the agenda.

30

My last army lecture had covered King Farouk's humiliating departure from Egypt followed by a takeover of that country by Muhammad Naguib and an upstart colonel, Gamal Nasser. That was ten years ago, and I had successfully avoided army lectures ever since. This one was to shatter that mould and my complacency over world affairs; the blame for not being prepared for what I was now about to hear and witness rested solely on me. I had even sat slightly tongue in cheek a year previously when the Russian Gagarin was reported to have circled the Earth several times before breakfast. What was to be revealed to me in the next hour was to make me seriously consider just what I had been doing to remain so ignorant as to what had happened in my cosy little world since I began my working life at the end of WW2. Quan Ling raised her eyes from her notes; the merest hint of authority had now entered her voice.

'Welcome gentlemen. You have now entered a new phase in the history of mankind. You will all learn in the coming days how the last global war and the regional conflicts that followed it have opened up new and awesome potentials for mankind. Some of you are familiar with certain advances in science and technology, like the transistor radio and the miniaturisation of other forms of electronic equipment. Many of you may have coloured television, or are even becoming familiar with computer technology. Now you may have wondered how after five years of worldwide conflict, plus 17 years of regional unrest, which is still continuing in some parts of the world, such things could come about. The answer is simple. War is a race to get one over on the other side, and as a consequence, scientists, on both sides, work on weaponry and other systems which they hope will defeat the enemy and bring an end to the conflict. In short, technology moves in leaps and bounds to achieve those ends. There are spin offs ..., as the Americans say, that result in all kinds of labour-saving gadgetry.' She glanced down at her notes again and shuffled the pages before continuing.

'This establishment, which you have all agreed to become part of, was commissioned to further the development of what was achieved by all participants in the last war; yes even by the Russians and the Germans.' She permitted herself a brief smile at the sharp intakes of breath. 'Even now, as I speak, German scientists who developed the V1's and V2's which created so much uncertainty towards the end, are collaborating with the Americans and the Russians in the development of rockets which

31

not only defeat earth's gravity but will travel in deep space. I think I can safely leave you to ponder on what that could lead to.'

I was loath to ponder at that point. "Hello Mr Martian", did cross my mind; there was still more to come.

'Our function here though is not to advance rocketry. Our brief, if you like, is far more important.' She paused once more, but not to refer to her notes; it was prior to dropping a bombshell. 'We are in the process of making contact with those who already have the ability to travel anywhere in space, and believe it or not, have contributed considerably to our current technology.'

There were no sharp intakes of breath; I think we were all holding it.

She moved to the side of the stage and held conversation with someone who remained out of sight. I fidgeted. It was contagious; several feet shuffled. That's it, I thought. Someone is taking the piss, or they are completely off their trolley. Next thing, Quan Ling will change into a little green man with an aerial stuck on her head and we'll all have a good laugh and go home; not so.

She came back to the centre stage and once again addressed us.

'I think that we've reached a suitable point to stop talking and start seeing.' She then raised her head and looked beyond us. 'As soon as the screen is in place then sir.'

I glanced back, two men stood at a cine projector.

She hopped off the stage and sat down on the end of the front row, where she fumbled with something. There was a muffled click. Curtains at the back of the stage drew apart and presented a white expanse of cinema screen. The lights dimmed and behind us the cine projector whirred softly.

The screen went dark, and then a pinpoint of light appeared roughly in the center. It grew in intensity and size as it bobbed about. I craned forward and saw that she was holding a microphone. I looked across the floor in the direction of the stage for the lead; there was none. Puzzled I turned back to the light bobbing around on the screen; Quan Ling took up the commentary.

'Lights like this have been appearing in the night sky in the Americas and also in Britain and Europe ever since the cessation of hostilities. Due to continuing reports of these phenomenon,

32

the majority of people today are becoming familiar with the terms 'flying saucers' and 'UFO's'. Periodically there are rashes of newspaper reports of sightings and alien encounters, and individual stories of abductions. Strangely though very few of us have actually seen a UFO or know someone who has.'

I for one, I thought, and up til now I wondered if I did actually want to see one. Although I had to admit that I did find the phenomenon fascinating. I hoped that this wasn't going to be a boring rehash of things I had already heard of and reluctantly laid to rest.

The image on the screen seemed to dart across to one side and remained there until the camera refocused and brought it back to centre screen. So this was what an actual night sighting of a UFO looked like; it didn't seem much to go on.

'As you can see they appear to move sometimes at speeds that seem incomprehensible to us, and in the years from 1945, as far as the general public is concerned, they have remained a complete and somewhat fascinating mystery. Certain elements within the British and American military intelligence services have however, since 1947, been involved in the downing and retrieval of flying vehicles and personnel that are not of this Earth.'

The image on screen continued to dart around, while I tried to take in what she was saying, sometimes disappearing from one spot, and reappearing in another. It bothered my eyes so I closed them and concentrated fully on the speaker. What was this lovely young Oriental saying?

'Now although there must be some of you that know, or think you know, about what is supposed to have occurred in the United States in 1947, for the benefit of your ongoing tuition within this organisation I will briefly recap on an event known as the Roswell Crash. Up until then UFO and flying saucer sightings hadn't received much attention by the press. We are aware that this was mainly due to pressure being brought to bear on it by the intelligence agencies, both here and in the United States.'

'In 1947 however there was a breakthrough. A farmer with a property near a US Air Force Base at Roswell New Mexico came across some strange metallic looking wreckage. He reported it to the local sheriff's office. The sheriff and he drove out to the site and the sheriff then reported what he had seen to the US military. In no time at all they descended mob-handed on the scene and cordoned off the area. It would appear that a plan of action was already in place to deal with this sort of eventuality.'

'After at first admitting that the wreckage appeared to be some sort of flying vehicle, and certainly not of this world, this admission was later retracted and an official denial of any such incident was released to the general public. All evidence was removed and the whole thing covered up. Early eyewitnesses were intimidated into silence and any leaks were dismissed with ridicule and disinformation. Great pains were taken to conceal the fact that alien, humanoid bodies were also found at the scene.'

I pinched myself, and it hurt; yes, I was definitely hearing this. Is this what Ganymede meant when he said, "Things to blow your mind"?

I was in the Merchant Navy in '47 and I spent that memorable bitter winter on a Swedish ship plodding around between the Baltic and the West coast of Norway. I think that, and a shaky romance had much to do with my decision to give National Service a try. News of this Roswell thing had never reached my ears, or the ears of anyone I knew at the time. Not surprising really; the cover-up had obviously been effective. The commentary continued.

'The Roswell crash appears to have been one of several in the general area at that time. One at least resulted in the recovery of a live crew member from a crashed vehicle. This also followed the US Military into obscurity. Once again eyewitnesses, both among residents of the area and the military personnel involved in the recovery were sworn to secrecy, intimidated, and otherwise threatened if they didn't keep their mouths shut and forget that the incidents ever happened. What I wish you all to know is that the Roswell Crash did take place as those first on the scene described it; not only that, but there was more than one craft brought down in that area.' A murmur went through the room; I opened my eyes again; Quan Ling, although only her back was presented to us, continued to have my full attention. She paused and appeared to refer to her notes before continuing.

'There are available, affidavits by witnesses in existence, and photographs that are purported to be of alien bodies, and ... also official denials and a great deal of misinformation issued by the US military and Intelligence agencies. All this is not particularly privileged information. It has been in the public domain since these occurrences took place, it's just that it's been batted around so much that people no longer know whether to take it seriously or not. The Americans are happy to keep it that way, and the British government, because it might lose out on current and future information are also prepared to keep the lid on it. In the course of your work here you will have every opportunity to make up your minds as to the truth or otherwise of these opposing claims.'

Despite the fact that she had her back to most of us, she now had the undivided attention of everyone in the room. If what we were hearing had even the glimmer of truth in it, how was it that I, and by the look on the other faces, no one else in the room had heard of all this? I had to assume that whatever had occurred in New Mexico, if indeed it had, it had been successfully concealed from everyone except those who had been directly involved. I came back to the speaker.

'Since then of course our government, having discovered what had been going on stateside, wanted in on the action. Commendable? In view of the ongoing Cold War yes, because there still remained the suspicion that all these 'strange lights in the sky' and crashed space vehicles, if such they were, might be Soviet secret weapons and a threat to national security.'

I could see the justification for that, after all war, whether winners or losers, makes everyone a little suspicious, even of allies.

'The upshot of that, is that the Americans are cooperating with our government and exchanging as much information as they feel fit, or as much as MI5 and MI6 can squeeze out of them, or discover by other means. In the interim the general public must understandably be kept in ignorance both for national security and their own peace of mind. In the meantime reports will still flow and people will accept or reject the reality of UFO's and extraterrestrial beings accordingly.'

I watched the little blob of light again for a while but it did things to my eyes that I didn't like. I closed them again and leaned back in my seat waiting for what came next; and come it did. I heard a combined gasp and opened them again. The blob of light had vanished, and in the now lightened screen a figure had emerged.

'This is a picture of what is believed to be one of our space relatives.' I opened them again; what we had seen and heard so far paled more than somewhat.

The image that appeared on screen was not *so* unbelievable as those beings I could recall from the science fiction comics of my youth, but its resemblance to a human experiment gone wrong sent a shiver through me. It was not something I would care to meet on a dark and otherwise deserted street.

'This is the live alien that was recovered from one of the New Mexico crashes and he, she, or it, spent several years in a US base. They gave it a name, Extraterrestrial Biological Entity, EBE. Unfortunately EBE became ill in 1951 and because of an inability by the medics available to treat an alien constitution, it died in 1952.'

It occurred to me that had all this been the subject of one of my last army lectures, instead of Farouk, I might not have given them the elbow.

I looked in awe at this my first glimpse of an alien being. It looked a bit like a long skinny kid. It had a big domed head with its large slanting eyes and ridiculously small features. It looked only remotely human. It did occur to me that it might be some sort of mock up; a dummy of some sort. Once again I was made aware that at least one person here seemed to anticipate what I was thinking.

'Now you are probably thinking that this creature is so unreal as to be unbelievable. I hasten to assure you that EBE does exist; in a preserved state. I have visited a US military base in the Nevada desert, and but for the glass container in which it now resides I could have touched it.'

The idea sent a slight shiver of revulsion through me. It was not connected in any way to EBE's physiology, only by how he or she was being treated as a laboratory specimen. But I had to hear this through. I still wasn't prepared for what followed.

'Since the mid 50's it is rumoured that alien spacecraft have also landed intentionally in the United States, and that President Eisenhower has actually conducted a dialogue with alien beings that are, unlike EBE, quite human looking.'

That just about did it for me; pull the other one; this lecture seemed to swing me between sceptic and believer, but I still felt the need to hear it through.

'We have, so far, been unable to confirm this as the Americans are being very cagey on that matter.'

Yeah, I'll bet they're laughing their heads off, I thought. I was thankful the cine camera stopped whirring and the cine session was over. Quan Ling reappeared on stage and the remainder of her talk was about things that we were, thanks to, or because of, unrelenting media coverage, more familiar with, like the Cold War and the Korean situation, which had put the extra six months on my National Service, and the still ongoing controversial war in Vietnam. It submerged me in a familiar state of boredom

The Korean conflict and my broken romance had jointly been a somewhat pivotal experience. Although not directly involved in it, the extra months of service imposed over Korea had kept me in the army long enough for me to assess the benefits of becoming a regular soldier. I was only now beginning to realise how some of the decisions I'd made, albeit at times quite inadvertently, had shaped my experience in life. Right now it seemed that I had landed in quite a cloak and dagger outfit. I was wondering how all this might turn out when the lecture came to an end.

After thanking everyone for their attention Quan Ling came across to me as I stood undecided as what I was expected to do next. I looked around, but there was no sign of whoever it was that had been sitting in the front row.

'It's time to catch up with Ganymede and the others David. Do you feel in need of refreshment?' I could have murdered a pint but I didn't say it. As we were only a couple of hours into the day; I compromised.

'I think a coffee wouldn't go amiss.'

'Coffee it is then.'

Chapter 5

Ganymede, Arthur C, and Philo Makris were obviously in the same mind; they were already in the cafeteria, which appeared to be fully functioning again. Good, I thought as Quan Ling and I took our seats, perhaps I would have a chance to ask questions about what I had witnessed and heard at the lecture. I stirred and sipped my coffee before jumping in headfirst.

'These things called UFO's, is there really a link between them and those crashes in New Mexico?' Four pairs of eyes immediately focussed on me; I felt very much like a new boy on the block; I stumbled on. 'I mean, I've been inclined to take things like that with a pinch of salt, and as for contact with beings from space, it just sounds more like something out of a comic paper.'

Ganymede was first to speak.

'That just about sums it up David. The vast majority of people would be tempted to laugh it off as some kind of joke.' He looked at the others; they nodded agreement. 'And that, at the present time, is all to the good.' If I wondered why, it must have showed. Quan Ling reached out and placed a hand on mine.

'There is a need to avoid any widespread panic David. Can you imagine how people might react even suspecting that we weren't the only occupants of the solar system, even perhaps the universe? And not only that, that some of those beings were so advanced in their technology that we would be defenceless should they attack us.'

'So we keep it under wraps as far as that is possible.' Arthur C gave a knowledgeable wink. 'It really is a case of ignorance is bliss Dave.'

I could accept the sense of that. When I was eight years old, or thereabouts, an American radio program had put half the world into a panic by broadcasting alarming bulletins of a Martian invasion of Earth.

Arthur C leaned forward with his arms on the table.

'It's all very old hat to my people Dave. They always knew that there were others out there.'

'So why not us...we...?'

'Ever read your bible, Dave?' He appeared to have changed the subject; it puzzled me. What had that got to do with anything?

38

'I...well, a bit I suppose, when I was a kid. My family weren't much for religion; we got some of it at school though.'

'A bit, you say; what bit?' Arthur C paused to re-light a stub of cigar, studying me as he did so. I was beginning to feel uncomfortable; my need for answers seemed to have turned into an interrogation.

'Well nothing much at all really, our teachers basically told us about it, you know, about Adam and Eve and Noah and the Flood and all that stuff.' I wondered why I, at 32 with a couple of years in the Merchant Navy at the tail end of the war and 12+2 years army service I should have to feel guilty over my lack of any religious beliefs. Arthur C sensed my discomfort for he waved his cigar stub in dismissal and grinned.

'It's okay Dave. It's not the Inquisition; you're not on trial here. The point I wish to make is that most religion is imparted through teachers and priests and those who accept what is said because it has been around for a long time and therefore must be true; The average follower of the faith rarely reads anything or even investigates anything for themselves.'

What he said made sense, of course, but I didn't feel inclined to start reading the bible. I decided to leave it there and not pursue any further questions, just wait and see what other mind boggling events I would be presented with in this strange world I seem to have blundered into. I wondered what would be coming next.

'You're with me,' said Ganymede rising abruptly. 'We leave these good people to get on with whatever they usually get on with when they are not lumbered with the likes of us.' I followed him from the cafeteria; I felt three pairs of eyes boring into my back.

'Don't let the Yank bother you, David, he's one of the top dogs here, and he's well clued up, not only with what goes on here but also in the States. I guess you've sussed that he and I are related?'

It would have been ridiculous to disagree. I hoped as we paused at yet another door with an electronic keypad and he turned and looked at me, that my face registered diplomatic agreement.

As we passed through the doorway I was confronted by a vehicle about the size of a family saloon car, Ganymede slid back a door and motioned for me to get in. I slid across to the far side and he followed me in and sat before a control panel.

It was left-hand drive like the American vehicles that were becoming increasingly rare since the bulk of their servicemen had returned home. The actual operation of the vehicle was all done through a control panel.

We left the lighted area and moved off down a track-way into pitch blackness. With the soft light afforded by the illuminated control panel I could see how close his profile matched that of his natural father. I still had questions that I needed confirming answers to, if only to get my head in some sort of order.

'Is all what I'm seeing and hearing true, guv; this Roswell stuff and beings from space, I mean?'

'It's as true as you and I are sitting here David.' Without looking at me he said. 'Those are only the thin edge though; there have been others since, and without doubt there will be many more.'

'And beings like EBE have actually landed here and made contact with the American government?'

'Not all are quite like EBE, there are those more like us in fact.' He glanced my way. 'Nordic looking, blonde hair and blue eyes apparently, in ordinary clothes, you wouldn't know the difference if you passed them in the street.' He turned his attention back to the console.

'So what really happened at the meeting between them and Eisenhower?'

'It's rumoured that they offered some of their technology in exchange for certain concessions on Earth, but Eisenhower declined.'

'What kind of concessions?' Ganymede turned his head again and tapped his nose.

'Bases on Earth perhaps, who knows, the Yanks have clammed up on that even to our government. One of our functions here is to find out exactly what is going on behind the scenes over there. We are funded by Whitehall and our brief is to pass back whatever information we can glean from across the pond.' He went back to the console and pressed buttons, the vehicle slowed as it left the tunnel and entered a large brilliantly lighted area and slowed to a halt. A familiar face approached as we stepped out. It was the elusive one from the lecture room

'I believe you two know each other.' Ganymede waved a hand towards the newcomer.

I found myself face to face with the back of the head in the front row. The cheeky grin in a freckled face topped by a shock of ginger hair advanced towards me with outstretched hand. He looked marginally older now, more mature to be correct, and the ginger had faded, looking slightly grey at the temples. Like me he had the merest hint of a pot in the belly department.

'Hi David, long time no *sea.*' It was the accent he put on the word that clinched where I had met him before.

'Hi...'I groped for a name to put to the face and the rotund body.

'Bill Reynard, surely you haven't forgotten the old Carnarvon Castle.'

It all clicked in then and I was shaking his hand. I turned to Ganymede.

'This guy used to tell fortunes on a ship I was on once. He reckoned it was some sort of a gift. He told me things about myself that only I could have known about.' I turned back to him. 'You even tried to hypnotise me once, remember? It didn't work though.'

'There was a very good reason for that.' He and Ganymede exchanged glances. 'I'm glad you persuaded him to join us, G.'

'It was hardly a chore sir. I think despite himself he was hooked by curiosity soon after he got here.' Ganymede looked at me for confirmation; I smiled and nodded.

'Can't tell how pleased I am to see you here David. It was a shame we lost touch soon after we packed up the sea and copped for the call up.' I nodded agreement although I didn't know that giving up the seafaring life had been in any way mutual. I could see over his shoulder a knot of uniforms, all gold braid, and red tabs, obviously waiting for him to conclude his business with us.

'If you'll excuse me now, I have a meeting with some brass hats. He looked at me. 'I'll catch up with you later David, chew the fat, eh? Have fun.'

'Is that about the, you-know-what sir?' Ganymede said, nodding in the direction of the brass. Reynard turned towards him.

'It is G. There have been new developments; I'll discuss them with you when I get back. I'll be out of the country for a day or two.'

'In the meantime, do I have your permission, now that he's joined the fold, to put David wise regarding the purpose of the Complex and similar installations?' It was not difficult to realise that my new guv'nor was treating my old shipmate with certain deference.

41

'That's okay, carry on by all means.' With that Reynard turned and with wink in my direction walked off, I couldn't have imagined in my wildest dreams how our next meeting would turn out.'

As Ganymede ushered me into a small office and sat me down, I said. 'Does Bill Reynard outrank you in some way guv?' I was thinking of the *sir* he had accorded him.

He sat down on the other side of the desk opposite me. 'Colonel Reynard is running this section David. I am no longer a serving officer so rank doesn't enter into it. But my association with him, unlike your own, which was an informal one in the Merchant Navy, means that I acknowledge his position in the hierarchy here. Past and current ranks like your own, count only in the wage scale. Here we are basically civilian operatives, bound by the Official Secrets Act of course, but among ourselves our respect is for the man rather than a uniform or previous rank. Bill Reynard is our boss in that he has a measure of control over our actions here, but I've always found him open to discussion and to accept an idea that he considered better than one of his own. Incidentally, you in particular will be seeing quite a lot of him in the future, he rates you pretty high.'

My surprise must have been obvious, Ganymede seemingly ignored it. He looked briefly at a paper on his desk then tapped it.

'He appears to be out of the top drawer as far as shrinks go.'

'A shrink? Able Seaman 'Ginger Reynard, a trick-cyclist?' I couldn't help a laugh; it triggered a sobering look from Ganymede.

'I think we need to be a little serious, for a while at least, Major. He broke from the army at the end of his National Service and went for a degree in the mind business. According to his CV he then re-enlisted and was commissioned. He then spent several years helping troops traumatised in battle. Not surprisingly your old shipmate's rise through the ranks was fairly meteoric.'

I was becoming increasingly aware of how the switch from David to Major and back was an indicator of his mood; I shut up and sat back. It was obvious that he had something important to impart. I didn't know to what extent it would soon have me reeling.

'It's now time for you understand why you were recommended for this particular project and for certain abilities you have which will not only be of benefit to the project itself but could well be of benefit for the human race as a whole.'

At last it looked like I was to learn why I was actually in this place.

'You've lost me guv; I don't have any special abilities.'

'Not that you are presently aware of I agree, but that's because they became buried quite early in your life.' If I didn't look a bit bewildered I certainly felt it.

'Just who was it that recommended me on the strength of these abilities of which I have no knowledge?'

'Your good friend Foxy Bill, who else?'

'He never liked being called that.'

In view of my past association with him I was only mildly surprised that Reynard might know more about me than I did myself, but I wanted to hear this out.

'He still doesn't, so it's not for his ears.' Ganymede seemed to reflect on something. 'Thing is that's quite a compliment; they called the German General Rommel the desert fox. Colonel Reynard is a different kind of fox though.'

'In what way?' I thought I knew part of the answer to that but I wanted him to carry on.

'Apart from being a classic shrink and the hypnosis bit which you say he tried on you, he is able to project himself, out of body to locations that are of interest to those of us working on this project.'

'Out of body? I've heard of that, it's something to do with near death experience, isn't it? People involved in accidents and badly wounded soldiers say they've experienced it.' I felt a need to show that I wasn't a total ignoramus.

'I think Bill Reynard does what is sometimes referred to as 'remote viewing'; he is able to project his consciousness and observe events in places where he is not physically present.' Was there no limit to revelations to boggle my mind? I looked at him. Was this some sort of leg-pull?

'A sort of fly on the wall, spy, eh guv? So are you saying that Bill did a bit of remote viewing inside my head and discovered these abilities of which I know nothing about?' My amusement was not reflected in Ganymede's stony stare.

'You can laugh, but we are only now discovering some of the hidden potential of the human brain, for instance do you know anything about telepathy, have you even heard of it, can you spell it?'

43

I assured him I had and I could spell it, but that I knew sweet FA about it.

'Well it may surprise you to know that Reynard knows that you do know about it, and at the age of approximately four or five years old you were actually practising it.'

'Oh come on guv, a joke's a joke but this is turning into a bloody musical comedy. I haven't seen Bill Reynard since the day I left that ship back in '48. All those years ago. So where has all this stuff you're on about come from?'

'When he didn't manage to hypnotise you?'

'That's right; it just turned into a big laugh.' He appeared to consider this before changing tack.

'How did you rate him?'

'What Bill, back then? Bit on the serious side, I think, for a sea-faring bloke I mean. We thought his hypnotist thing was a bit of a joke, but apart from that he was one of the boys; knew his job too.'

'Now that you've met him in a totally different capacity, how do you rate him?'

'That's a difficult one. From the little I've learned about him now, as a psychiatrist and a high ranking army officer and …that remote viewing thing you're on about … that's a bit awesome, to say the least.'

'Does he strike you as an honest man, someone you can trust?'

It seemed an odd question. Although it was Bill Reynard in the flesh, it was difficult to link the Able Seaman with the high-ranking army officer I had just passed the time of day with, let alone him being a psychiatrist to boot. But Ganymede was waiting for an answer.

'I don't see why not, I never had any reason in the past to think otherwise and there doesn't appear to be any side to him now.'

'Good. Because for what it's worth, in the years that I've known him, I've never had cause to doubt his integrity or sincerity.'

'So why all the mystery about something, a bit of a lark really, that we had donkey's years ago?'

'I think that's something that needs to come from Bill, not from me.'

'But you know, don't you, and have done even before I walked into this bloody shambles of a camp.' It was beginning to

44

get my back up this withholding of information from me, about me, and it obviously showed. 'Although I was more or less Shanghaied into this I did accept in good faith what you said about my reason for being here even though the reference to these abilities I'm supposed to have didn't make a lot of sense; it still doesn't.' He could see that I was getting heated and attempted to diffuse the situation.

'Believe me David, I don't have all the answers, and I don't want to say anything that might be misleading. In a very short while I'm sure Bill Reynard will put you fully in the picture. He spent some time in the States going round UFO crash sites and the like before coming back with a plan, or more correctly, an idea. At the time he didn't confide in me, I was instructed to locate you and get you to join the outfit. It was several months before I finally tracked you down. He felt that there was enough going on here to interest you.'

'He was right about that anyway, I still am, very much so.'

'Then perhaps you'll find that what Bill needs your cooperation for is even more interesting than what you've experienced so far.' He raised his hand before I could utter a further word. 'No that's it David, I'm sorry, you'll just have to wait until he puts his ideas and plans to you.'

I felt drained, mentally numbed. There was no physical pain, but I sat for a while with my head in my hands; this crazy world I had stumbled into was getting crazier by the minute. I needed to get somewhere where sanity reigned, if only for a while.

'Are you okay David?' There was an edge of concern in his voice. I lowered my hands and looked up.

'I think my head needs some alcoholic lubrication, guv, I could murder a drink, several in fact.'

'No problem.' He rose abruptly and looked at his watch. 'But we'll have to move it; the pub closes in half an hour.'

I decided that for a couple of days at least I had no option but to stay cool and await the words of my master. I needed to realise that Bill Reynard was now something more than an old shipmate of mine.

45

Chapter 6

'We won't be going topside at all today, David.'

Ganymede's voice interrupted my study of the pictures on the walls of the office in which he'd given me the shocks the day before. I had been so riveted on what he was saying at the time that I hadn't been aware of them. I turned and looked at him. He anticipated my query perfectly and once again I got the feeling that it wasn't my look of dismay or the fact that it was very close to eats time and my stomach was asking questions.

'It's okay; we do have the cafeteria in the Complex.' He laughed. 'Fingers crossed. I'm afraid the old camp cookhouse has joined the other defunct messing facilities.' He was smiling. 'The food is probably much better down here anyway. Personally I prefer its friendlier atmosphere, and it's a gathering place for interesting people.'

'As interesting as these pictures and maps? I waved my hand, indicating the walls. 'I've not recognised one of them and yet parts of them seem vaguely familiar.'

'That's because they are familiar in a basic way, for instance, this one.' He pointed. 'What would you say that was?'

'Well...' I hesitated. I had studied it earlier but hadn't come to any conclusions. 'It's a planet,' I said cautiously. 'A pretty dead looking planet.' He nodded slowly.

'It is in a way I suppose, but I think satellite is the common description; it's the moon.'

'It doesn't look like any moon that I'm familiar with.' I, like a good many others, had done a bit of astronomy in the sixth form at school so I was well acquainted with its major features none of which were present here; in fact the whole surface was gloomy and indistinct.

'It's the dark side David.'

'But how...?'

'Ways and means, of which you will shortly become acquainted with.'

I realised I would have to be content with that and I moved to some outline maps which were once again strangely familiar, but not quite; all the continents looked a bit pushed together.

'The two on the left represent the world as it moved through two distinct phases of change; continental drift and changes in sea levels etc.'

46

'And this one?' I pointed to one on the right. 'All these islands?'

'That is a big question mark David. We've been doing our sums, and that, combined with information that's been gleaned from various sources, including the space vehicle crashes, is what the world may look like in the future.' He looked and sounded serious; I felt the need to be too.

'It's just a collection of islands?'

He nodded.

'Some bigger than others of course.' He went to a shelf and removed a transparent sheet with outlines of all the major continents. He pinned it carefully over the map of islands. Now what do you see?'

I studied it for a while then took a deep breath; I needed it for the – wow! I could see that the islands in most cases lined up with the various mountain ranges throughout the world.

'I suppose that could be Ben Nevis?' I placed a finger on a mere isolated speck roughly in the area of the Scottish highlands.'

'That's right on David.' He replaced the transparency on the shelf and turned to me. 'Thing is we won't be around when that comes about, will we?' It was a sobering thought. From the look of things only 10 to 15% of the Earth's surface would be above sea level. It was time for my stupid question of the day.

'What happens to the people, guv, there's a few billion of us now I believe?'

'Nearly four billion and rising, and by the year 2000 the prediction is at least six billion.'

'Bloody hell!' I indicated the map. 'When is all this supposed to happen? It'll be standing room only.'

'If this does come about it'll be more like swimming room only.' His serious look relaxed allowing a smile. But you must understand that predictions are dodgy things, they are not always true to form or end result. We are learning that the future, any future, is flexible; it's not set in stone. It could happen in fifty years, or a hundred, or even thousands of year's time, or not at all.'

'But it's a possibility?'

He returned to his chair and settled back before answering; it was not what I expected.

'There is always the possibility. Six months ago David, what sort of future did you contemplate for yourself.'

47

'Hard to say really.' I had a few months to go to the end of my service. I was looking forward to a bit of pension ... I don't recall having any definite plans ... just wait and see if anything interesting turned up. Being a free agent again seemed to be enough; I would more or less take it from there.'

'Now give it a bit of thought. Everyone at any one time has a vague idea of where they are heading or would like to be heading.' He held his head slightly to one side, expectantly.

'Yeah I suppose so. Like I said, I had no definite plans, but there were things I felt I'd like to do when my time was up.' Ganymede smiled knowingly and encouragingly. 'A nice long holiday for as long as funds permitted certainly appealed, including travel of course. The possibility of meeting someone who would bring a bit of romance into my life. Maybe even get married and have kids in a place I could call home. I think the main thing I looked forward to would have to be the freedom to do all those things without being on a twenty-four hour -- seven days a week beck and call in the army.' He was grinning widely now.

'And what have you got now? Those things you mentioned were all possible predictions at that time. By joining up with me you have changed to a greater or lesser degree your expectations of the future. You have also committed yourself to certain restrictions.' He saw my look of alarm and raised his hand. 'I don't mean that you are on 24 hour – 7 days a week call out. You do an eight hour working shift at the moment which will on occasion be on a twenty-four hour rota basis. Off duty you are free to do as you please. You will need permission to go on your own personal travels and excursions at times, and of course your ID implant will locate you anywhere in the world. In short, you have freedom within certain parameters, but that is also true in everyday life; so, nothing new. So you see, joining with us has altered your future. You may still realise whatever dreams you may have had but in an entirely different way.' Still smiling, he said, 'And you will certainly travel to places beyond your wildest dreams...'

There was a knock at the door and a head of red hair was thrust into the room; much less unruly than in the past. The lowdown on my life was finished pro tem and I wasn't sure what I was about to be presented with now. I can't say I was all that happy about what Ganymede had conveyed to me regarding what had happened back there on the high seas with Bill

Reynard; in fact I felt it was more than a little frightening. Bill Reynard's breezy smile did little to put my mind at ease

'Right David, time for you and I to get together for a while. He turned to Ganymede. 'The brass has given us the go ahead. They weren't exactly cock o' hoop but there are no budget restrictions as long as we can show results.'

'That's good, but I must warn you, I've only told David here the bare details and nothing about what you hope to achieve by his being here.' It seemed to take the wind out of Reynard's sails, but only for a moment.

'Right. Perhaps that's as well for now.'

Chapter 7

'Where to now Bill...sir?' Reynard looked askance at me and winked.

'Bill will do fine David. The army game ended at the old wooden door into this place, and you and I go back a ways. Some people here will address me as sir, but that is merely recognition of my place in the hierarchy. By the way, you'll be putting your rank as major into mothballs shortly.'

We were passing a sentry panel and I let my arm slide over it. This time a huge steel door slid silently open before us. It was a moment before I realised what he had just said.

'But I've only just got it.' I was taken aback; to put it nautically.

'Not to worry, David, it will not affect your pay or status. Like I said, the army game is over; you are now a civilian working in a top secret installation. We know that you are a responsible and conscientious person or you wouldn't be here. There could be times when you can strut the major's crowns; sometimes we need to feed a little British bullshit to foreign nationals, especially those that can hardly walk with the weight of their medals and gold braid. You will be on civil service pay which I'm sure you'll find quite substantial and you'll find that you'll be able to choose your own accommodation in the outside world.' He held out his hand. 'Welcome aboard shipmate. And now I'm going to show you a ship that you've never seen the like of before.' All the while he was talking we were walking within a large hangar; we stopped in the centre. A door opened in one of the side walls and walking towards us was yet another vaguely familiar face. His lanky six foot frame headed straight for Bill Reynard. He acknowledged me with a slight nod before giving his full attention to him. I knew I had definitely seen him somewhere.

'I understand you want it brought up sir?'

'Yes please.' Reynard turned to introduce me. 'This is David Kent; he'll be working with me for a while. David, this is Major Derek Collins, retired.'

Another retired major. I took the proffered hand and shook it, all the while groping mentally; where had I seen this crew-cut six-footer before?

He was aware of my puzzlement.

'Hi! 2nd Lieutenant Derek Collins, Intelligence Corp Cyprus 1951. I don't think we were ever formally introduced.'

I remembered then. I was being quizzed by the CO with regard to my future if I signed on and extended my army service. He had suggested that the future was in electronics and that I should seriously think of taking courses in that. It didn't appeal much at the time; I was only a wireless operator special with the vaguest idea of how the sets I operated actually worked. In the latter years of my service I hadn't done much of that, being mainly employed in instructing the up and coming. Better brains than mine at that time were still grappling with what they were still calling the electronic brain.

'You were taking notes at my interview with the CO at 2 Wireless?'

'That's right, you were quite impressive. I thought at the time that someone might have persuaded you to switch from Sigs to I Corp.'

'I was never approached.' I must have looked as puzzled as I felt.

'That's typical, someone obviously filed my notes in the bin, or you would have been well up the promotion ladder before now. Anyway you're here now and I'm sure that what you are about to see will interest you.' He removed small keypad from his pocket, similar to the one Ganymede had used at doors, and fiddled with the buttons as he came and stood beside us. I watched fascinated as a great rectangle of the hangar floor descended out of sight before us. Reynard gave a reassuring wink as I looked at him. Machinery whirred softly from the void below as the lift, or whatever it was, made its return journey. When it came to a stop I was looking at something that made my mouth go into fly-catching mode.

'What the fuck is that?' I couldn't help it. It was Derek Collins who supplied the answer, but I was hardly the wiser.

'It's the most modern flying machine you'll ever see David.' Beside me Bill Reynard grunted and Collins glanced quickly in his direction before adding. 'At least for the time being.'

'How the hell does it fly?' I stared at it with disbelief. 'It's got no wings or rotors.' I started to walk around it but I could see already that there was no evidence of a propulsion system; it was just a circular disc shaped object that could conceivably be some form of giant casserole dish.

51

I had been doing a bit of homework and had read some literature on new concepts concerning flight being developed in the States since Kennedy promised to get a man on the moon by the end of the decade. Like many others, I had filed that in what I fondly considered my Hollywood dream box, especially after seeing pictures of what appeared to be an unreliable flying contraption nicknamed the Flying Bedstead. Nevertheless questions tumbled through my mind and found voice. 'Where's it from?'

'It was made here, in the Complex,' said Reynard.

I touched it. It was cold but I felt it becoming warm under my hand, I snatched it hurriedly away and I looked from one to the other.

'What's it made of?' They were both looking at me with mild amusement.

'This is made of a form of plastic called dense polystyrene.' Collins looked towards Reynard who gave a nod of approval. 'It's a replica made from blue prints we were supplied with by the Americans.'

'So what is it a replica of exactly?'

'This is the kind of machine that the Yanks have recovered from crash sites in New Mexico. It is this type of craft that is continuously being reported in our skies.'

'So it does actually fly?'

Reynard gave a derisive snort.

'This one doesn't. Like Collins said, it's a replica. The Yanks are still trying to analyse the metals used in the construction of these things. It's really weird stuff, almost paper thin but it has incredible strength; flexible too.'

'You say this one doesn't fly, does that mean there are some that do ... I mean apart from the crashed ones?'

'Our intelligence at the moment is that yes they have built a machine like this that does fly, and they have back-engineered a propulsion system. We suspect, suspect mind you, that they have received help on this from a source that we can at present only speculate on.'

'From the people that actually fly around in these things?'

Reynard shrugged.

'The strength of that speculation is based on how we view the alleged meeting between Eisenhower and those alien visitors.'

'I see.' The words didn't really clarify anything much in my mind. In fact the immensity of what appeared to be going on in

52

this world behind closed doors, and of which people in the outside world were totally ignorant of, tended to have a numbing effect on what little grey matter I possessed. I certainly wasn't ready for what came next.

'How would you feel about coming face to face with an extraterrestrial being David?' I looked at both in turn. Reynard was serious, unsmiling. I detected a flicker of amusement on Collins' face.

'I...I'm not sure.' I wondered if they were having me on, I decided to play along. 'I've no doubt that it would be an interesting experience, I suppose it's something you can arrange?' It was a facetious remark and his face hardened a little.

'It depends how far you are prepared to go to cooperate.' Not for the first time did I wonder where all this was leading; cooperate in what? His face relaxed into neutral again. 'If you will be in my office first thing after lunch tomorrow then, David, I'd very much appreciate it. We'll finish up here, and Collins will show you how to get out of this section. With that he walked away to disappear through the doorway from which Collins had emerged.

The gleaming silver, non-flying machine, descended out of sight and moments later the floor of the hangar resumed its normal appearance.

'So what's the point of making a replica?' I said after it had gone.

'I asked exactly the same question.' Collins chuckled. 'It just seems an exercise in stupidity.'

'And what was the answer?'

'Simply something to add to the confusion. Officially these things do not exist. The idea is to plant this thing in an area where there has been a reported sighting. The press and UFO researchers will swarm to the location, and then two men in silver suits will appear on the scene, pick it up, and walk around with it. Big joke. UFO debunkers jumping for joy.'

'I see, and the general public getting more deeply into the hoax syndrome?'

'That's right. The Americans have already set up a string of these deceptions or similar that has proved after investigation to be a hoax. One of the main problems these days is that there are so many reports that even with a little ingenuity anyone can fabricate a sighting or an encounter, or even abduction.'

'I see, so where do you stand in all this, the reports, the rumours, the uncertainties?' He grinned and shrugged.

'I just get on with the job David, and try to keep an open mind.' It sounded like good advice.

After leaving Collins I made my way back to Ganymede's office, which appeared to have become my second home, and sat down to ponder on these things I was continually witnessing. There was a lot to think about. It was late by the time I realised he was unlikely to turn up again that day. I headed for the cafeteria. I looked around half hopeful, but there was no sign of Genna Rees. To add to the disappointment hot food had finished for the day and I had to settle for ham rolls and coffee.

Ganymede still hadn't put in an appearance when I got back to the hut, and there was still no sign of him when I settled down for the night.

**

Back in Ganymede's office next morning, I found he hadn't arrived yet. I sat down to await his appearance. I must have dozed off. I looked at my watch as I came awake and breathed a sigh of relief. There was still no sign of my guv'nor. I wondered where he had got to; he never missed meals. But I still had time to eat before my meeting with Bill Reynard.

The cafeteria was only sparsely populated but I spotted Genna of the laser ID in a far corner, alone. She looked up and smiled; I decided not to eat alone. As I approached she indicated an empty chair. I took it to be a welcome gesture and slid my plate onto the table and sat down. I was glad to see she was only a little way into her meal.

'Hello David Kent.' I was met with bright blue eyes and the hint of a lopsided smile, and she had remembered my name; it was all pluses.

'Hi Genna.' I had already rated her attractive, but because she had been in uniform and I was groggy during our previous meeting I had failed to appreciate how attractive she really was.

'How are you settling in?'

'In a very unsettled way actually, there's a lot to take in.'

'So I believe.'

'You sound as if you're not acquainted with some of it.'

'My clearance doesn't cover some of the restricted areas.'

'Then I'd better be careful what I say.' Her smile went impish; it made her look even more attractive, if that were possible.

'Of course, I could be a Russian spy.'

'That's ridiculous you wouldn't have got in here.'

'Perhaps I'm a very good and resourceful Russian spy.'

'Well whatever you are, you're a very pretty one.' I turned to my meal, her rising blush made it plain I had embarrassed her. She remained silent for a while. I looked up at her; I wanted to make amends. 'It was meant as a compliment, I'm not on the make,' I said. I took refuge in my meal again.

'That's okay David, you're not so bad yourself.' She laughed then, and it eased the tension.

What we needed was some common ground as to what we could talk about. According to her she was new here, that made two of us.

'How about if you told me what you know about the place and that might give me some idea of what I can talk about.'

'Well you don't have to be particularly bright to know it's not concerned with what we call ordinary things in life.' I nodded agreement. 'I get the idea that it's got something to do with what happened in America back in 1947,' she said.

'So you know about that?'

'I have a cousin who lives in Florida. He wrote me of rumours that were circulating about some weird incidents that occurred in New Mexico at that time. That was it really, it was never mentioned again.'

'Considering it almost immediately went under wraps it's not surprising. I've only just heard about it for the first time since I arrived here. I still don't know if I'm free to talk about it. What else do you know or could have a good guess at?'

'My cousin has said that there are things going on in the north of the state.'

'Like, for instance?'

'Rocket launching for instance. There's talk that they've got German scientists, the ones that developed the V2 rockets at the tail end of the war working on rockets that will eventually reach the moon.'

'President Kennedy is looking that way I believe. From what I've already seen here perhaps it's not quite the pipe dream I thought it was.'

Talking and eating had brought us both to the end of our meal. I was reluctant to leave at this stage but my meeting with Reynard was closing in.

'Look Genna, I'd like to continue this later if that's okay with you but...' I glanced at my watch, '... I've a meeting with someone in about ten minutes.'

'I'd like that too David.' She raised a hand in a gesture of farewell as I rose to leave. I didn't know that it would be quite a while before I would see her again.

Chapter 8

'How are things, are you settling in all right?

I was seeing Reynard again for the first time since my meeting with the strange flying machine.

'It's all a bit strange, not like anything I've experienced before.' The question, I could see, was merely to put me at ease. I hoped he wouldn't continue with something as twee as a comment on the weather; he didn't.

'I have a confession to make David.' That surprised me, he'd never seemed the confessing type.

From the depths of an extremely comfortable recliner chair I heard the words and waited for what came next. Whatever Bill Reynard was about to confess certainly was not reflected in his face with any measure of contriteness; he was actually smiling. 'Years ago when we were at sea together, I hypnotised you.'

'It didn't work though, did ...' He interrupted

'It did David, but it scared the shit out of me at the time, I couldn't believe what I was hearing.'

I couldn't imagine Bill Reynard being particularly scared of anything much. It was my turn to smile, if only weakly. I had always been convinced that the hypnosis hadn't worked.

'So what actually happened?' I wasn't too sure that I wanted to hear what had been so frightening, but I knew I was going to anyway. He hunched forward in his seat resting his forearms on his knees.

'I don't know how much Ganymede has told you.'

'Something between very little and bugger all really. He said you would explain what this is all about.' I decided not to mention what he'd said about the telepathy, I wanted to hear it from the man himself.

'Of course. Ganymede on occasion can be the soul of discretion. Right then ...,' He relaxed back into his chair. '... Carnarvon Castle 1948, homeward bound from Capetown. After a little encouragement and a few beers in the 'Pig and Whistle' you agreed to let me hypnotise you. We sought the peace and quiet of the rope locker on D deck where we wouldn't be disturbed.' I laughed.

'I'm sure there were some in the Pig who gave a nod and a wink thinking we were off for a bit of shirt lifting.' Reynard fielded that with a chuckle.

'Well she was carrying quite a cargo of queers, if I remember. Anyway you went into trance almost immediately and that was a bit of a surprise for a start; it was the first time I'd ever tried to hypnotise anyone.'

'How come you knew how to go about it?' I didn't quite know what to say, it rattled me a bit. I'd always believed it hadn't worked.

'I had an uncle who was in the Royal Navy at the outbreak of the war. He was great with his sea stories to us kids and he told me about a guy on one ship he was on who used to hypnotise crew members into performing incredible feats of strength. He was a marine; he thought his name was Casson. It was mainly for a bit of fun and entertainment, but I found the idea fascinating.'

I had of course heard of Peter Casson from an ex RN bloke that I had sailed with during my time in the Merchant Navy. Apparently it was the same bloke who was now running what I'd heard described as greatest hypnotic stage show since Mesmer, but I remained silent, this was Reynard's story.

'At first I wasn't sure how to handle it. Here I was with a subject in trance and I didn't have a script.' He grinned, obviously recalling the situation. 'I fooled around for a bit, got you to pick your nose, do a few press ups, that sort of thing.'

'Hardly anything scary in that,' I said.

'Up until then no, but then I decided for some strange reason to try and take you back through the years to your childhood.' I laughed.

'And that was scary? I think my dad sometimes referred to me as a little horror.'

'No, it wasn't until I started to ask you questions about what you were experiencing at certain ages. It was at the age of four that it appeared to go off the wall; you seemed to get quite agitated and reluctant to tell me what was happening.'

'I've no way of knowing what I was doing at that age; that was donkey's years ago.'

'Of course, but in trance you had a total recall of quite a remarkable event that took place. I can say remarkable now, but at the time it really put the wind up me. I couldn't figure out what it was all about then, so I brought you out without you remembering once again what had occurred. I say again because up until then you yourself had already blanked it out successfully.'

'You think there was a reason for me doing that, it was something horrible?' He appeared thoughtful and he leaned towards me once more.

'In view of what we have discovered since, with this space vehicle phenomenon and alien beings, not in itself horrible, although to some it might seem so.'

He was still some way from making any sense. Was he at this point reluctant to let me in on my remarkable experience at the tender age of four; and what had all this space vehicle and alien beings to do with it?

'What are you trying to tell me Bill? Come on, if it was scary back then it wouldn't necessarily be scary now, would it?'

'Not necessarily I suppose, it would depend largely on what the individual would be prepared to accept.'

'Try me.'

'Okay. At the age of four you were visited by someone or something that was not of this world. It appeared in your bedroom while you were still in a waking state. You weren't particularly scared although whatever it was might not have resembled any human you were acquainted with at that time.'

'So I was in my bedroom with a strange creature and I wasn't particularly scared. Why can't I remember it?'

'I'm not sure. We have some knowledge of similar encounters and we are beginning to think that perhaps these beings are not unlike the EBE you saw at the lecture; they appear to be benevolent, but are able in some way to remove any memory of their visit; actually blanking out the whole episode.'

'So what is the point of the visit?'

'We believe, indeed we hope, their purpose is simply to share knowledge and information.'

'And then leave you with no memory of it, that doesn't make sense.'

'It remains in your subconscious David.'

'Where it remains, out of reach.'

'Not at all.' He suddenly became quite serious and leaned towards me again. 'Under hypnosis we can recover those memories. I got a glimpse of that back there at sea. You actually had a conversation with your bedroom visitor.'

'We spoke to each other?'

'Not in as many words.' He saw he had lost me and decided to be more specific. 'It was a telepathic conversation; you could read each other's minds.'

59

'I can't do that; I'm not in the least telepathic.'

'But you were then and I think you could be again, that's why you are here David, in this place at this time.' There was no mistaking his excitement. An obvious thought occurred to me.

'Is that something to do with this hidden ability of mine that people have been on about?' He nodded and leaned forward to emphasise what he had to say.

'I would like to re-acquaint you with that ability David. It would be invaluable in the project we are engaged in here.'

'And how do you propose to do that; re-acquaint me?' I suspected that I already knew at least half the answer to that.

'I'd like to take you back to that four-year- old period.'

'Hypnotise me again?' His nod confirmed what I anticipated.

'And if as you say, you could re-awaken this ability of mine, what then? Ganymede said locating me and drafting me into this set up was the result of an idea you had while you were in America.' He remained silent for a while before answering.

'That's true David, but I'd like to put that to one side until we see how things turn out. Are you prepared to cooperate in the experiment?'

'Do I have a choice?'

'What do you think?'

'Can I have time to think about it?'

'Take all you need, it's your play. We are going to make history here David and I'd like to think you'll be part of it.' There was no doubting the sincerity in his voice; I knew I would have to go through with it.

Next day I was back in his recliner, drawn by the same curiosity that supposedly killed the cat; I hoped it wouldn't be the death of me.

Chapter 9

'Where are you now?'

'I'm ... there are lots of trees.' It was my voice; it seemed distant, disembodied.

'What kind of trees?'

'I'm not sure.'

'If you were sure, what kind of trees would they be?'

'Just ordinary trees. It feels familiar here... I think I know this place'

'You've been there before?'

'Yes.'

How old are you?'

'I'm five,'

'How do you know that; are you sure?'

'I started at school today.'

'What is your name?'

'David.'

'Is there anyone there with you?'

'No, I am in my bed for the night.'

'I thought you were in the woods.'

'No I am in my bed.'

'I see...Are you alone there?'

'Yes.'

'How old are you?'

'Four, I think.'

'Now listen carefully David. I am going to move you forward in time one hour by counting down from 3. 3—2 – 1. It is now one hour later, tell me what you see now.'

'It is dark...there is only a little light from a street lamp outside.'

'There is no one else in the room with you?'

'No. I'm tired, I want to sleep.'

'Stay with me David. I am going to move you forward one hour more. 3 – 2 – 1. What do you see now?'

'It's the same as before.'

'Right. Now I want you to move to a time when something is happening in the room, something entirely different to what normally occurs there, do you understand?'

'Yes.'

'Fine. I will count down again and you will be there. I want you to remember all that happens when I return you to the everyday. 3 – 2 – 1. What is happening now?'

'The room is filled with light and someone is standing at the foot of my bed.'

'Can you tell me who is standing at the foot of your bed, is it someone you know?'

'It is a friend of mine; I see him when I'm playing in the garden sometimes.'

'I see. Do you know how he came to be in your bedroom?

'… He just turns up at odd times when I'm out playing usually. I look up and there he is.'

'Is the light in the room daylight?'

'I'm not sure; I don't think so.'

'So why is your friend there at this time?'

'I think he has something to tell me.'

'What do you and your friend usually talk about?'

'He doesn't actually say words like me.'

'So …wow! How do you speak with each other?'

'With our thoughts … I think.'

'Bloody hell…'

It was then that I became aware of being back in the recliner in Reynard's room. Ganymede was standing behind his chair, they were both grinning widely. It was taking me a little while to re-adjust.

'I think we could mark that one a success.' He was talking to Reynard but I felt he was including me.

'Even more than I could have hoped for. How do you feel David?'

'Not too bright. That was some experience.'

'You remember it then.' He appeared quite satisfied.

'Yes.'

'All of it?'

'More than I was able to tell you at the time, the mental exchange was fast; phenomenal.'

'So what was it about?' Ganymede came from behind the chair.

'It was mainly about me and what I'm doing here. They knew way back then where I was heading even if I didn't.'

'They. Who are they?

'His people I guess, I always knew he wasn't of this Earth. He seemed able to appear and disappear at will.'

62

'He said it depended on the people involved here as to whether this project would be beneficial to mankind. He told me there were people I could trust, but there would be times I should watch my back.' Reynard turned to Ganymede.

'What do you make of that Bill?'

'There's always an odd one in the woodpile.'

Ganymede looked thoughtful as he turned back to me.

'You will let me know if you get a premonition or even the feeling that someone is not a straight shooter here David?'

'Of course guv. I'll watch your back and Bill's too, as long as you both keep an eye on mine? They both laughed.

'So be it, In the meantime David I'd like to follow up on this again as soon as possible. You did jump about a bit in your recall, both age-wise and in location, but that does happen occasionally. I think we might be able to crack this and open up your ability to converse telepathically again.'

'You really think that's possible?'

'Let's just say that I wouldn't put money on it right now, but I have very high hopes; the potential is definitely there.'

'You mean I might be able to read minds?'

'Not necessarily, I think it has to be a two way thing and both parties need to be on the same wavelength?

'Right.' There goes the slim hope that I might get a chance to read Genna's, I thought.

Reynard got up, the session was over. He put a hand on Ganymede's shoulder.

'Can I have David for a few days to keep this rolling?'

'I've nothing definitely planned for him right now sir, and after all he is here for your reasons rather than mine.' Reynard appeared to accept that as no more than his due and turned to me.

'Right David, Tomorrow then, same time, unless something untoward occurs.' I wondered why there was the merest exchange of a glance between them.

'Time's your own David.' Ganymede said as I was leaving. He remained behind and I got a strange feeling they had something to discuss that was not for my ears. Or was it just me? I had never before considered the possibility that I was in any way neurotic. I set out for the cafeteria. Hunger was my excuse, but a chance meeting with Genna was the main reason.

There was no sign of her in the cafeteria and I realised that she hadn't been around for a day or two. Perhaps she had assignments elsewhere; it was no consolation, I felt miffed. I had taken to eating in the cafeteria in preference to the austere facilities in the camp or the messroom in the Complex. It had a friendlier atmosphere, and was as Ganymede had said an excellent meeting place. I felt more a part of things there.

On my way back to the billet in the fading light I was surprised to see that the cookhouse and dining room appeared to be boarded up. Puzzled I walked past the billet I was sharing with Ganymede from which the only light in the camp glowed from the windows. I carried on across the scrap of parade ground to the main gate. It was bolted and barred. I tried the guardroom door which was closed, that was also locked. Not for the first time did I wonder what kind of a merry-go-round I was on. Perhaps Ganymede had some answers, it was about time somebody did.

He was flaked out in his usual position on his bed as I entered the hut. His belongings were heaped at the foot of it. From the look on my face I didn't need to ask him what was going on.

'They have closed the camp down David.' 'We won't be using it any more. As far as the general public are concerned it will be a contaminated, no go area. It will be isolated completely from the Complex and as far as the world outside is concerned they never have and never will know of its existence.'

'What about my freedom to choose where I want to live?' I felt the edge of panic, it felt like I'd let myself in for a jail term. Isolated, locked in. 'How do I get in and out this place, visit the pub, take in a movie, mix with ordinary people and return to sanity now and then?' He waved his hand in a familiar gesture of dismissal.

'Don't get in flap David everything is provided for. We have a nice little office in the village from which we can come and go as we please without arousing suspicion. It's an information bureau actually with an extensive ground floor and a first floor club and bar solely for the use of our personnel who don't particularly want to use the village facilities. It is connected by a tunnel like the ones we use to get around the Complex.'

'Well that's a relief, I thought for a moment I was doomed to serve a life sentence down there.'

'No in basic terms you're as free as a bird and it might not be long before we have you flying like one.'

'How do you mean?' He tapped his nose and raised the finger.

64

'All in good time David. Meantime just get your gear together and get your head down, we are out of here first thing tomorrow.'

As I settled down for the night I was in half a mind to mention Genna's absence, but I doubted that it would be any concern of Ganymede's anyway. Perhaps, as I first thought, she had business elsewhere. I knew very little about her really. She might already be attached. The only thing I could be certain of was the attraction she had for me. I felt distinctly smitten.

Chapter 10

'Is this the place?' Reynard eased himself down onto a carpet of beech leaves and rested his back against the trunk of the parent tree. It was his suggestion that we come to the spot where my experience as an infant had taken place. We had passed the hamlet where I had grown up a hundred yards or so down where the track led into the woods. 'I'm surprised your parents let you play up here so young.'

'I suppose they were safer times Bill, it was a tight-knit rural community; it still is.'

'Everyone knew one another and what went on here. I can understand that, a dodgy looking stranger would stand out. Tell me about the first time your playmate appeared here.'

'I was sat over there.' I pointed to where a stream ran through the wood a few yards away. 'I used to sit on the bank watching for minnows. It seemed wider then.' I laughed. 'It's barely a trickle now.'

'Everything is big when you're little, go on.'

'I saw a face staring up at me from the water; it made me jump. Then I heard a voice. I looked up and there he was sitting across from me.'

'He spoke to you?' Reynard was leaning forward and looking at me rather oddly.

'Well that's the funny bit; the words seemed to be in my head.'

'So you saw his reflection in the water first, you didn't see or hear him arrive?'

'That's right.'

'You say you jumped, were you scared?'

'No, more surprised. I can't remember feeling threatened; he meant me no harm, I seemed to know that.'

'Did he say for you not to be afraid; in your head?'

'I don't know. He was about my age, I felt we were friends. Thinking back it all seems rather like some sort of dream ...' Reynard was shaking his head.

'That was no dream David, that really happened, you just found yourself linked into another reality. Have you realised what you are actually doing right now?'

'What do you mean?' I wondered why he was beaming brighter than the winter sun that cast faint shadows off the bare trees.

66

'You are recalling all this without being in a trance state; you are not hypnotised.'

'Then how...'

'I wish I knew, I don't have all the answers, but for a moment there you had a spontaneous recall of your first meeting with ... did he have a name by the way?' I shook my head. I wasn't sure what he was on about; it was if a spell had been broken, he noticed my concern.

'Something wrong David?'

I wondered if I could explain, he obviously wanted an answer. I needed to try.

'I know why we are here Bill, I remember my meeting with ...' I paused grappling with the memory. 'We didn't seem to need names, and I remember we didn't use words to communicate. I think that when you said that I wasn't in trance my mind just blanked.'

He appeared to consider that, and then he stood up and rubbed his backside with both hands.

'I don't know about you, but I'm getting cold here. Is there a pub in this hamlet of yours?'

'The Plough, real ale and home cooking if I remember.'

'Come on then I'm getting a local call that I'm hungry.'

**

He put the car in gear and drove out from the forecourt. We had dozed by the log fire after steak and ale pie, I seem to have become addicted to the stuff, and a pint of best bitter, and I was still half dozy; I wound the window down a shade just enough feel the chill air on my face.

'I think it's showing real promise David.'

'The pub or the wood?'

'Both.' He chuckled. 'I would certainly like to do the pub again,'

'And the wood?'

'That was bloody interesting. I need to give that some thought, we may come back to that at a later date, but in the meantime I would like to continue with the regression programme. We are breaking into something new here David.'

'What, the telepathy?'

'Oh, that's not new, well in us perhaps, but animals use it all the time. Have you ever watched films of the way lions stalk and ambush their prey; they work as a team with never a sound passing between them.'

67

'I have yes, but it never really occurred to me. I stood on Brighton sea front once at dusk and watched thousands of starlings performing an aerial ballet, is that the same thing?'

'Maybe David, maybe. I think we have a lot to learn. Somewhere along the line I believe we've lost the ability to communicate with the natural world. We are so wrapped up in believing we have a monopoly on intelligence. There is ample evidence now that we share this world, and the universe, with beings that are far more intelligent than we imagine ourselves to be.'

I shut the window again; enough was enough of the chill December air.

'Where is all this leading Bill; this UFO business and visitations from aliens and what goes on with the Complex and what the Yanks are doing?'

'It's leading to the exploration of space David. To taking a walk on the moon; finding out if it is possible to row a boat on a Martian canal. I think in the main though it's about coming to terms with our neighbours or more importantly perhaps, that they are as much a part of creation as we are.'

'Long live Dan Dare and the Mekon.' I looked across at him. He didn't appear to share my amusement.

'All is probable, even possible David. You have already had your eyes opened; this is not the time to close them again.'

They were words that would ring in my ears for a great many years to come.

Chapter 11

A Mental Journey

My outside accommodation was fixed up in surprisingly short
time. The flat on the first floor of a semi-detached, brick built,
turn of the century house afforded all I required in the way of
conveniences. Located at one end of the village in easy distance
of both the railway station and the information bureau, it had a
large living room furnished with a three-piece suite of
indeterminate vintage and shelves set in recesses alongside the
fireplace. The bedroom was just big enough to take a double bed
and a wardrobe and a blanket chest, and still without banging
elbows on the walls, a bedside locker. The place had received
some modernisation, and the rear room had been fitted as a
kitchen and extended sufficiently to accommodate a bathroom
and toilet. Access was through the front door and up the stairs to
my very first own front door.

It was cold, only just above freezing when I moved in, which
took some of the shine off things. I lit the gas fire in the living
room and realised I would have to invest in a couple of electric
fires for the rest of my warmth and comfort over the coming
winter months. Initially there would be a healthy dent in my
finances.

I mentioned this to Bill Reynard soon after I was once more
back in his comfortable recliner.

'Not to worry David, the department can give you a loan and
supply any additional comforts until you get straight and get
some sort of budget working.'

'Really?'

'Yes really. I don't think you realise what a potentially
valuable property you are; we all are.'

'You still think you can bring out the telepath in me?'

'There is a distinct possibility. While I was away I had a
chance to discuss your case with a regression therapist and a
clairvoyant, there is a link between clairvoyance and telepathy
you know.'

'No I didn't, in fact I don't know much about these things or
how they work. I've heard that spiritualists say they can talk to
the dead, and mediums can tell you things that only you could
possibly know about. You did some of that before you

hypnotised me at sea. I've heard that you can do other things too.' He looked at me strangely.

'Who told you that, Ganymede?' My face confirmed it. 'What exactly did he tell you?'

'He said you can project your mind out of your body and be somewhere else.' It sounded a bit daft even as I said it.

'With practice it is possible for most people to do it, it's called remote viewing.'

'Be somewhere you ain't.' Even coming from him it sounded a bit daft; I kept a straight face. He straightened up from what he was doing and came around the desk towards me. I looked for any sign of annoyance; there was none, he just sat down on a chair beside me and picked up his notebook. I genuinely hoped I would again see my childhood friend. He said something and then his voice sounded far off.

'I'm going to count down from three,' '3 – 2 – 1.' I was drifting, and Reynard's voice sounded soft, soothing, and distant.

'Where are you now?'

'I'm in a vehicle of some kind; a bus, I think.'

'Are you going somewhere, is the bus on the move?'

'Yes.'

'Are there others on the bus with you?'

'It is quite crowded.'

'Good. Do you know any of those present, are they familiar to you?'

'No I do not recognise any of them. They are mostly military personnel, officers, and other ranks but there are some civilians too. They are not people I know. I feel they are mostly Americans but there are conversations being conducted in other languages.'

'I see. Do you know where you are going?'

'I'm not sure but there is an air of expectation in here.'

'Where do you think you are, what kind of countryside are you passing through?'

'I … don't know… the windows are all blacked out; it's most odd.'

'Okay, okay David. I'm going to take you forward in time to your destination. 3 – 2 – 1, you are now at your destination, what do you see?'

'I have left the bus and we are heading out towards … some sort of craft … it's … like the one I was shown in the Complex!'

'Easy David. Is it the same or just similar?'

'Similar, much bigger.'

'Look around you, tell me what else you see; take your time.'

'There are military type vehicles and tents, two of them. It appears to be a very barren place, very little vegetation.'

'Are you able to approach the craft that you have been brought to see there?'

'No. That is cordoned off. Several have tried to duck under the tapes, mostly the civilians, but have been herded back at gunpoint.

'David. Listen carefully; I want you to do something for me. Duck under the tape and move a few paces towards the craft. ...'

'But I'll be spotted.'

'Trust me David. You will come to no harm there. Have you done that?'

'Yes.'

'Good. Is there any response from those guarding it?'

'No. They look my way occasionally but don't seem to be much interested.'

'That's because they can't see you. I want you to approach the craft and take a good look all around it ... Tell me what you see...'

'It's a disc-shaped craft like the mock- up but this one is big; at least 100 feet across with what looks an observation dome on top.'

'Are there any access points, can you get inside?'

'The surface is smooth, unbroken.'

'Take your time, walk all the way around it.'

'Ha! Ha!'

'What is funny?'

'I nearly bumped into one of those guarding it, we are face to face, and he is quite unaware.'

'Pass him by; is there still no sign of access?'

'Oh wow!'

'What are you seeing?'

'The whole of this side is smashed in, badly damaged.'

'Can you see inside?'

'No, they've blocked off what might be an opening.'

'Okay David, you're doing fine. You said there are tents, can you take a look in them and tell me what you see ...?'

'One looks like it might be used as a mess tent, there are several people eating at tables there.'

'What about the other one ...?'

71

'Oh my god!'

'What is it?'

'A body. It's on a table, I think it's dead.'

'Why do you think that?'

'There are people there, poking it around, and discussing it.'

'Will you move in and take a close look at the body; tell me what you see …?'

'It is still alive, but in a pretty bad way. There is what looks like others but they are covered and placed against the tent wall. I don't like it here …'

'That's okay David, I'll bring you back, you will have total recall of this experience … 3 – 2 – 1.'

I was back in the reclining chair with a headache. Reynard was standing over me, grinning. He looked as happy as a dog with two cocks.

'How do you feel David?' How indeed. I couldn't understand what had happened to me.

'Where was that?' What did it have to do with my so-called telepathic abilities?'

'A great deal; more than I could have hoped for.'

'I went somewhere, saw things, crazy things.' Reynard was shaking his head.

'You never went anywhere David you've been here along with me all the time, you were just picking up on everything that I saw on my last trip to the States, we linked David, we linked telepathically.' He was over the moon and I felt as if the moon was actually affecting me; what the hell was he babbling on about?

'You mean you were actually in that place and saw those things; the craft and the bodies?' He nodded, beaming like he'd just bedded the girl of his dreams.

'And in trance you picked up on it; we communicated David; or you did.'

'We were on the same wavelength then.' He seemed to consider that and then shook his head.

'It wasn't exactly two way David. You were hypnotised, in trance, and able to tune in to my experience there. I confess that I am at a loss to explain it. All I can say is that it happened, how or why is beyond me. There are obviously phenomena that still remain to be explained, roads we yet have to travel. I think we should wrap up now and leave something for another day.

**

I sensed they had been discussing me when I walked in on them. Ganymede's face was set serious and Reynard appeared considerably sobered from the day before, but they both had that guilty look. I stood uncertain.

'Sorry I didn't ....'

They exchanged glances, as if in unspoken agreement and turned back to me.

'Take a seat David.' Ganymede waved towards a vacant chair and looked again at Reynard who gave a barely perceptible nod.

'Yesterday's session David, it wasn't an unqualified success. Oh it proved that you are capable of receiving transmitted thoughts and that's a plus.'

I suppose I had been feeling on a bit of a high because of the experience of picking up on Reynard's thoughts, Ganymede's words brought me down a tad.

'There's a minus?'

'Not a serious one. Given time we may well overcome it. The point is Bill is not a telepath, it was a one way thing; you were reading his mind.'

'Isn't that what you were aiming for?'

'Only partially, and don't forget you were under hypnosis, it wasn't a spontaneous, conscious telepathic communication, which is what we are hoping for.'

'Back to the drawing board then.' I was surprised at feeling more than a little deflated.

'Not completely David.' Reynard took over. 'Let's just say there's a little more than halfway to go. You can receive even better than we could have hoped for, what we need is someone who can conduct a two-way conversation.'

'How will that be possible?'

'That's what we were discussing when you came in.' Ganymede interceded. 'We are working on it. Take a few days off David. Relax; do your own thing, we'll give you a bell when we come up with something.'

It sounded like a good idea, real time to myself. I wondered where Genna had got to; she hadn't been in evidence for several days now. I seemed to be on overload and time was out the door. It would have been nice to get to know her outside of this place.

'I've still a few things to sort out at the apartment; the décor is suffering a lack of imagination.'

'That's fine, but don't feel you need to be housebound.' He took something from a drawer in his desk and handed it to me.

'Here, you might as well have one of these; if it buzzes head for the Complex.'

I looked at it and turned it over. It was about the size of a cigarette packet and made of something like black Bakelite.

'What is it?'

'The American's call it a ... page boy?' He looked at Reynard for confirmation.

'A pager actually. They'll be on the market in about ten years. It has a good range David it will keep us in touch. We need to continue with the regressions too.'

Chapter 12

On looking around the décor of the flat I decided that perhaps I could live with it a bit longer, I had other things on my mind that needed attention. I needed more information on this UFO thing in order not to feel always at a loss with some of the things going on in the Complex. It was to that end that I spent the first afternoon of my time off scouring the local library and browsing among the magazine racks of local newsagents.

The outcome resulted in me settling down for the evening with bottle and glass, a publication called FATE magazine and a book by someone named Arthur C Clarke from the library. It was not the title, 'Childhood's End' that attracted me but the quirky coincidence of Arthur C and how it related to Ganymede's natural father.

In the course of consuming well over a third of my bottle of Glenfiddich I gleaned a considerable insight, thanks to a Walter Germain, into clairvoyance and telepathy and extra -sensory perception.

Arthur C Clarke's contribution I could have read well into the night but for the influence of the whisky on my eyelids. But up until the time when I actually dropped off I was enthralled by his imaginative tale of friendly visitations of beings from space. It tells of a peaceful invasion inasmuch as it is designed to eradicate wars, and bring about a world free of dissention, in short to prevent humanity from self-destruction due to the escalation of atomic weaponry.

I wondered how much the author's imagination had been triggered by UFO sightings and the things that were allegedly happening in the United Sates. On waking late the following morning and feeling as hung-over and depressed as the weather which beat relentlessly against my bedroom window from a leaden, December sky, I decided nevertheless to finish Clarke's book in the comfort of the bed.

Rising seemed hazardous, and the idea of breakfast, for the moment anyway, caused a sensation in my stomach best described as extremely unsettled. It was noon when I finally emerged fully into the land of the living.

I fixed myself some cheese on toast. It was years since I'd had to find my own meals and that and beans-on-toast was roughly the limit of my expertise in that direction. I daringly added several bacon rashers to the assortment. It was in the middle of what the Americans, ever inclined to introduce new words for, refer to as brunch that there was a knock at the door. Placing my half eaten meal under the still warm grill I plodded downstairs to open the door to a bedraggled and soaked semblance of Derek Collins.

'I was out and about,' he said by way of explanation. 'I got caught in this lot, thought I might beg a bit of warmth and a cuppa.'

He sat quietly nursing and sipping the mug of coffee I provided him while I finished the rest of my meal. Between sips he passed the time gazing idly around the room. He waited until I had poured the remainder of the coffee pot into my own mug before he asked.

'Has anyone else visited you since you moved in David?'

'No, why do you ask?'

'Just wondered, that's all.' He continued to let his eyes wander the room. I was beginning to feel that there was something I wasn't quite getting when he put down his mug and rose abruptly. 'Is that a new telephone David?' he walked across and picked up the receiver. Now I was sure there was something.

'Why are you here Derek, what's the drum? It's not about being caught out in a rainstorm, is it?

He ignored me and unscrewed one end of the phone and removed the metal diaphragm before putting a finger to his lips and offering it to me. I looked at it and raised my eyes inquiringly. He shook his head and put his finger once more to his lips before reassembling the receiver and replacing it in its cradle. He then led me by the elbow from the room closing the door softly behind us.

'What the fuck is all this about Derek?'

He moved his head so close that for a moment I thought he was going to kiss me. Before I could move my head away he whispered, 'Your phone is bugged.'

'Bugged?'

'Yep. The phone definitely, I don't know whether it covers the whole room.' I turned back to the door intending to open it.

'Then let's get the bloody bug out of there. Why should anyone want to bug me?' He restrained my hand.

'It's the nature of the game David. You're a new boy in a very hush, hush business and they'll keep you under surveillance until they are satisfied you aren't a risk to their operation. If we remove the bug they'll know they've been sussed. He indicated

76

for me to follow him and we passed through the kitchen and into the bathroom.

'We can talk here, bathrooms are difficult to bug, nowhere to hide one and very little in the way of conversations are held here.'

'How did they get to bug me anyway?'

'Did you find this flat off your own bat or did someone recommend it to you?' So that was it, the sanctity of my English castle was compromised before I moved in.

'Philo Makris, some sort of bodyguard.'

'Philo is a man to watch. I have no proof, but I have heard that he is the last person you will see in this life if you are suspected of betraying this organisation.' It sounded unbelievably sinister.

'Why should I want to do that?'

'Who knows what form persuasion might come.' his eyebrows raised. 'Pillow talk is very often more productive that any amount of money.'

'Oh you mean the Soviets would be interested in what goes on here?'

'Very much so. They recruit the prettiest girls; they know the value of a pair of open legs.'

'I have heard.'

'The Americans are also familiar with the same tactics; they have some pretty good-looking dames too.'

I don't know why but Genna sprang to mind. But Collins hadn't quite finished, and it didn't put my mind at rest.

'Us Brits are well versed in dirty tricks too.' He was buttoning his coat as he spoke. It was obvious he had completed what he had come to do and intended to move on.

It occurred to me that, being a mine of information, he might be able to throw some light on Genna Rees' absence.

'Oh, some sort of refresher course, I believe. They are always coming up with some new gadgets or techniques. I think she's back here again tomorrow.' He looked at me, grinning for the first time since he'd arrived. 'Fancy her do you David? No don't answer that. Hope you do better than I did; she turned me down flat.' I remained silent. I sensed his feeling of relief as he changed the subject. 'I wouldn't worry too much about the bug, just take care. When they decide that you're not a security risk they'll come and remove it. Just check it out occasionally, and when they've done the business change your locks.'

'I'll keep that in mind,' I said as he left.

77

The rain had given way to a weak glimmer of sunshine, but the wind still blustered; it needed pressure to push the door closed behind him.

I ignored the beckoning of the Glenfiddich and brewed more coffee; there were things I needed to think about.

I could make no secret of feeling a little uneasy after Collins had left. Being watched was one thing but knowing you are being watched is quite another. I had to assume that only members of the team would know my number; I would keep it that way. I picked up the phone and unscrewed the mouthpiece. The bug was attached by what appeared to be a double-sided sticky pad. I was sorely tempted to remove it and face the consequences, but angry at the intrusion and not a little unnerved by it, I decided to heed Collins' words. But I would never use this phone to make calls out. I would get a new line installed and go ex directory, bugger them! Hell! I was acting like a scared rabbit in a car's headlights not knowing which way to turn, calm down Davey boy. I jumped as the phone jangled.

I stood looking at it for a moment before picking it up.

'Hi there gorgeous, it's me.' It was a male voice, it sounded steeped in liquor and lechery; it irritated.

'Piss off. I'm not your gorgeous.'

'Sorry pal, wrong number.' There was a click and the line went dead. I wondered if it was some sort of a wind up, or maybe a check to see if the bug was working.

It took the rest of the morning before the feeling of vulnerability began to wear off. I had decided to leave things as they were, for the time being anyway. By mid afternoon most of the cloud had given way to a blue sky. The bright sun lacked any vestige of warmth but I decided to go out, if only to get away from the phone for a bit. I picked up Arthur C Clarke's book on my way out. I needed more in the way of real UFO information; everyone in the Complex seemed well up on the subject. A further scouring of the library shelves yielded a big zero so I returned the book and left. What now; time to kill, always the worst part of any day?

An aimless walk along the street produced nothing in the way of inspiration. The cheese on toast and bacon combination was failing to sustain me, so confronted by a tearoom I sought to remedy the situation; it was unexpectedly fruitful.

Quan ling was seated alone at a table for two, she looked up and smiled as I entered and indicated the vacant seat.

'David, how nice, you are looking a little lost.'

'Only up to a moment ago, at a loose end really.' I explained my mission into the village and my need to catch up on the UFO phenomenon.'

'Is it something I can help you with?' Her meal arrived. It was an omelette, fluffy and mouth-watering; I ordered one and a coffee. She nodded approval.

'I come here once a week, just for the omelette.'

'Don't let me interrupt; they are not the same cold.'

She then proved her ability to strike a delicate balance between eating and talking. Only one of the other six tables was occupied and that by an elderly couple well beyond earshot.

'UFO reports are no longer a priority in our work David. Oh we do record those for which there appears to be a definite contact; an actual landing or abduction, but sightings are coming in increasing numbers throughout the world.'

'You make it sound 'old hat'.'

'I think that's because we, that is the Americans and us, have had ongoing contact with space vehicle crews. EBE you know about of course, but there are others who actually have bases on Earth.' She noted my wide-eyed look of amazement and rested her fork. 'This is not the time and place David, for me to go into details. You will get all this from either Ganymede or Bill Reynard at some future date. Meanwhile, rest assured that you are a participant in a reality that people in the street know nothing of.'

My omelette arrived as she finished her own. She drained her coffee and rose. 'I'll leave you to enjoy your meal.' She placed a hand on my shoulder as she rounded the table. 'You don't need to sweat the small stuff David; you will in time, see the bigger picture.' Her face clouded briefly. 'By the way, we never had this conversation; I'm not in the habit of talking out of turn. I'll see you back in the Complex when you're called.'

I watched as she paid her bill and as she passed out into the street; she didn't look back.

My call from the Complex, via the pager, came the next morning, but not from Bill Reynard, It was from Ganymede. The American trip is off David,' he said as I entered his office. 'Bill Reynard has been called away. He apologises and says it's not cancelled, simply postponed.'

I was disappointed but it was because Ganymede who had sent out the call, and I had half expected something else from him. Like where Genna Rees was. I hoped my disappointment didn't show. He searched my face, and just for one fleeting second seemed about to say something but changed his mind.

Instead he handed me a booklet. Apart from a Ministry of Defence logo it had a plain cover, I looked at him enquiringly.

'Computers David. Operators for the use of.' I still looked at him enquiringly. 'The other string to your bow, old chap. You are to be introduced to the vagaries of the electronic data base.'

'Oh well, duty before pleasure, what's that all about?'

'Broadly speaking, the logging, collating, and analysing of UFO reports, encounters, and abductions. A considerable amount of incoming data will be encrypted, but we have people who will deal with that.'

That's how I came to be sitting in the holy of holies with one of the women who had been working on the computers during my grand tour.

Evangeline Frobisher was all that her name suggested. She was a thin and homely woman, already greying, possibly ex WRNS. With the book of words, and under her tuition, I was fully conversant with the data processing function of my computer in a matter of days. I say mine because she disappeared on completion of my tuition. The explanation offered by Ganymede was that along with the other operator who had been absent during my course, she had only been on loan from Bletchley Park.

'It's your baby now David. I'll sit in if you get on overload or when you are otherwise engaged.' He removed papers from a drawer in his desk. 'Here's a couple of things I'd like you to have a read through when you've a spare moment David.' He handed me two slim bundles of stapled A4. I took them and glanced at the titles and then back at him. He explained. 'The first one, The Philadelphia Experiment, is about a wartime experiment in evading radar detection. It went sadly wrong. There were countless rumours and allegations made at the time and over subsequent years. It's a pretty damning document and one you'll need to make up your own mind about. The second one, The Montauk Project is equally sinister and is about experiments in mind control conducted at a secret base. I'd like your feedback on that too.'

'You say these were conducted during the war?'

'That's right, and that of course is the justification for anything deemed necessary, regardless of how diabolical it is. I

80

think the bombing of Hiroshima and Nagasaki falls into that category.' It was the first time I had seen him even mildly incensed over anything.

'It put a quick end to the war guv, saved thousands of lives.'

'And killed over 250, 000 others, mainly innocent non-combatants.'

The direction this was taking was making me feel uneasy. I tapped the papers and turned to go.

'I'll give this a going over then, guv.'

I had a great deal of food for thought as I headed back to the flat. My childhood from the age of nine until fourteen had been encompassed by war and it had taken on the appearance of being the norm. The full horror of it had only been revealed in the aftermath and the Japanese atom bombs had been felt to be justified. Now I wasn't so sure, perhaps it could have been handled differently. Hindsight was a wonderful but sadly misplaced thing. I poured myself a drink and picked up the stuff Ganymede had given me.

I stared at the title page for a considerable time before turning it and entering the horrific world of the Philadelphia Experiment.

The account alleged that in October 1943 in Philadelphia, a warship, the USS Eldridge was rendered invisible in an attempt to enable ships to avoid detection by radar. The invisibility was allegedly achieved by high frequency generators driving electricity through a complex system of cables throughout the ship.

The Eldridge was seen to actually vanish from her berth, followed by reports that she had reappeared in Norfolk Virginia over 200 miles away, a fact that was witnessed by crew members of a merchant ship berthed there. From Norfolk it vanished again and reappeared back at its berth in Philadelphia.

Personnel boarding her were horrified at the mayhem they discovered.

Disorientated crew members suffering obvious mental distress staggered around or were sunk in stupor and babbling insanely. Even worse, some of them were physically fused in the ship's superstructure.

The Naval authorities denied that such an experiment had ever been conducted and dismissed it as a hoax.

I sat and stared into space after emptying my glass, and considered that. The Navy would have been hard-pressed to admit to something that had ended in such a disaster. On the other hand it sounded an almost impossibly elaborate hoax.

I fixed myself a light meal before tackling the mind control stuff.

The Montauk Project was commissioned to conduct experiments in psychological warfare. It didn't have the full backing of the US Congress but this was apparently sidestepped and it went into operation with the blessing of the US Ministry of Defense.

There were hints of involvement by ex-nazis who were also involved in similar research during the war. The areas of research included, mind control, and actual reconditioning of minds, and memories; a highly sophisticated method of brain-washing.

When discussing these mind control items later with Ganymede he mooted the possibility of a system that could produce zombies programmed to do their master's bidding; it was a frightening concept. With regard to the warship experiment, while suggesting the possibility of an elaborate hoax, he also said it was difficult to understand the rationale of creating such a fabrication. In his words. 'Make of it what you will David, but we humans do play around with things we don't rightly understand.'

Chapter 13

I was about to leave the cafeteria for another session with Bill Reynard when Ganymede stuck his head round the doorway. Spotting me he entered the room and came across, sliding into the seat opposite me and resting his arms on the table.

'I'm glad I caught you. Bill's been called away, there's a flap on so your next session is postponed.' I thought, bugger I was hoping to get back into it. What little I could remember had made me curious, I also wanted to see more of this playmate I had known in my infancy. As always Ganymede seemed to pick up on my reaction.

'Don't worry David; Bill should be back in a few days. We get these flaps occasionally. They don't usually amount to much but we have to follow up new developments.'

'Flap?'

He could see that he needed to explain further.

'We've just had a whisper on the grapevine of an unusual UFO event in the US; Bill has flown over to find out what it's all about.'

'What is it, a sighting? He gave me the kind of look you gave dumb clucks.

'Sightings are two a penny David they are streaming in daily from every country in the world. You'll realise that when you get going on that computer.

Most of them are found to be identifiable, weather balloons, atmospheric conditions, or simply the sun reflections off conventional aircraft,' he laughed, 'and at night even Venus has been reported.'

'So the one Bill's looking into is a genuine sighting?'

'More than that David. The bod reporting this one reckons it actually landed and he was invited aboard it.' It was my turn to laugh.

'What is it they say guv, take more water with it?' He appeared to ignore my remark.

'Apparently he was with half a dozen other people at the time and there was no booze involved.'

After Quan Ling's lecture and the cine show I suppose I should start to take things more seriously. Bill Reynard's sudden departure could hardly be taken lightly either.

'So there were several witnesses and it's unlikely that they were all hallucinating. When is this supposed to have happened?'

'A few years ago; mid 50's, thereabouts.'

'Crikey! Pretty ancient then?'

'I think the guy got so much flak and ridicule at the time that he went low key.'

'And now he's stuck his head up again?'

'Apparently it happened again, has done several times since the first contact.'

'What does Bill hope to achieve?'

'Get an interview, I guess, really sound the guy out. There's nothing he likes better than to get inside people's heads

'Hypnotise him?' Ganymede shook his head.

'I don't think there's a need for that, the guy was always fully conscious of what was taking place.'

'If this turns out to be true guv, what does that mean to us?'

'It means that we most certainly lose our cock-of-the-walk position in the universe.' He was watching my face for a reaction; I didn't give him one, I'd already figured that one out, and more besides.

'It means that if there are definitely people out there who can just drop in on us willy-nilly we could be in deep shit.'

'That hardly needed spelling out guv; they would have a capability that we don't.'

'How does that grab you?'

I was surprised that it didn't. For some odd reason I didn't feel it constituted a threat. Taking into account what I had already learned since I arrived here, the lecture, the strange being floating in formaldehyde somewhere in the States, and my own recall of what I supposedly experienced in my infancy, I figured that we had nothing to fear. If anyone out there had it in mind to take us over they would already have done so given the technology they possessed.

'I find the idea that we are not alone in the universe sort of acceptable. I think I even welcome the idea'

'It's not acceptable to a lot of people David, but it's for real, and there are some who will bust a gut to keep it under wraps.' He was leaning forward, his expression underlining the words.

'In the interest of national security and the avoidance of a general panic?' I thought it was a sensible offering.

He gave a derisive snort and shaking his head he removed his arms from the table and sat back in his seat.

'For fear of losing power David. If they allowed what they know and what we know to get into the public domain they

84

would lose control. You think you live in a democracy?' I nodded. His expression saddened. 'There is no such thing my friend, and nothing happens by chance or coincidence, but mainly by design' He sat relaxed, his eyes staring fixedly into mine. 'There are those who set the scenes and choreograph our performance both here....' He waved a hand..., 'and out there in the wider world.'

I felt the urge to raise my hand with a question, in schoolboy fashion, but instead I said.

'But we vote our governments' in, that's a democratic process.'

'In theory, and that theory has become a myth. By political rhetoric, religious conviction or otherwise, and various protocols, people are persuaded to vote for what they assume are in their best interests, right?

I couldn't argue with that. In listening to opposing candidates I was often bemused by how each in turn could convince me that they were the one I should vote for. In consequence I rarely if ever voted. I waited for him to continue, I wanted to see what he was getting at.

'What's the most useful commodity in use on the planet David?'

I hesitated; it could be a catch question, but a quick wrack of the brain produced a hesitant answer.

'Money...?'

'Money David, what would we do without it? The jingly, crispy, folding stuff that feeds and clothes us, pays our bills, and if there's any leftover it provides for our pleasures and fun times. It's money that gives those in power the means with which to control us.'

'Surely they are there to govern us, the governments I mean.'

'The key words that define 'govern' are 'control' and 'order'; the power you give to others David leaves you with little or none. Do you know where governments borrow money from when they've squandered and misused what they've relieved the taxpayer of?' He could see I didn't, I'd often wondered though; but not seriously.

'The banks of course, and the little banks borrow from the bigger banks and so on up the line until you get to the biggest banks of all, and there at the top of the heap are the absolute money moguls. The richest families, nearly all in the banking and investment business. The industrial giants and the

85

consortiums that control the commodity markets, they are the ones that crack the whip and squeeze the windpipe of the odd government now and then.' He looked at his watch. For the first time I noticed that he had one on each wrist because he looked at each in turn. He looked up at me and saw puzzlement. He tapped his right wrist.

'From a friend of mine, it's a new development. It's a new generation David, battery operated. He said they'll be all the rage one day. What time do you make it?'

I looked down. The sweep hand on my watch had stopped; I had forgotten to wind it the previous night.

'Perhaps I'll invest in one of those.' He shook his head.

'They appear to be affected by some of the equipment down here. I should remember to wind yours and to hang onto it. It's nearly 10 o'clock by my H Samuel Everite,' he waved his other hand, 'time to take advantage of your missed appointment, there are still things I have to show you.' He stood up and pushed his chair back, the lecture was over. It was already giving me a lot to think about. He indicated over his shoulder towards the tea bar.

'I think there's someone over there that is of some interest to you,' he said as he moved off.

I looked across; Genna Rees was already heading in our direction carrying a cup of tea and a bun. Ganymede muttered something to her as their paths crossed on his way out. Genna laughed and continued towards me.

'Hi David.' She placed her tea and bun on the table and I eased out a chair for her.

'Hi Genna.' I nodded towards the retreating Ganymede. 'What was all that about?'

'Search me. Something about me putting you out of your misery and you catching up with him ASAP; what did that mean?' She was grinning as she sat down.

'Well, seeing you back again has certainly dispelled the gloom around here, but I'd better do my master's bidding. I was wondering if we could meet up later and perhaps go for a meal this evening.'

'I think I would like that very much David. I have things to catch up with here but I could drop by your place around seven?'

'Great. I think you've done wonders for my misery, I'll see you then.'

**

Ganymede was on the phone so I slipped into a spare chair until he'd finished; it took only a matter of seconds.

'Right, thank you. I'll get things moving here and get someone over there.' He replaced the receiver and looked across at me. 'Sorry David, something's turned up, you'll just have to carry on with the UFO reports. Perhaps we can get back together in the morning.' He picked up the phone and was dialling again as I left to continue the now boring task of swelling the UFO database. With a sigh of relief at the stroke of 5 o' clock I closed down and headed for home, joyfully anticipating an evening with Genna. I was only barely aware of the odd air of desertion about the place as I left.

By eight o' clock that evening deflation was beginning to set in; no sign of her. I picked up the telephone directory and thumbed through the R's. I rang the only Rees but got an answerphone. The woman's thick Scottish accent was a far cry from Genna's Welsh lilt. Either she wasn't listed yet or was ex directory. I gave it another hour before deciding I'd probably been stood up. But that somehow didn't make sense. I had no address for her and it was getting past a reasonable time to eat out. I decided to go to the Complex; someone might have an address or a means of contacting her.

I realised it was a foolish move even as I entered the information bureau. The grill was down over the reception desk so I passed on through. When I entered the Complex the futility of what I was doing hit home; the place was deserted. I was about to leave when I remembered the sick bay, there was just a chance that it was manned and someone there might know Genna's whereabouts. It was, but the nurse on duty couldn't help me. She didn't know Genna Rees as she had only been drafted in as a temporary replacement while she was off on her course; she was due to leave next day. There had been a flap on just before she came on duty that evening but she didn't know exactly what it was about apart from there being an incident somewhere near Winchester in Hampshire.

I had to be content with that, so I returned to the flat, and the bottle, and bed. There was nothing further to be done until morning.

**

I looked into Ganymede's office; he wasn't there. He either hadn't arrived yet or had been and gone and was probably around somewhere. I tried the door of Reynard's office, it was

87

locked. He was obviously still away doing his thing in the States. I wandered towards the sickbay. I was reluctant to start back with the UFO's until I found out what had happened to Genna. The reception desk was just in the process of changing hands. Neither nurse knew the whereabouts of Genna Rees. There was one last place to look. The cafeteria yielded half a dozen people at breakfast; Genna was not among them.

On the way to my allotted task I spotted Philo Makris in conversation with one of the security men, but even as I made my way towards them Makris disappeared through the doorway of the tunnel leading to the information bureau. I retraced my steps. I needed to get a grip. Genna was bound to show sooner or later, and then I'd know the best or the worst; whichever.

Chapter 14

As a fully accepted member of Bill Reynard's team, I now had an office of my own. Also, as if to confirm my trustworthiness, the bug on my phone had long since been removed, and as a consequence of changing my door locks I now felt secure as far as invasion of my privacy was concerned, but it did have drawbacks.

I had packed up a bit earlier than usual as I'd brought the database up to date and incoming traffic had ceased for the day. I decided to read through the transcripts of my regression sessions. There had been a long break since the last of them, due mainly to Reynard having to dash off somewhere, his recent sudden departure to the States being a good example. There was nothing since our journey to the woods and the pleasantries of the Plough Inn.

I replaced the transcripts in their file, reluctant to admit that I had only been killing time, for despite the comforts of a place of my own it hung heavy. Service life had provided constant companionship of one sort or another, but apart from the comings and goings in the Complex I was experiencing very much the life of the loner. I had seen nothing of Genna or the team for over twenty-four hours.

It made me jump, but it was almost a relief when the phone rang; it was Reynard, He had been gone for almost a week. The only indication that he was actually back were his first words. 'Where is everyone David? The place is deserted.'

I suggested it might have something to do with an incident over Winchester way.

'Oh well, I suppose we'll know soon enough. In the meantime, I think I have something interesting to show you David. Can you be in my office by 1800 hours? I glanced at my watch; it was 5 o' clock.

'No problem, Bill.' I had already decided to eat out that evening so maybe I'd grab something in the cafeteria before I dropped in on him.
**

In the countdown to Christmas there was little to show in the way of preparation for the festival barely a week ahead. The previous year someone had managed to hang a few balloons and stick sprigs of holly in glasses as centre pieces on the tables.

89

My feelings were mixed. I wasn't religious and I wasn't particularly atheist. I knew that this winter festival had been hijacked from the Pagans. On reflection I could possibly be in the Pagan category. To me it represented a get together for a bit of a feast and a 'knees up' with friends I probably hadn't seen for a year or more. It marked the turning point of the year, and a time to try and change things that hadn't worked out too well in the past.

I wondered if Genna would turn up, it would be nice to spend some time with her, Christmas or anytime. Wondering what had happened to her was giving me a hard time, had I said or done something to get the elbow?

I paused in the doorway. She often sat on the far side of the cafeteria up against the illuminated mural that gave a very real impression of gazing out across a sunlit meadow set in a rural landscape stretching to a range of low hills. It was the only view of the outside world we were ever likely to see from the depths of the Complex. I imagined walking in a place like that with Genna Rees, I then dismissed the fantasy. Get a bloody grip Kent.

I settled for eggs, chips, and beans, something I normally enjoyed, it didn't even taste the same today.

I looked at my watch; time had already raced to within fifteen minutes of my meeting with Reynard.

There was still no sign of Ganymede. I couldn't resist trying his door on my way to Reynard. Perhaps Foxy Bill might know by now what this Winchester flap was all about.

He looked at me blankly when I asked and said. 'Haven't a clue. I arrived here just over an hour ago.' He grinned. 'I assumed everyone had skived off, the cat's away sort off.' He obviously wanted to get on with what he had come to show me. 'What do you think of this David?'

I was looking at a very small person sitting in a very big chair. There were several photos that Reynard handed me, some of which showed the person standing among what I could see were people of normal height. I arrived at an enlargement of a face that was far from normal; it was reminiscent of the one I had seen at Quan Ling's lecture, but perhaps more acceptably pleasant. The head looked out of proportion in the same way as an infant child's did. The eyes dominating the domed head were black ovoids. It wore what appeared to be a seamless skin tight uniform of metallic grey.

90

'Who is that -- what is that?'

'It's a survivor from a space vehicle crash just over a week ago.'

'Where?'

'America, New Mexico to be precise. I was invited to pay a visit to an air force base there after I interviewed that chap who says he had a trip in a space ship from Venus.'

'I wonder what the attraction is down there ... I mean for the UFO's. That's where that Roswell thing was, wasn't it?' My eyes kept drifting down to the photos.

'How about guitar music played by pretty girls, and food that sets your arse on fire?'

'How did the Venus flight thing go?' I asked purely out of courtesy, I really wanted him to get to the little guy in the metallic suit.

'Difficult to say really. In view of what we are privy to regarding ET's it all sounded quite feasible. He certainly didn't appear to be a nutter. On the other hand the witnesses to the first encounter weren't still around or available for comment. Subsequent meeting with the Venusians, if that's what they were, only involved him, and are therefore uncorroborated.'

'What's your conclusion?' Hopefully that would tie it up. I gave the photos a nonchalant wave.

'It's believable, but I'm afraid I'd need to be invited by people from another world to take a trip in one of their ships before I could endorse such an experience.'

'Did you actually see this ... whatsit?' I turned one of the photos towards him and tapped a finger on the little figure. 'And this, whatever it is, breathes and walks and talks?'

'All except talks David.' The Yanks are tearing their hair trying to interrogate this one. They wouldn't let me see it, they had it in quarantine at the time, and these are recent pics I was allowed to bring away with me.'

'I thought they had contact with others, couldn't they put them together?

'This one's different, they haven't come across it before, and they think it's a robot.' I stared at him.

'You're joking.' It was no consolation to realise that he wasn't. Was I now supposed to take science fiction seriously? I'd been weaned on comic books like the Eagle, and even some from America that were brought over by GI's were still doing the rounds in my schooldays.

91

Exciting though it was at the time it soon became accepted as a fun thing, something that succeeded 'cowboys and indians' in our gang games. The ray gun and the paralyser pistol supplanted our bows and arrows. There were robots too, scary and indestructible.

'How do you feel about a trip to America to see this ... whatever it is, for ourselves?' He tapped the photo. 'Since I've been back I've called in a few favours, pulled some strings, we have the necessary clearance now. I could see he wasn't joking about that either. He stood stiff-armed with his hands planted firmly on the table and his face thrust forward; challenging.

'When?' Even to me it sounded a somewhat ridiculous response, but it was all I could think of. It seemed to satisfy him; he relaxed and straightened up.

'In a couple of days. I'll contact a brass hat who owes me a favour or two to get us past the red tape, and I'll need to sort out your visa. I don't suppose you've got a passport, have you?'

'Never needed one at sea or in the army.'

'No, of course not.' He picked up the photos and slipped them into a drawer. His phone rang. He picked it up and listened, then said. 'Yes he's here now, do you want a word,' He looked up at me and mouthed "*Ganymede*". 'Not just now. Very well. Talk later then.' He hung up. 'Apparently he's up to his eyes, some sort of crisis. I've already told him of our intended trip, he thinks it's a good idea.'

'You knew I would go for it then?'

'David. You didn't really have a choice. You belong to the team and you are bound by what the team wants; we all are. Out of courtesy it asks rather than orders, and it says please and thank you.'

His words sent a little shiver through me. It felt as if a cell door had slammed shut behind me. I was free though, to speculate on what the outcome might be if at some time I refused what the team required of me. Philo Makris loomed large in the equation; with a silenced pistol jammed in my ear. But Reynard was smiling and I realised that perhaps it was simply down to my imagination; perhaps.

I hadn't been to the States during the time I'd spent at sea. Joining the ranks of the Cunard Cowboys lacked appeal. Apart from the occasional Union Castle run to South Africa I liked the small ships, the coasters, and the tramps, it seemed more what seamanship and being a seaman was all about. Tramp steamers, the ones I did get a berth on, never ventured that way.

Reynard's voice took on a more serious tone. 'We'll be under constant surveillance all the time out there. They don't allow anyone without a high security clearance within a hundred miles of what goes on behind the scenes. Just keep your head down and your eyes and ears open. You can take a couple of days off to pack whatever you'll need for a fortnight away and to attend to whatever other affairs need taking care of. I'm off to London first thing in the morning to get our travel documents sorted out. I'll give you a shout when we are ready for the off.'

I wasn't to know at that point that the crisis mentioned that Ganymede was involved in would have personal repercussions, and that the trip, like everything else promised by Reynard was already about to suffer postponement.

Chapter 15

Ganymede and Derek Collins were discussing something as I barged in. It was obviously something not meant for my ears for it stopped immediately and they both looked up at me.

Collins looked as if he'd been dragged through a hedge backwards. It was the first time I had seen him in uniform since the Cyprus days. It was ripped in places and there were the crowns on his shoulder tabs; the place was literally crawling with majors. Ganymede rose up and taking me by the elbow steered me back towards the door.

'Not now David, I may be occupied for some time. With Bill Reynard away in London sorting out your travel arrangements perhaps it would be a good time for you to get on with some of the input for the UFO database. I'll get in touch if I need you.' With that he returned to Collins and I was left wondering what was going on as I made off to do my master's bidding. Was there something going on that was being kept from me? I felt as if I'd been dismissed. Sod the database. I was coming to believe that it was just something to make my keep worthwhile until Reynard could bring out the telepath in me; and then what, what was the end game? There was nothing for it but to return obediently to my computer and smoulder away the remaining hours of the day.

On the way Philo Makris passed me going the other way, his sober face even more so. His brief nod was more an acknowledgement than a greeting as he hurried by. I looked back as he disappeared into Ganymede's office; something was going on.

Next morning I sat for a bit with a coffee and bun in the cafeteria in the hope that Genna might turn up; two days since I had last seen her. It was possible that she was on another assignment somewhere, but surely she would have let me know; I didn't like the thought that I was of that little importance to her.

I spent another day grappling with boredom and not a word from Ganymede. The input for the database was riddled with insignificant and easily explainable events. The public, it seemed, were almost seeing UFO's under the bed. But boring or not I dutifully recorded them. "I'll be in touch" had a very indefinite ring to it. I found myself at odd times wandering off into the cafeteria in the vain hope of seeing Genna. She had awakened something in me that I'd tried to avoid for nearly three years; I felt ready to run in the romantic stakes again.

There was still no sign of her, despite the fact that I sometimes sat in the cafeteria long enough to be charged rent. I went in search of Ganymede and drew a blank. His office was locked which was unusual. This part of the Complex, although never a hive of activity was completely deserted, I decided to take a look in the sick bay. My ID got me through the door.

I didn't really expect to find Genna there but it was still a disappointment to find someone else in the reception area.

'I'm sorry to intrude but I was wondering if a friend of mine was here.' I found myself face to face with a bespectacled, matronly woman dressed in the same kind of uniform I had first seen Genna wearing. She had been reading and she removed her glasses and looked me up and down.

'And you are?'

'Kent, David Kent.' Surprisingly it brought a smile to her face.

'There now, we spent best part of yesterday trying to get hold of you.' She indicated one of a row of cubicles with a flourish of her glasses. 'I think you'll find your friend in the second one down.' She donned her glasses again and picked up her book.

Do hearts actually leap like they say in books? Mine gave a very convincing yes to that as I crossed the floor. That was it, she'd been ill and it didn't appear to be serious.

My heart stumbled and fell at the sight of Collins wired up to a monitor. He was sitting up and gave me a weak smile; I hoped my disappointment didn't show.

'I'm glad they got hold of you David, take a seat.'

I had got over it by the time I was seated. A glance at the monitor revealed a steady row of peaks. I could only assume that was how it should look.

'What's been happening to you? You looked a bit rough the other day when you were talking to my guv, and now this.'

'They think I might have had a mild heart attack.'

'At your age, you can't be much older than me?'

He looked at me a bit strangely before blurting it out.

'It's about Genna; I think you've a right to know. She spoke of you before it happened.' A finger of dread traced a pattern somewhere inside me.

'Before what happened?' It sounded strangled. I recalled how Collins had looked in the office and now this. 'Where is she, dead?' I had to force the word out. He was shaking his head, it seemed like a reprieve.

'No... we don't know ... it all went wrong. I'm not making much sense, am I?'

You can say that again, I thought, but I could see he was distressed. The peaks on the monitor screen looked a bit wobbly. I was feeling a bit like that too.

'OK Derek. Take it easy, there's no rush. Take your time; tell me what this is all about.' There was the sound of footsteps approaching

'Are you all right Mr Collins?' It was the woman from reception. She came in and stared at the monitor for a moment. The peaks had settled back uniformly. She turned to Collins. 'I think you should rest sir and see Mr Kent later. To me rather sternly. 'Two minutes, no longer.'

I turned to Collins as her footsteps retreated.

'What now?'

'I'm not well David; she's only looking after me. I really wish I could say that Genna is alive and well. People have been known to survive these things and turn up none the worse for it.'

'What things? What happened to you two? Was it some sort of accident? Turn up! What the hell does that mean?' I was already wondering if I really wanted to know.

'I think she was abducted; right under my nose. I couldn't do anything.' It came out with a sob, and the footsteps were back; in a hurry. The peaks on the screen had gone wild again. I had barely time for what he was saying to sink in. She said just the one word to me as she hurried in like an avenging angel.

'Out!'

I avoided the trolley that hurtled through the doorway accompanied by two more silver uniformed angels of mercy. I just had time to notice the monitor at the side of the reception desk as I left; it didn't look good. I hoped Collins wasn't going to cash in, for my sake as much as his; I wanted to know what had happened to Genna. Ganymede's office was still locked, and the same air of desertion hung over the area. I went back to the computer and forced myself to see my shift out. I stood for a moment in the corridor outside the sick bay. In there was the answer. Collins was far from being a well man and I wasn't game to face the wrath of the matron type; I decided to head home to the flat.

"Abducted", he'd said. What was that supposed to mean. Kidnapped? Held for ransom? A bewildering array of possibilities crowded my mind; all except *the one*.

In the manner of bad news it arrived a few hours and several whiskies later with a knock on my door. I still had a glass in my hand as I let Ganymede in. He looked directly at the glass.

'I could use one of those too David.'

I poured a stiff one and handed it to him when he was seated. I had a fair idea what was coming. 'Derek Collins died an hour ago.' I nodded instinctively.

'Damned waste. Brilliant career ahead of him; could have gone all the way to the top. A Major you know. Twenty eight years old and a bloody major.'

'What happened guv?' I didn't wish to ask about Genna directly, that was a personal need. I figured that knowing what had happened to Collins would bring that up anyway.

'I was told that you spoke with him … at his request.' It was obvious that I wasn't being blamed for his death. 'What did he tell you?'

'Very little really, or perhaps too much. I got turfed out of there pretty quick. He said that Genna Rees had been abducted.' Ganymede tilted his glass before continuing, he obviously appreciated the contents.

'That's right. Look, we know…that there is some chemistry at work between you and Genna Rees, and I can understand your concern. I'm sorry I gave you the bum's rush yesterday but we, that is Collins and I, were trying to put together a clear picture of what had happened, so let's not play mind games. I'll give you a brief outline of events leading up to her… disappearance. Collins by the way was not very clear about the closing stages of the incident.

'Disappearance? You make it sound like she vanished into thin air, guv.' He nodded.

'It appears to be very much like that. I'll try to give you it as it was reported to me. We received information that a body was allegedly dropped from what was described as a black helicopter in a field adjacent to a stretch of road between Chilcomb Hill and the A 32 at Winchester. The event was seen by a cyclist on his way home from work. By the time he reached the spot, a matter of twenty-five yards or so, the helicopter had disappeared behind a hill. He approached the barbed wire fence and saw what he then described as a body lying about 20 feet in. That information was relayed to us by a branch of the local police that is briefed to report any incidents involving flying vehicles that are not fixed wing aircraft. We sent Collins out, he's our man for investigating

97

weird goings on, among other things, and Miss Rees went along routinely in case a casualty was involved. We were informed that there were no helicopters up that night; it was foggy all over the south.'

'So it might not have been a helicopter?' I was still having a bit of a problem getting my head around what he was saying.

'We were inclined to consider that possibility, and in the light of subsequent events we concluded that it was an assumption by the witness because the craft had a hovering capability.'

'Helicopters are pretty noisy things.'

'This has been discussed with the witness and he is rather unsure about that. He works as a band-sawyer in a car factory and his hearing is not the best just after work.' He took another swallow of whisky and studied the glass for a moment before continuing. 'We haven't ruled out the helicopter though as there have been reports both here and in the States that they have been sighted, mainly in the vicinity of cattle mutilations.'

'Is there a connection between black helicopters and UFO's?' Among the data I have been storing black helicopters were also described as sometimes being seen in the vicinity of UFO sightings.

'We've been shoving that around for some time too. They could be one and the same. From the way these UFO's perform, travelling, and manoeuvring at blink-of-the-eye speeds, I don't doubt the possibility; it doesn't take much to assume that physical laws as we understand them don't apply to these things. It has even been suggested that they can appear in any guise they wish. Some abductees have described being confronted by tractors or a bus before finding themselves back in their cars, having experienced missing time. It is only under hypnosis that they have recalled where that missing time was spent.' His words were leaving an emptiness inside me. It was mind numbing to think I would never see her again; Genna disappearing without trace. It was thinking the unthinkable.

'Has Genna Rees definitely been abducted by one or the other of these things guv?' The empty feeling in the pit of my stomach was already confirming that.

'Collins' report states that his last recollection after the 'body', which was identified as a mutilated calf wrapped in black plastic was removed, and the police had departed, they were suddenly enveloped in a blinding white light. The next

98

thing he remembers is being on his own struggling back through the barbed wire fence.'

I poured myself another drink and offered the bottle. Ganymede shook his head.

'Better not, I've got some driving to do.' He rose to go and paused at the door, his face reflected both our feelings. 'It's a bad business David; I'll let you know of any developments. I've been in touch with Bill Reynard he should be back in the morning. I was no longer looking forward to the American trip with this hanging over me. I must have looked pretty down.

'He'll probably postpone the Yankee trip until this is cleared up. Chin up David.' Then he was gone. I don't know whether that made me feel better or not.

Chapter 16

'David! A word?' I recognised the voice, it was Makris. I was heading for Ganymede's office, I stopped and turned and waited for him to catch up. There was the suspicion of a smile on his normally sober face.

'Bill Reynard asked me to let you know that Genna Rees has been found safe and well.' I resisted the urge to hug him. Instead I let the feeling of relief soothe away the anxiety of the past days.

'Thanks Philo, I needed that, where is she?'

'At the moment she's being looked after by the Winchester police, I'm on my way to bring her in, would you like to come along?'

There was only one answer to that.

Light rain was falling as we emerged from the information bureau and headed out of the village. Low cloud contributed to cloaking the early afternoon in premature gloom but I was feeling the radiance of an inner sun; the words "safe and well" had set the seal on feelings for Genna that I had become increasingly aware of.

Traffic was light to nonexistent. In a country barely out of the grip of post-war austerity cars were mainly the privilege of the privileged or the rich; who were both. My own mode of transport was still a pushbike or shanks. Futuristically it might attain the dizzy heights of a motor cycle. I certainly didn't envisage anything in the order of a left-hand drive BMW with a needle nudging 150 kph most of the time, whatever that was; my school maths were never up to much, and my decimal and fraction conversions abysmal.

Makris was a lead foot driver, and the only noticeable concession he made to our passage through villages was a marginal flicker of the needle back to the 100 kph mark. The rain had cleared by the time we entered the city.

Genna looked up from the magazine she was reading as we entered the reception area. She looked pale but smiling. Makris moved across to where the duty sergeant stood behind his desk. I stood looking down at her.

'Hi.'

'Hello David.' She put the magazine to one side and stood up. 'Have you come to take me home?'

'I guess so. I was wondering where you'd got to.'

'I'm still wondering David.'

'You don't know?' She shook her head. I sensed Makris beside me before he spoke.

'Not now you two, there's to be no debriefing before we return to the Complex.' His tight grin did little to mask the warning in his eyes. 'They too had orders not to question her.' His thumb flicked in the direction of the desk sergeant. To Genna he said. 'I'm glad to see you are all in one piece Miss Rees.' With that he turned and headed for the door; we followed him out into the persistent gloom of the overcast, I felt Genna's hand creep into mine.

I studied her face as she slept through the return journey; I felt the tension of the last few days had lifted almost to the point of weeping with relief.

Still drowsy, she accompanied us to Reynard's office where coffee and Ganymede awaited us.

'Glad to have you back Miss Rees. You had us all worried sick. Mr Reynard should be along in a minute, he cut short his trip the moment he was informed that we had contact with you, in the meantime make yourself comfortable.' He turned to Makris.

'Do you want to sit in on this Philo?'

'I think not sir; I'll wait for the report.'

'As you wish...and Philo...thanks.' Beyond the door he was intercepted by Reynard. There was a brief exchange before he continued out of sight and Reynard came in. He nodded briefly to Ganymede and me before sitting alongside the recliner and giving his full attention to Genna.

'Welcome back Miss Rees. I have no doubt that you have been through a particularly harrowing experience. I would like to establish just how much you do actually recall.'

'Very little I'm afraid sir.' She sat, rather tensely I thought, with her hands in her lap. He smiled reassuringly

'No matter, all information is valuable. Start if you can from your arrival at the incident.' She appeared to make a visible effort to get her thoughts in order.

'We were met at the scene by police...I had to be lifted over a barbed wire fence.' I detected a weak smile. 'I was informed that it wasn't a human body; it was a dead calf, so my services were not required.'

'Can you remember exactly who was at the scene?'

'Two police officers in uniform, Mr Collins, and myself.'

'No one else?'

'No... unless you count the calf.' She permitted herself a further weak smile

'Tell me about that, did you examine it?'

'Only superficially.'

'What did you find?'

'A small incision in a jugular vein and some excisions in the lower abdominal area.' Reynard appeared to consider that for a moment.

'How about blood, any evidence of blood?'

'None as far as I could see; in torchlight, that is. There was something odd though.' She seemed to be reaching into her memory.

'What was that?'

'The wounds, the edges appeared to be sealed somehow.'

'Cauterised?'

'Not in any way I have seen.' Reynard made eye contact with Ganymede who gave a barely perceptible nod.

'Okay. What happened next?'

'I think Mr Collins arranged with the police to have the calf removed, for further examination in Southampton University's Medical Facility.'

'Leaving you and Mr Collins at the scene?'

'Yes.'

'Tell me what happened after that.'

'Mr Collins suggested that we have a look around in case we had missed anything.'

'Which you did, look around I mean?'

'Yes.'

'You were together at this time?'

'No, we chose different areas to search.'

'Were you in sight of each other?'

'Oh yes.'

'How far apart at any one time?'

'Fifteen, twenty yards, maybe a little more.'

'Now think carefully... Genna. You were both having a look around a scene where a passerby had seen something dropped from what he described as a black helicopter. What happened next?'

'The whole area was suddenly illuminated by blinding, white light.'

'Did you see anything; where the light was coming from?'

'Just the light.'

'And after that?'

'After that I found myself alone; there was no sign of Mr Collins I called out but there was no reply so I struggled over the fence wondering what to do. I flagged down a car and asked the driver to take me to the police station. It was there I was told that Mr Collins had returned here, and that didn't make sense, we had been together only a short while before.'

'It will make sense Genna, I can assure you, but it may take a little time. Meanwhile I think you should take time out, get yourself something to eat and get some rest. I would like to discuss something further with you in the morning.' He looked over to me. 'Perhaps you wouldn't mind seeing Miss Rees home David and dropping her off here tomorrow. I would rather neither of you discussed this business with anyone outside.'

'His 'rather' had a ring of, -- you'd better bloody well not.'

Chapter 17

She seemed refreshed after a further coffee with her meal in the cafeteria. She toyed with her empty cup, I almost sensed what she was about to say.

'Do you think I could have a word with Derek Collins before we leave here David?'

She obviously wasn't aware that she had been missing for nearly five days. It might have to be left to Bill Reynard to tell her that. The answer to her question would take a great deal of diplomacy, something that I definitely lacked. She looked at me, puzzled by the delay my thoughts were causing.

'Well, do you?'

'Derek Collins died of a heart attack soon after he arrived back.'

It was out, and she looked at me horrified; it was some moments before she collected herself. 'Why ... should he do that ... I mean ...this is all crazy, one minute he's with me and then the next he's back here having a heart attack and I'm still out there.' She reached across and gripped my hand. 'What is going on David?'

'Take it easy Genn. Let's get out of here and I'll try to explain.' I hadn't a clue how I was going to do that without telling her what, or what we thought, had happened to her. 'I'll take you to your digs, we can talk there.'

'I'd rather not David. I don't feel that I want to be on my own right now; can I come to your place? There is something going on that doesn't make sense to me.' Her hand still maintained its grip on mine.

**

'Whisky okay?' I lifted a bottle from a shelf.

'Yes please I could certainly use one; it feels as if I haven't had a real drink for ages.' She sat back in the depth of her overstuffed easy chair. I poured it and handed it to her then poured a measure for myself before sitting down opposite her. The electric fire was already bringing the room up to welcome warmth.

'That is nearer the truth than you think.'

'What truth?'

'That you may not have had a drink for ages, an alcoholic one anyway.'

She placed her glass on the side table and leaned forward with earnest appeal in her eyes.

'Please David, don't play games. I'd like to think we are friends, good friends and I need to know what's going on.'

I could see the situation was causing stress for her; I had to tell her what we suspected had happened. I knew it would hardly be likely to interfere with what Bill Reynard was obviously planning for her in the morning.

'We, that is Ganymede, Bill Reynard, Makris, and me, believe that you were abducted.' My diplomatic foot was right in it, but there was no gentle way to explain her absence and the confusion it was causing her.

'Abducted? You mean ...?'

'You know about that sort of thing?' I could see she was working on it. I gave her a moment before reaching for that morning's newspaper and handing it to her; she looked blank. I pushed it towards her; prompting.

'What day is it?'

She looked down at the front page then up at me, 'So it's Christmas Eve.' She looked at me puzzled, and then it dawned on her; she was visibly shaken.

'Oh my God!' She looked again at the paper and back to me for some kind of confirmation.

'That's right Genn; it was over five days ago that you and Derek Collins answered that call.' She reached for her drink. It was almost empty; she drained it and handed me the glass. I didn't know whether she was going to laugh or cry.

'I think I need more drink David; lots.' She smiled weakly. 'It is Christmas after all.'

I poured a healthy double and repeated it for myself. She sipped hers and settled back in her chair nursing the glass in both hands.

'What happens now? What happened to me?'

'We wait until tomorrow and then we may find out more.'

'How will you know that?'

'My guess is that Bill Reynard will suggest that he hypnotises you.'

'How will that do any good?'

'He says that much of past experience is stored in the subconscious, and under hypnosis it can be accessed. I've been having sessions with him.'

'Why?'

105

I wasn't sure how much I wanted to tell her.

'Some sort of experiment, he thinks I might recall something from my past that might make a useful contribution to the work we are engaged in here.'

'Such as?'

I knew she was puzzled, and that she was looking more for some sort of reassurance; it wasn't an interrogation.

I wasn't quite sure how to proceed but I decided to tell her about my previous association with Reynard and what had happened at sea, and the sessions I'd had with him since coming to the Complex. She listened taking occasional sips from her glass. I could see she was finding it difficult to believe what she was hearing. I could see too that the late hour, the whisky, and recent events were vying with her ability to stay awake.

'So you see he's trying reawaken some ability that I'm supposed to have had all those years ago.'

'Why would he want to do that, what sort of ability?' It seemed that for a moment anyway she had shelved her own predicament. I decided that there would be no harm in her knowing what Reynard hoped to achieve.

'Sounds creepy,' she said, 'the telepathy.'

'I thought so too at first but after the sessions with Bill Reynard, the actual recollection of experiencing it felt … sort of … natural.'

'I'm not sure I'd like to be hypnotised David.'

'I know the feeling Genn, but you would like to know where you've spent the last few days, wouldn't you?'

'Do I have a choice?'

'Of course, but it can't be easy knowing there's a time gap in your life that you can't fill.'

'Will you be there David?'

'Let's say I intend to be.'

Her glass was empty and I leaned forward and took it from her. I drained my own and stood up; it had been a long day, it was time to call it one.

'Come on, you need bed.' I helped her up and led her to the bedroom. She looked at the bed and then at me. I answered the question that flickered in her eyes. 'It's okay I'll kip on the settee, I dragged a couple of blankets from the chest at the foot of the bed.

'But David …I can't …' I placed my finger on her lips.

'You can and you will. I'll be okay; you just get a good night's sleep.'

I settled down for what proved to be an uncomfortable night feeling quite noble, and not a little stupid at perhaps having missed out on something the Welsh called bundling.

Chapter 18

I accompanied her to Reynard's office. If she was nervous she did well to conceal it. Ganymede was already there, seated in one of the two chairs up against one wall. He nodded a greeting and Reynard led her to the recliner, adjusting it once she was seated. Satisfied he turned to me and indicated the chair next to Ganymede.

'I felt you would like to sit in on this David.'

'Thanks,' I sat down and glanced across at Genna. She looked just a little apprehensive; I knew the feeling.

Reynard sat in a chair beside her. He assured her there was nothing to fear and told her the same as he had first told me, that if she experienced any situation she felt she couldn't handle she could move to one side and observe it as a spectator. He then began the induction, counting down with her taking deep breaths, each one moving her deeper and deeper into relaxation. With me, he had moved me by stages back to my infancy but with Genna he took her back to where her journey had begun that day nearly a week ago.

'You are on your way somewhere, can you tell me where?' His voice was pitched low almost intimate. Genna, eyes closed, answered as if in a dream.

'I'm not sure...' she sighed. 'I am going to attend a casualty ... there has been an accident.'

'Are you alone?'

'No.'

'There is someone with you?'

'Yes.'

'Can you see who is with you?'

'It's Derek ... Derek Collins.'

'I see. Genna I'm going to move you forward in time. I will count down from 3 to 1 and you will be arriving at the scene of the accident; 3 – 2 – 1 you are now at the scene of the accident.'

I could see that Genna was getting agitated.

'It's not an accident ... it's ... Derek ...' her voice tailed off.

'Derek, what about Derek?'

'He told me it wasn't an accident.'

'When did he tell you that?'

'On the way here.'

'If it isn't an accident, what is it?'

'Something ... strange.'

'Is there anyone else present where you are now?'

'Derek is talking with someone.'

'Can you see who he is talking with?'

'Police officers.'

Reynard turned to us and gave thumbs up. I wondered why because Genna was only relating what she had already consciously remembered right up to the intense light.

'Genna I am going to bring you back from that scene. I am going to count down from 5. On the count of 1 you will wake up feeling fresh and wide awake, feeling great.'

Genna opened her eyes, smiling. Reynard patted her shoulder.

'That wasn't so bad was it?' Then to us all, 'I think that will do for now, we'll call it a day.' He consulted his watch. 'I have to dash off now if I'm to make it to my dinner date. I'll see you all again on the day after Boxing Day at 9 am. In the meantime a merry Christmas to you all.'

I wondered about Reynard's 'dinner date'. He never mentioned a family but I supposed he had one. Anyway his private life was no concern of mine. Ganymede, on the other hand, deeply embroiled in the cloak and dagger world as he was, tended to represent the typical, confirmed bachelor; a rootless adventurer, an errant knight who took his pleasures wherever he found them. My own private life appeared to be on the up now that Genna was back in the fold.

We headed for the canteen for our Christmas dinner. It looked like being a quiet affair. There were only a very few people present, most having gone on leave to their various family do's. Genna took a seat and Ganymede and I went to collect the festive meal. I voiced what was on my mind while we waited to be served.

'She already knew all that guv, what's the point?'

'Don't worry David. Bill discussed that before you came in; he knows what he's doing. It's to inspire confidence, a trusting relationship between Genna and himself. We don't know yet what she went through while she was absent. If it was definitely an abduction by ET's it may have been pretty hairy, even terrifying.'

Out of consideration for Genna we managed to avoid the subject of UFO's and ET's; until pudding time, and then it was her that brought it up. Perhaps it was the wine, but it was obvious that she was troubled by her recent experience. She looked at each of us in turn.

'I seem to be the only one here who knows little or nothing about these UFO's and ET people that just drop out of the skies but officially don't exist. I've been told nothing except that I was missing for five days after attending an incident at which I was abducted. As a result I was left in a confused state and Derek Collins is dead.'

I could see the start of tears and I reached out and placed my hand over hers.

'We don't know that Derek's death was a direct result of what happened, he did have a heart condition apparently,' said Ganymede. He looked dismayed at Genna's condition.

She wiped at the tears with a napkin. 'It doesn't alter the fact that he is no longer with us.' She appeared more composed as she looked directly at Ganymede and said quietly. 'You know, don't you sir, about these people, these ET's?'

He appeared to mull over that before replying. 'We know quite a lot about them Genna, but I'm afraid not nearly enough. The fact that you are here, delivered safely back, is a fair indication that most of our space visitors mean us no harm. What happened to Derek Collins is a tragedy, but we can't say it was the direct result of what happened near Winchester. His condition suggests that any situation of extreme stress could have triggered his heart attack. As a qualified medical person you would of course understand that.'

She nodded. 'I wasn't aware that he had that problem sir.'

'I'm sure none of us did.' He seemed relieved that there were no further tears. 'To get back to the ET's. There is a lot of speculation, even among those who are in daily contact with the situation, as to the reason behind their constant visitations. They seem to come in all shapes and sizes and they vary in their likeness to human beings. The overriding factor is that they possess a high degree of intelligence and they have been coming here, on and off, since biblical times.'

I looked sharply in his direction. Up til then I had been watching Genna.

He noticed my added attention. 'You wanted to say something David?'

'Not really guv. It was just that Arthur C said something once about visits to his people by space beings in the distant past, and that I should have a read of the bible. I wondered what the connection was at the time.'

Ganymede chuckled. 'I remember, and now you've made that connection?'

'Only that there were some weird goings on in those days, with people dropping in from the skies or popping up in odd places for a chat with the locals.'

'Give it time David,' he was laughing openly now, 'and you'll not only clinch the connection but maybe come up with the bigger picture.' It was at that point that Genna interrupted.

'I was brought up Chapel you know, and we were fed bible for breakfast, dinner, and tea, and if we didn't behave, for supper too. But I can see a connection. You're saying that the ET's visiting us now are, or could be, similar to what people perceived as angels in the past?'

'If their technology was on a par with what we are experiencing today, even revered as gods.'

'Gods?'

'Why not, they reputedly performed miracles.' He smiled. 'Lesser gods perhaps.' He looked around. 'Our discussion seems to have emptied the place, perhaps we ought to be making tracks.' He stood up. 'I have an engagement this evening and it's quite a drive from here.' He winked at me before leaning down and giving Genna a peck on the cheek. I'll see you both the day after tomorrow.' He straightened up and shook my hand. 'Take care of each other. We may one day discover that it was lesser gods that somehow created man in their image.' He turned and headed for the door without looking back.

'What was all that about David?'

'The wine probably.' I helped her to her feet. Time to go Genn.' I drew her towards me and kissed her. 'Merry Christmas Genna Rees, my place or yours?'

She responded to the corny line with a laugh. 'What do you think David Kent?'

111

Chapter 19

Reynard handed me a teleprinter printout almost as soon as we assembled in his office. It was the autopsy report on the mutilated calf. It mainly confirmed what Genna had reported; it had been electrocuted prior to the procedures carried out on it.

Once again we took up our former positions, there was one difference; Arthur C White was also present. He made it clear that he was only there to observe.

'It's your show Bill.' He tapped a small box on his lap which I took to be some sort of recording instrument. 'I'll get copies of this to each of you later.'

Back in the recliner Genna looked much more composed than she had previously. It took just the key word Reynard had already primed her with to put her back in trance.

'Genna I am going to take you to the point where the policemen have just left and you and Derek are checking the area.' I glanced at Ganymede, he was staring intently at Genna; my mouth had gone dry.

'It's the light, it's blinding me.' In the chair she seemed to recoil deeper. I felt rather than saw Ganymede lean forward beside me.

'You say that the light is blinding you. Can you see anything at all? Reynard's voice sounded soft, relaxed.

'It's gone out now.'

'Can you see anything now?' There was a long pause before she answered.

'There is a soft glow... over everything ...,' her voice was almost a whisper.

'Can you see Derek Collins, is he there with you?'

'I... oh dear.'

'What is it Genna?'

'It's Derek ... I can see him ... he's just lying there, I must go to him.'

'Is there anything or anyone else there with you, can you see where this glow is coming from?'

'I can see something above me ...' There was a sharp intake of breath ... 'It's coming down, it's glowing all over... it's getting bigger ...' There was panic now in her voice ...

'It's all right Genna, you're safe; nothing to fear.' Reynard's voice was low, controlled, almost caressing. Genna's voice, when she spoke, once again had that dreamy quality.

'I can't move. I can't go to Derek. He is lying quite still.'

'You can't move, why is that?'

'I ... don't know. I am floating now ... it is so peaceful.'

'Listen carefully Genna, I want you, if you can, to tell me what is happening to you, do you understand?' She made no acknowledgement. It was as if she was preoccupied. It was several seconds before she spoke again.

'It feels strange, there are people floating with me, they are helping me, they are saying there is nothing to fear.'

'They talk to you?'

'No ... this is funny ... they are putting words in my head.' Reynard's glance in my direction was significant.

'How many are with you?'

'Two, but I feel there are more around.'

'Can you describe them?'

'They are quite small, shorter than me, like children ... Oh!...'

'Is something wrong?'

'We have been joined by a much taller one; different than the others. While they have large heads and strange eyes, this one looks much more human.'

'Does he speak with you?'

'Only in my mind, like the others. I ask him about Derek and he says he is well.'

'Can you ask why this is happening to you?'

'He says they are on a study mission. He is leading me towards a large screen; we seem to float towards it. He touches something and the screen lights up and I can see Earth. It is beautiful, it ... we are moving away from it, and it is getting smaller. He tells me not to worry; we will only be away for a short while.'

'You are leaving the Earth, where are you going?'

'I ... don't know ...' her voice was fading and she remained silent for a while. Reynard sat making notes apparently unconcerned. Ganymede relaxed back in his chair. I sat, still tense, waiting for what might come next; it wasn't long coming.

'What am I doing here?' Her voice was shrill; insistent.

'Doing where, Genna?' Reynard put his notes aside.

'I am on a table. There are three of the little people around me. The tall one is standing behind them, he says they only want to examine me and then he will show me around the ship.'

'How does that make you feel?'

113

'I … feel … that I will come to no harm.'

'What does the examination consist of?'

'I am being poked and prodded.'

'Are you in any pain?'

'There is no pain. I can feel what they are doing; it's like when I've had minor ops under local anaesthetic.' There is a long silence. Reynard is back with his notes. The minutes dragged like waiting for a kettle to boil. Then she was speaking again. 'He tells me it is a mother ship he is showing me, it is not like the one I was lifted up in. There are three like that in the hangar; this place is enormous, there are these small people everywhere. They would like to take me to their home, but I am not prepared; I would not survive in my present form.'

'Do you know why that is?'

'No. He tells me they must take me back now as they have other business to attend to. He shows me the screen again.'

'What can you see now?

'I'm not sure. There were stars but they were passing quickly; now everything is a blur, I think we are travelling very fast.' Once again she was silent for a while.

'What is happening now Genna?' Reynard broke the silence.

'I'm floating. There are lights below… now they are passing by '... Derek is nowhere in sight.' Reynard looked puzzled for a moment, and then he appeared to catch up with what I was already thinking.

'Are you in the field you and Derek first went to?'

It was when she confirmed that, that Reynard seemed satisfied and brought her back to the present.

'Okay, I think we'll wrap it up there.' He looked to where Arthur C was replacing his box in its bag. 'Is that all right with you sir?'

'I guess so Bill. I think the little lady has had quite enough of an ordeal.' To Genna he said. 'If you do remember anything at a future date honey we would like to hear about it.'

Twelve hours later Genna was admitted to the sick bay suffering from abdominal pains and a severe headache. Arthur C White ordered a full body scan.

I had never heard of such a thing, and I stood open-mouthed wondering what that entailed. Reynard however appeared to be up to speed on the concept. 'Do we have such a thing?'

Arthur C said. 'Not right now.' He looked at each of us in turn as if weighing something up in his mind, and then he turned to Ganymede. 'I think it's time, don't you?'

'Yes sir.'

'You'd better brief them then, it'll be tonight if they get the coordinates right.' He was grinning as he left the office.

'We are expecting an unusual visit tonight.' Ganymede was answering the unspoken query on our faces. 'I think it best if I don't go into details at the moment, perhaps nearer the time. David, I would like you to rendezvous with me in the wood at the end of the old runway. In the MT shed in the old camp there's a covered three tonner; this will get you access.' He handed me a small box similar to the one he had called the door key of tomorrow; it had just one button. It was another gadget that was to become very familiar in the future. 'I want you do drive it to the rendezvous at 2 am in the morning.' He turned to Reynard. 'I'm sorry we couldn't let you into this earlier Bill, but General White has only just got permission to release certain information.

'Well David,' Reynard said later as we sat down for a coffee, 'What do you make of that?'

'It's a rum world Bill. Sometimes I wish I was back in the one of the innocent, ignorant seafarer.'

**

It was a clear cold night. I turned the collar of my greatcoat fully up, grateful for the woolly balaclava's added protection against the chill breeze. A full moon cast eerie shadows as I entered the old camp from the door to the Complex.

As I turned the corner and passed along the front of the MT shed I stared across in the direction of the parade ground, towards where the house and the bulk of the camp buildings had been; all that remained as far as the camp main gate was an empty area literally covered in coil upon coil of razor wire.

The rattle of the garage door as it rose sounded like a prolonged thunderclap in the silent night. I ran the motor of the sole three-tonner within for a while before setting out on the four hundred yards to the wood. Ganymede and Arthur C were already there, their breath clearly visible on the cold night air. Ganymede waved me through a gap in the trees and I came to a halt at the edge of a large clearing. I joined them on the ground despite my reluctance to leave the comparative warmth of the cab.

115

Arthur C was scanning the sky with glasses. I figured it would be an aerial drop although the clearing was hardly big enough for that, so I asked anyway.

'What now guv?'

He too was looking upward and without turning said.

'Our scanner is on the way David, by a very special delivery. In a very short while you will become one of a very few privileged people on the planet.' I was already feeling chilled again and I resented his maintaining an air of mystery.

'Privileged to what?' But he had no time to answer as Arthur C lowered his glasses.

'Here she comes!' There was uncharacteristic excitement in his voice. Ganymede gripped my arm.

'Here comes history in the making David.'

Looking up all I could see at first was a clear starlit sky, and then I saw it. Slightly larger than the surrounding stars it quickly increased in size until it resembled the mock up I had seen in the Complex, but this one looked alive and glowing like phosphorescence in a dark sea.

'Is that ...?' I didn't really need an answer as it descended with barely a whisper of sound in the centre of the clearing. The glow diminished to a pale grey as it settled. It appeared to be supported on legs and I watched with hairs standing on the back of my neck as a figure emerged from beneath it. There was an air of eerie unreality about what was happening. The figure beckoned and moved to the outer rim where a ramp was descending.

'Drop the tailgate David, our package has arrived.' With that, Arthur C and Ganymede walked across to the disc. I did as asked and watched from the side of the truck. There was a brief exchange between Arthur C and the bulky looking figure that had emerged from the craft, and then they were returning with a crate which they carried between them. It needed my help to get it up on to the bed of the truck. I slipped the tailgate into position and joined them for the craft's departure. It was already surrounded in a luminescent glow. I had to pinch myself once again to make sure all this was really happening. It rose soundlessly to about 300 feet and then at incredible speed diminished to a mere speck of light on the distant horizon.

Ganymede and Arthur C followed me back to the old door of the Complex where they unloaded the crate and carried it inside; Ganymede reappeared in the doorway.

116

'That's it for tonight then David,' he said. 'Take the truck back, and go home and get your head down.' Arthur C brushed past him, and held out his hand and crushed mine warmly. 'Despite what you've just seen Dave, we are still a long way even from reaching our local planets, right now with a little help from our friends we have a propulsion system equal to none, but we still haven't got the radiation shielding necessary for a trip into outer space.'

'I'm trying not to think that far ahead sir.'

'Good man, but we'll get there; just don't hold your breath.' He laughed as he and Ganymede disappeared through the doorway and the door closed silently behind them.

We assembled, minus Arthur C, in Ganymede's office the next morning. He held a forefinger down on a sheet of paper before him. Genna, as far as I could make out was still in the sick bay.

'The scan on Miss Rees was conducted in the early hours of this morning; she was not found to be suffering from anything more serious than female period pains. She has been granted a day or two of rest.' Then he raised his eyes and looked in our direction, 'There was however something that we have been made aware of in the past but have never up to now actually come across; the scan located an implant of infinitesimal size. The odd thing is there was no evidence of any wound, which may indicate that it's been in situ for some time. This we have been able to retrieve and it is being examined in order to ascertain its function.'

'I believe it may be a location device.' All eyes looked towards Reynard. 'Like the leg tagging of birds and the tracking devices they attach to animals to track their movements over a time period. Far more sophisticated though, even than our ID implants.'

'I'm inclined to agree Bill. It would explain how they are able to locate those they have visited before.' Ganymede looked across at me. 'Perhaps David here ought to be scanned; he's had several rather unusual visitations.' Reynard nodded.

'We have had countless reports of contactee regressions where contact has been made at various times throughout their lives. I'm sure David here would be only too pleased to cooperate.' Ganymede accepted that with a proviso.

'I would like to wait and see what the lab turns up on Miss Rees's implant, if that's okay Bill?'

117

'No problem. In the meantime I think I'll drop in on her for an informal chat. I'm sure David here would like to come along.'

She had a small plaster low down on the left side of her neck. She didn't appear to be in any discomfort, in fact quite the opposite; quite cheerful.

'Hi David. Where are the flowers and chocolates?'

'Damn! I knew there was something.' She tutted and looking past me acknowledged Bill.

'Mr Reynard.'

'Hello Genna. How are you feeling?' He took the only bedside chair. I moved around to the other side and sat on the bed; it felt like a proprietary action.

'Fine sir. When can I leave here?'

'I should think tomorrow, we can't afford to keep healthy young women in dock. I'll arrange for you to have a few days off, and David here too so that he can keep an eye on you.' With that he got up to leave. He paused at the door. 'I'll also arrange a time for your scan David; it'll be sometime tomorrow morning.'

I stayed until the dragon at the reception desk all but threw me out.

**

'Your scan has proved positive David.' Reynard eyed me solemnly. 'Take a seat; there are a few things we need to discuss.'

After the scan that morning I had taken Genna to her place to pick up a few things she might need. She still didn't feel she wanted to be on her own for a while. I certainly wasn't going to dissuade her from staying with me. We were on the point of leaving when the call came for me to report in. I gave her the key to my apartment and told her to make herself at home before heading back to the Complex.

'Problem, Bill? I'm bugged, is that it?' He nodded. It seemed ridiculous to think that I had been a marked man even before coming to the Complex and getting an ID chip.

'I think you may have been carrying the implant from very young.'

'You mean ...?

'That's how your childhood friends were able to locate you; they could come in any guise they wished.'

After already having been acquainted with much that went on in what could only be described as the secret world, what Reynard was saying made sense.'

118

'So, you think it's been there since then?'

'From the many reports we have from contactees throughout the world there is no doubt that a very high percentage have been visited at various times since very early childhood.'

'Is Genna Rees also one of them?'

'I never regressed her back that far as you know, so I can't say. Her implant is still being examined but the technology is far in advance of anything we are capable of at present, we may still learn nothing.'

'Can you take mine out?'

'Ah! That's a real problem. Look David, I won't beat about the bush, yours is located close to an area of the brain called the amygdala and could well be inoperable.'

'What's that when it's about?'

'Difficult one, and I have very little expertise in that area, but we have been taking advice on it. It's a part of the brain that does have something to do with the sympathetic nervous system, with emotional memories, and even producing them; including those associated with fear. It is also linked with things like sexual orientation. I could go on David, but it all comes down to being a dodgy area to operate in.'

'Don't worry Bill that last bit is quite enough for me to give the thumbs down on any attempt on recovering something that causes me no trouble or discomfort. And whoever is monitoring me from 'out there' hasn't caused me any harm to date. I can live with that.'

It did occur to me that it might have been implanted in that area for a reason and I said so.

Reynard laughed. 'It could indicate that you are something special and they didn't want it to be removed.' He appeared to consider that before continuing with some amusement. 'They probably think we are still struggling with the hammer and chisel days of trepanning. Brain surgery has made considerable advances since those days but like I said, it's a dodgy area. He was attempting to make light of it and I accorded it a laugh.

'Yeah, I read that somewhere; even in the Stone Age they knew how to let the devil out.' It eased the situation out of gloom and doom.

'We'll have to leave it there I'm afraid David ... oh by the way, our American trip has been rescheduled, we take off in a week's time.'

I can't say that at that moment I felt any particular joy at the prospect. Being re-united with Genna after her ordeal seemed to have altered my perspective of life in general. Not that I wasn't interested in what I was discovering about the world in general and the covert activity behind the façade of normality, but its importance had dropped more than a degree or two.

Quan Ling passed me as I left Reynard's office. I realised I hadn't seen her around for a few days. She looked pale; we exchanged smiles of greeting.

Genna was there waiting for me when I got back to the flat; it didn't seem to have been quite so bad a day after all.

She was reading as I entered. She put it to one side and made as if to stand up, I waved her down.

'No. Please, you give this place atmosphere.' She laughed and settled down again.

'How do you mean?'

'I'm not sure, but it wasn't here before you came. What's that you're reading?' She held it up showing the cover.

'An Everybodys, it was under the pile over there, I hope you don't mind.'

'Oh that. No it's an old one; I think Ganymede gave it to me.'

'It's quite interesting, isn't it?'

'How do you mean?' Even from where I stood I still couldn't see how Rex Harrison dressed as a sheik could be called interesting.'

'You haven't read it then?' I explained why. She ruffled the pages and folded them back before handing it to me.

The article was headed 'We were shadowed from outer space'. I looked at the date on the magazine December 11th 1954. I skimmed through it. It was about a sighting of a mother ship attended by six smaller craft, by the pilot and crew and several passengers in a BOAC Stratocruiser, over the Atlantic. The craft remained in sight for 18 minutes, until the arrival of a fighter plane sent to investigate. The date of the sighting was June 1954; 8 years ago. I remembered Genna's mention of a mother ship during her regression. The UFO input I was getting for my database had never come up to this standard.

So that's why Ganymede had given it to me; he wanted me to catch up on the reality and enormity of space craft in our skies. It was mortifying the way things took so long to catch up with me.

'Half the world would have known about this Genn, Why does it make me think I joined the wrong half?'

120

'Not to worry David. I used to feel the same when I first came to the Complex, but we sure know differently now, don't we?'

'I'll say.'

I spent just one more night of discomfort on the settee before, as if by mutual consent, we decided that the Welsh custom of 'bundling' could only have been a credit to their intelligence. Using our own measure of commonsense we dispensed with the customary central obstruction. I can't say I missed being either noble or stupid.

Chapter 20

Reynard moved away from the two men he was conversing with as I entered.

'What's with Quan Ling Bill, she's looking a bit peaky?'

'She was at a crash site; messy business, no survivors. I'll tell you about it later.' He led me over to the two men. 'Meanwhile I'd like you to meet Major Gessler and Sergeant Shelman who are to accompany us on the American trip.' The introductions made, I felt I could get along with Gessler although he was in uniform. Tall, slim and crew cut, his Glen Miller spectacles gave him the same academic look as the popular 40's bandleader, but the eyes behind them were as sharp and alert as a German guard dog. Apart from Arthur C he was the only American brass I had met. Having been virtually shanghaied from the army into my civilian role, I now felt some parity with senior ranks in the services; they no longer outranked me.

Shelman I wasn't sure of. He was in uniform, and sported the chevrons of a sergeant. He wore pistol at his hip and I assumed rightly that he was Gessler's bodyguard. He was cap-less, so there was no way of knowing what branch of the service he was. His close-cropped blonde hair contrasted sharply with a deeply tanned face. His smile only barely reached blue-grey eyes as we shook hands, and then he stood back with his hands held lightly in front below his waistline. It was a deceptively relaxed pose, probably a split second away from blasting someone with the sidearm he wore. Little did I know that one day I would be grateful for him to do just that.

They had already reached the end of what they were discussing before I came in, and after pointing them in the direction of the cafeteria, Reynard turned once again to me.

'The major and Shelman brought Quan Ling back with them from Dreamland.' He saw my puzzled look. 'Ah! Sorry David. It's a name, in fact one of the names they've given to one of their top secret sites in the Nevada desert, and it's where they take some of their crash retrievals. It can't be a pretty sight; jars of pickled aliens or their remains.'

'It certainly doesn't sound too choice. If she witnessed that I'm not surprised she found it disturbing.'

'That wasn't the hard bit, she's a pretty tough cookie really, but they also retrieved human body parts from the wreck?'

'Humans?'

'That's right. The situation is still being evaluated. We have no clues as yet as to why they were dismembering and dissecting humans.' He looked grave and shook his head. 'Some appeared to be young children.'

'My God!'

'Exactly. I'm afraid we are faced with the distinct possibility that not all of our visitors from space have our best interests at heart.'

It was a shocking revelation. Up til then I had assumed, from my own experience and that of Genna's, that these space beings were, at the very least, benevolent. Bill Reynard agreed that from the contacts and abductees that he was aware of, that appeared to be the case. We were obviously working on the wrong assumption.

'We may learn more from this trip.'

'Is it to this Dreamland place?'

'Not sure David, but it's either there or somewhere similar. The way these Yanks operate we probably won't even know exactly where we are when we do get there. Their military and the intelligence agencies are paranoid over security.'

'Anyone else going on this trip?'

'Ganymede is going on ahead with Arthur C. They have some different business initially, but I believe he plans to meet up with us at some point.'

'Who'll keep shop here?'

'The redoubtable Quan Ling, who else? That reminds me she may be in need of counselling after that experience. I'll fit that in before we leave. Makris too will be here. I'm sure they will be able to take care of things between them. How would you feel about Genna Rees going along with us?' There was a hint of amusement in his eyes. My look of pleasure was obviously all the answer he needed. Genna was equally as pleased when I told her the news.

We travelled north a few days later, arriving at Greenham airfield in Berkshire at midday. It was shared jointly by the USAF and the RAF. Security was almost as tight as in wartime. American military police, nicknamed 'snowdrops' owing to their white helmets, were everywhere. We sat in a hangar which served as the departure lounge accompanied by the muted roar and welcome warmth of hot air blowers. The trip in an unheated vehicle had left us rather chilled. Although spartan, the hangar was, in true American style, furnished with a fine refreshment

123

bar including the traditional doughnuts, and coffee by the gallon. American servicemen including the brass stood around in mixed groups apparently maintaining the myth of a classless society. I was yet to be exposed to the hypocrisy of democracy, but right then, as I sat waiting with Genna for the order to board, I was a very happy bunny.

Reynard joined us and informed us that we would be flying over seven miles high at 500 mph by Boeing B47E Stratocruiser. I wondered, with beings shooting around space at incomprehensible speeds, if that was really in the realm of achievement. For people who had been brought up to believe we were the acme of creation we seemed to be rapidly losing the plot.

After the comfort and warmth of the plane it was only a matter of minutes for the effect of the chill night air of the desert to find a way past my outer clothing. Reynard stating that eight degrees above freezing was a lot warmer than England at this time did nothing to dispel the chill. As we stood beneath the wing trying to get in the warm aura of the jet engine Gessler apologised for the delay of the bus arranged for our onward transport.

'A last minute decision as to where would be the most suitable for your visit I'm afraid. It sort of caught them with their pants down.'

Once in the warmth of what I assumed was our destination I was able to take stock of our surroundings. I estimated we had travelled down about three levels to get here but you never could tell with lifts; the ones here ran silent and at speed, leaving a momentary feeling of weightlessness. We were shown through to a fair sized dining area where we were immediately under the scrutiny of those already in the process of their evening meal. There was a definite shortage of smiles as Gessler led us to an empty corner table.

'This is where we leave you for a while Mr Reynard,' he looked at his watch. 'We move on again in a couple of hours, that should give you time to get some eats and any other refreshments. We keep a well stocked bar and I can see a waitress is already on her way to take care of you.' With that he rejoined Shelman waiting watchfully nearby, and departed.

Despite the late hour, we voted unanimously for steak, egg, chips, and peas; always an overseas favourite of mine during my sea-going days, and forever thereafter. The beer was however

124

too cold and gassy for me, I settled for coffee, Genna and Reynard also declined and went for Californian red wine. It took some believing that this was how the service personnel in these underground bases lived.

The general assembly soon lost interest in us and as they finished their meals and drifted away in two's and three's until finally we had the place to ourselves. Reynard had been here before and was familiar with some of the set up.

'This section is a sort of hotel complex, residential mainly for those who work in the installation and a tourist stopover for dignitaries like us,' he laughed. 'We will, on the surface anyway, be treated as VIP's but they'll watch us like hawks and they'll only show us what they want us to see; a bit like royalty but without the red carpets and flower posies.'

Gessler and his shadow showed again in due course and wheeled us off to our quarters for the night; it was 4 star by any reckoning. Genna and I found ourselves in adjoining rooms with a communicating door; it was unlocked. It occurred to me that Major Gessler was both a tactician and a diplomat. My room had an ensuite shower and toilet and Genna's went overboard with the addition of what I soon learned was a Jacuzzi. We tossed a mental penny and decided it was big enough for two; I wondered as we luxuriated in the bubbling water if we were already under surveillance. Both rooms had a double bed; we settled for just the one in the smug belief that any surveillance ended with lights out; fortunately at that time I had no knowledge of infra-red technology.

As we sat at breakfast next morning we were joined once again by Gessler. Shelman sat alone at a nearby table and feeling his eyes on me I looked at him. His lopsided grin and a slow wink of the eye puzzled me for a considerable time. Gessler sat half-turned with his back towards us and conducted a brief low-toned conversation with Reynard before turning back to face us. It was a moment or two, during which Genna and I were exchanging little eye messages like a couple of lovesick teenagers, before we realised Gessler was now including us in the conversation.

'We are going for short flight today to a place we call Paradise Ranch. It has other names which I won't go into; suffice to say that I have been assured that you all have clearance for a visit there. I need to stress at this point that although we have no equivalent of your Official Secrets Act; once you enter any

125

military controlled installation here you are automatically under the jurisdiction of our intelligence services. The penalties for the disclosure of any classified information can be painfully severe.' Here he looked at each of us in turn with a disarming smile. 'In actual fact when you visit Paradise Ranch or any similar installation, you have seen nothing, heard nothing, and for your own good health, you say nothing.'

Our destination appeared as a vast bowl-shaped depression almost completely surrounded by ranges of hills, some of considerable height. We came in low over them and landed on what appeared to be a dry lake bed. Reynard caught my questioning look.

''Groom Lake, I was here last year on a very tight leash, perhaps we'll get to see more than I did then.'

'What actually goes on here?'

'Officially it's designated as a design and test area for advanced aircraft. The hangars you can see from your window house some like the one that flew in the scanner to the Complex.'

'And unofficially?' I was getting used to the idea that nothing in this strange new world I now inhabited was really as it seemed.

'Unofficially I can't honestly say. There are rumours ranging from the bizarre to the unbelievable, I think it best we just go along with this and see what the score is.'

'The score being only what these people are prepared to show us.'

'Exactly. Better unbelt now, here comes the man who probably knows all there is to know about this place.' We rose from our seats as Gessler and his shadow approached. I felt Genna move alongside me and slip her hand into mine; we exchanged a reassuring squeeze.

It was hardly the tour I had expected, it was almost as if seeing one flying saucer, a name that certainly seemed to have caught on, you've seen them all. Ganymede joined us in the closing stages. According to my watch it was just after noon. He took me to one side leaving Genna and Reynard to continue on with Gessler and the hovering Shelman.

'I think it's time for you to know what is really going on here David. Gessler will rejoin us in a bit and Bill will stay with Genna and show her around the less restricted areas.' He took my arm and guided me to a door set in the side of the hangar.

126

Outside was a four-wheel drive containing a driver, and what could only be an armed escort.

We had encountered a number of these characters, they seemed all to be cast in the same mould; khaki drill overalls, middle-aged, slightly overweight and carrying a side-arm and a communication device.

'They just keep an eye on who goes where and why.' Ganymede supplied. 'This is where it really gets interesting David, it's a pity Genna doesn't have our level of clearance.'

'What about Bill?'

'He's probably seen all he wants to of what's down here. Bill's interest is in the people who bring them here especially those who crawl out or are dragged out alive.'

'Dragged out?' I looked at him sharply. His gaze was steady as it met mine. He indicated for us to keep our voices down.

'Bill got something from a reliable source about a crew of little guys who were brutalised because they wouldn't give up their individual control boards. Apparently they clung onto them for dear life. According to Bill's informant, an oil surveyor who was in the area at the time, the panels looked to be flat metallic plates with deep impressions into which the operator's hands fitted. That was the best he could make out through field glasses. He didn't hang around; he didn't wish to be caught up with the military.'

'Especially a mean shower of bastards like that.'

'Exactly.'

We were driving down a ramp into a tunnel at the end of which steel doors opened as if by magic as we approached them. We came to a halt in a natural arena containing saucer-shaped craft; but these were different from any I had seen so far. They looked to be at least 100 feet in diameter and all with similar peculiarities; they were, without exception, all badly damaged.

'These are the real thing, aren't they guv?'

'All genuine ET vehicles David, all crash retrievals.'

There were five of them and it was evident that some had been worked on.

'What happened to the crews?' It seemed under the circumstances a genuine question; the answer sent a little chill through me.

'The live ones are here on this base.'

I had heard rumours that there were some survivors from crashes apart from the EBE that Quan Ling had mentioned at her

127

lecture. But to hear there were some actually here, in this place, actual people from other worlds, what price Flash Gordon? I was wondering how it would feel to actually come face to face with one.

'Have you seen them?' Of course the answer shouldn't have surprised me.

'Just an hour ago as close as you are to me. They are dodgy lot though according to Gessler, their demands for sharing their technology are way over the top.'

'You mean they are not being held as prisoners?' It was here that he studied me thoughtfully for a moment before answering. We had walked some distance from the Landrover, and out of earshot of the driver and the escort.

'It could almost be said that it might be the other way around.'

'You mean ...' I was having difficulty with this, and the way the conversation was going.

'David,' he sounded almost fatherly. 'These people are thousands of years ahead of us. They travel the stars for crissake, something that could take us thousands of years to even attempt. Most of these...' he indicated the crashed vehicles; 'were brought down quite by accident; our radar equipment caused some malfunction of their power sources. Others were struck by lightning which also affected their control systems. On the surface they represent a potential threat to our world; we've no idea what forces they could bring to bear if they were so minded. That is why the US government has thought it prudent to establish a treaty with these ET's.'

'But you said earlier they were a dodgy lot.'

'In spades. They've already broken their word on several occasions.'

'How many of these beings are there?'

'That's a problem. We know now that they have long established secret bases that we have been unable to locate, and those we know about have proved to be impregnable.'

'So there have been attempts to dislodge them?'

'Absolutely futile, their force fields are formidable. We had an operative who approached too close to a space vehicle once that obviously wasn't up to being examined; he lost the use of one arm when it made contact with the force field.'

Seated once again in the Landrover I was able to let my thoughts run wild for a bit. It was no consolation to realise the potential threat these space visitors posed. Even Ganymede's assurance that according to most people who had been contacted by them throughout the world they had appeared to be benevolent in their dealings, was barely comforting.

**

'Now gentlemen, you have seen their machines, I think it is time for you to become acquainted with those who operate them.' Gessler's words set the butterflies in motion. I looked at Ganymede, he just grinned back.

We left the Landrover and entered a lift that seemed to descend forever despite its rate of descent. Gessler looked at me and answered the unasked question.

'We have come down seven levels Mr Kent. The odd thing about our visitors is that despite their ability to travel in the far reaches of space they seem just as happy to be deep underground.'

He ushered us into a cavern of considerable size, the walls of which was lined with what I assumed were laboratory benches. There was no ignoring the dominant feature however, despite the fact that we were immediately confronted by a man I estimated to be at least seven feet tall. At six feet I rarely had to look up at anyone. He was decidedly human. Long blonde hair reached narrow shoulders encased like the rest of him in a close fitting pale grey overall. His face had an angelic cast and the blue eyes icy and staring were otherwise devoid of expression; my first face to face contact with an alien being, he could have represented friend or foe equally. I felt no inclination to reach out to prove he was real, in fact I felt intimidated. I looked past him at the huge vehicle. It stood at least two stories high and looked to be twice the span of anything I had seen so far. There were others like the one before me standing around it.

'You have permission to come here major?' He was addressing Gessler, and his voice indicated that our presence was an affront; the resentment was barely concealed.

'All I need Jarl. We still have the right to prove your existence here to a select few.' Gessler's tone was far from conciliatory. I could sense an air of antagonism between them. 'I see you have made a great deal of progress with your project.'

'More than in your wildest dreams major. Perhaps you would like to take a trip with us when we are completed.' He lifted one hand in the direction of the giant vehicle. It was a moment before it registered; the four digits on his hand had nails that curved

129

inwards like claws. The sinister undercurrent to Jarl's words could have been imagined; I decided I didn't like this guy.

'Thanks no, I like my feet on terra firma, I know where I am here.'

'Ah! But do you major – do you?' With that Jarl turned on his heel walked arrogantly off.

'Well gentlemen you see what we are presented with here. We are working on ways to control these guys, but so far without success. Let's get the hell outa here; quite frankly they give me the creeps.'

'That craft they're building, what's that all about?' I looked forward to being back in the fresh air; I wasn't too happy with the feel of this place. I was curious as to how they were going to get that massive vehicle up into the open anyway.

Gessler said. 'We can only sit back and wait. They may be still developing their technology and it may be some sort of experimental craft. They do toss us a few scraps now and then which enable us to repair some of their crashed vehicles. They even help sometimes in their reconstruction.'

'So it's not all bad?'

'That's the puzzle Mr Kent; they can switch from arrogant disregard to friendly cooperation. Recently they have been teaching some of our top test pilots how to fly their craft.'

'That can't be bad surely?'

'One of those crashed vehicles you saw earlier cost us one damn good flyboy and two others we never saw the going of; their craft just blew up, vaporised minutes after take-off.'

'So you think…?'

'It's difficult not to. I don't think we will ever know for sure just what we are dealing with here. Throughout the world as you know meetings with these Nordic types as they call them have been regarded as friendly. One guy claims to have met some from Venus and to have taken trips into space with them.'

'Yeah I've heard about that, I believe he was very convincing,' I assumed that was the one Bill came over to investigate. 'I'm getting to the stage where I no longer need much convincing,'

Gessler said without turning his head as we followed him back to the lifts, with Shelman bringing up the rear. 'Okay I thought the same, and subsequent contacts with these people have substantiated his claims.' He turned towards us as we stopped at the lifts. 'We think that what we have here are not true Nordic types; we think they could be hybrids.'

'Sounds reasonable, cross breeding has been practised on Earth for thousands of years, why not elsewhere in space?' said Ganymede.'

'That's right. The problem is, who the cross-breeding has been between. We know that those on base here control a species called grays, small guys, skinny with big heads and wrap-around black eyes.'

'I saw pictures of them back in England. I heard that some people abducted by them had a hard time,' I said.

'That's true, but there are also what are known as tall grays, they are about the same size as people like Jarl; make a good match for cross-breeding wouldn't you say?'

There was little more to discuss. Sometimes on Earth crossbreeding brought out the best of the participants, sometimes the reverse. Dodgy was an eminently suitable label for the likes of Jarl, I thought.

The following day we left Paradise Ranch by army transport, flying roughly south east. I wasn't told our destination. I was reunited with Genna and Reynard. This time we were minus Gessler and Shelman.

I asked Ganymede the leading question.

'Gessler and Shelman have gone on ahead apparently to somewhere in New Mexico.'

'Is that where we are headed guv?'

'I believe so. Gessler wasn't very forthcoming on that.'

'How do you rate Gessler?'

'I'd say he was a worried man.' Reynard's remark caused us to turn abruptly to him.

'Why do you say that?' Ganymede asked.

'Call it gut feeling if you like. Something is bothering that man, but I can't put my finger on it.'

'He seems a pretty cool cat to me Bill considering the knowledge he is carting around with him.'

'That could be the problem David. Even the bit we are sharing with him is a bit heavy, don't you think?'

'Things the general public have no knowledge of.' He gave a thoughtful nod.

'I think despite his outward acceptance of what goes on in these places, and remember we will probably never know the full extent of that , he may be finding it difficult to keep the lid on.'

'He might blow the whistle, you mean?'

'Think about it David. These places are alive with strange beings and their craft and goodness knows what else we may never be privy to. The governments of the world are pooh-poohing and spreading disinformation about the very things that we know are reality. It's not surprising that there may be some who may be thinking, only thinking mind you, that people have a right to know what's going on in their world.'

'And create mass panic?' Ganymede from across the aisle was listening to the exchange.

'That is the assumption and the excuse for keeping it all under wraps. Governments always assume that everyone on the street is an easily controlled moron incapable of reasonable thought.'

'I'm beginning to wish I hadn't agreed to come on this trip.' She tried to make it sound light-hearted, but Genna's comment may have reflected the thoughts that most of us were having. For myself I was beginning at times to think I was at odds with a reality I had grown up with, and but for those visitations during my childhood that Reynard had uncovered I might have been tempted to back away from this whole thing.

Nevertheless I was intrigued by what was being revealed from behind the scenes of normality. My companions on this strange odyssey, on the surface at least, appeared to be normal if not everyday people; I decided, in Gessler's words, to hang in there; a decision I was later to very much regret.

We touched down at Stapleton airfield in Denver Colorado and spent a few hours kicking our heels as we waited for onward transport to our final destination. It came in the form of a helicopter.

'Are we going in that?' asked Genna in an awed whisper. She stated my own thoughts exactly.

'Unfortunately, yes.' Ganymede confirmed our fears. 'They don't look much I agree, but I have travelled in them and they do the job. The place we are headed for has no airstrip as such and these things can land virtually anywhere.'

'Where exactly are we headed Guv?'

'Somewhere in New Mexico, place called Montaña de panal.'

'I've heard of it,' said Reynard. 'Can't remember where or how, on an Indian Reservation, isn't it?'

'That's right, Apache' Ganymede nodded in confirmation. 'A place of rumours. Lots of UFO sightings and disappearances; cattle – people -- domestic pets.'

'Sounds a fun place, what does that mean; Montaña de panel?' I said, and I could see by the look on Genna's face the same thought had occurred to her.

'I never knew there was a base there.' Reynard looked puzzled. 'But then I seem to be in the dark about one or two things.' There was no mistaking the pique in his voice.

'There isn't yet Bill.' Then to me. 'It translates as Honeycomb Mountain. The Indians keep well away believing it's inhabited by evil spirits.' He turned again to Reynard. 'Look I'm sorry we haven't kept you up to speed Bill, but everything comes from higher up; they make the rules, it's a Yank show. I only learnt we were heading for this Honeycomb Montaña place myself whilst in Denver'

'So if there's no base there, why include it in the tour?' Reynard still sounded slightly miffed; not quite in character, I thought.

'It's something to do with negotiations, Bill. Up till now it's been all up to the Yanks, but it seems that that certain elements in the British Government have been putting on the pressure and we are going for a bigger share of the action.'

'You mean we Brits have actually got some clout in this?'

'That's right; the aim is for a shared base.'

'In Montaña de panal?'

'That is my information, when and where is still to be worked out.'

'So where do we fit in guv, are we in the negotiations?'

'We David old chap are once again here as observers. We look and listen and are seen and not heard. This little town, which is of the one-horse variety takes its name from the nearby mountain and is little more than an old mining settlement. But it will be buzzing with brass and military intelligence bods from both sides of the pond. Many of them will be totally unknown to us even from our side, and will remain that way. The negotiations will be highly classified and we may be excluded at times, especially when some of those involved are never seen on the public scene.'

'Faceless men?'

'And women, David; the female of the species, eh? Sorry Miss Rees, present company excepted.' Genna nodded graciously in Ganymede's direction.

'Right, let's get aboard then and be on our way.

133

There were three crewmen; pilot and co-pilot, and a loader, and two occupants in a forward passenger bay already on board. They had their backs to us. There was no mistaking the aura of CIA that hung over them. We had ample space for us and our luggage and were barely seated before we were executing what I would describe as a very unstable take off; like being in a small boat in a rough sea.

I had experience in small boats; I found I didn't like helicopters much either, they were too lively for my stomach.

Chapter 21

Honeycomb Mountain

The immensity of America's arid deserts hold a strange
fascination, but at the same time a sense of uneasiness for me. It
was similar to my reaction once watching an Indian snake
charmer with a cobra. Behind the fascinating façade danger
lurked. This one we had been flying over for roughly an hour
finished almost abruptly against a mountain range which at first
glance appeared just as barren. Scattered at its foot a sprawl of
ruins and a drunken derrick indicated ancient abandoned mine
workings. We landed close by and stepped out into what would
pass for a hot summer's day in Britain, and it was good to feel
something stable underfoot again.

The two agents in their garish Hawaiian shirts, dark
sunglasses, and identical grips moved rapidly towards a low
adobe building and disappeared inside.

'I wonder what those two are all about.'

'These two will probably know,' said Ganymede. I spotted
Gessler and his faithful sidekick heading towards us in a
Landrover. He loaded us on and we skirted the mine workings
and headed for a narrow opening in the foothills. From there a
limestone track led us for about two hundred yards to a
cavernous opening in the cliff face. Then we were underground
in the cool. The cave was as big as any sports arena and
artificially lit. Stalactites festooned large areas of the roof, and
corresponding stalagmites reared up in their efforts to join them.
An area had been cleared and levelled to afford parking for a
number of vehicles.

'It's beautiful.' Genna's comment hardly needed condoning;
the place sparkled like a jeweller's window.

The temperature had taken quite a dive compared with the
world outside, and I couldn't suppress a shiver as Gessler and
Shelman led us through double glass doors into a foyer with
doors leading off in several directions. I looked around trying to
comprehend the incomprehensible.

'Welcome to the Montana Hilton folks,' said Gessler. 'I'm
afraid we don't run to a receptionist or room service yet, but I
think you'll find the accommodation and the chow up there with
the four stars.' He pointed to one of the doors. 'Through there
you'll find a series of rooms, just take your pick, and make

135

yourselves at home.' He pointed to another door. 'Through there is the eatery. We'll have to leave you to it I'm afraid. We have a major security alert on at the moment, some environmental nut on the loose. Nothing for you guys to worry about. We'll apprehend him and relocate him where he won't be troublesome.' He and Shelman were leaving through yet another door when he paused. 'This door is out of bounds by the way, unless you are accompanied by us or a security officer.'

'Our first 'no go' area,' said Ganymede as the door closed behind him. 'I wonder what they're hiding in there.'

The room Genna and I chose was carved out of the living limestone, which had a slightly pinkish iridescence, it was everything Gessler had promised right down to the headboard lights on the king-size bed and the en suite shower- cum – toilet annexe. It was compact, like a liner's 1st class cabin, but who'd want to swing a cat in a room with a king-size bed. I think the thing that really sold it, if it needed to, was a recessed wall heater to raise the temperature above the 50f found in most underground caves. Ganymede and Reynard were already eating by the time Genna and I had unpacked and made some use of the facilities provided. She was proving to be the bonus in my life that had long been denied.

At lunch we opted for a cold choice; a ham salad. Ganymede and Reynard appeared to be deep in conversation; we decided not to intrude and chose a table some distance away. A slight tremor underfoot caused us to look at one another. I looked across at the other table, their heads were raised; they had felt it too.

'It's not volcanic here, is it guv?' I called across.

'I shouldn't think so David. They are hoping to build a base here, that's probably some preliminary blasting. '

'Nothing to worry about then.'

There was movement at the door and Gessler poked his head in, and more or less confirmed Ganymede's comment.

'You may feel an occasional tremor folks. It's nothing to worry about. Most of the work here is done by tunneling machinery but we occasionally need to enlarge some of the cave system with explosives. It shouldn't be too troublesome, most of the activity is a good half a mile from here.' He grinned. 'Now that we have guests to consider I promise we won't blast at night.' He had a few words with Ganymede and Reynard and left again. They rose soon after. Ganymede stopped on his way out.

'We have a meeting David. No need for you to attend. You're off the hook for now. You can get back into civvies if you like. I think you're free to look around, you might find some of the old mine buildings of interest. They're not in the security net; in fact I believe there was a move afoot at one time to preserve them.' With that he followed Reynard out of the door.

'Nice as it is in here I think I'd like to take advantage of the sunshine David,' Genna said as we arrived back in our room. 'People are spending money on trips to Spain for weather like this and we've got it for free.'

She sat on the bed while I changed. I no longer placed much importance to the uniform; I'd wear it when required. Right then I was only too glad to get out of it.

**

'It looks as though they had this earmarked for a museum.' I said as we wandered around the ruins. As a first we had picked a solid-looking sandstone building, but apart from what appeared to be reasonably new shelving and stacks of timber it was empty of artifacts apart from an open crate containing handheld mining implements. We moved on to a two story building. It was timber-framed with adobe panels, and it looked as though it had received some TLC since its construction. The carved lettering over the door stated 1870. It had a pitched roof that was connected by a gantry linked to the remains of a tower. Inside a substantial looking wooden stairway linked the two floors. Only dim light filtered down. I started to climb.

'I'll pass on that David it looks a bit spooky.' She sounded light-hearted but I sensed that wild horses wouldn't drag her.

I stepped into a spacious open area furnished solely by the burlap sacking that was cutting down the light from a single window. In the gloom I could just make out a door in the far wall; it was slightly ajar revealing nothing but darkness beyond. I moved to the window intending to pull aside the burlap to let in more light. There was the merest whisper of sound behind me and a man's voice said. "Leave it." I froze.

'Anything up there David?' Genna called from below.

'Who's that?' The voice again; barely audible broke the spell and I turned around. My eyes had become accustomed to the gloom, and I registered the gun first, then the wild-eyed face above it framed in long unkempt dark hair. 'I said who is it?' This time a hint of menace.

'Friend of mine.' I tried to sound casual but it came across as more of a croak.

'Is there someone up there with you David?' I wanted to yell for her to run for it but he had moved a step closer, the gun levelled at a point between my eyes. It wasn't a hero situation, but I could feel anger beginning to overcome my initial shock at the confrontation. I realised that this was possibly what the security flap was about. There was a flutter of sound from above me, sounded like wildlife. I was vaguely aware that there was a trap in the ceiling, the usual access to the roof space.

'Get her up here – now!' the gunman hissed.

It was a time when events seemed to slow down or the mind speeded up, I'm never sure which. Whatever it was I didn't want Genna involved. If this guy was a terrorist of some sort I didn't want her in a hostage situation.

'David!' there was concern in her voice now. 'What's going on up there?'

I knew she was at the foot of the stairs and could possibly see me but the joker with the gun remained out of her sightline. It was then that I knew what to do, or rather what I had to do.

'It's okay Genn, be down in a minute. You go ahead, I'll catch you up. I think there's something here that might interest Bill.' I locked eyes with the gunman as I spoke, fighting to remain calm. He was not reacting to my refusal to do as he said. It occurred to me that it might be possible to get some measure of control over this situation.

'Don't be too long then.' I heard her move out of the building. Now I only had myself to worry about, but it was little consolation.

'You bastard!' He waved the gun in my face and then retreated a few steps, grinning. 'You silly bastard!'

I knew then that he was reaching the same conclusion as me. If I was a hostage then I was his only bargaining power and that's why he wouldn't shoot. Unless he was stupid or completely round the bend; although that remained a worrying possibility. He pointed to a spot on the floor under the window.

'Sit down David. You don't mind if I call you David, do you?'

'Be my guest.' I felt the tension had eased as I lowered myself down. 'What do I call you?'

'That's not important.' He backed away and crouched against the wall opposite, and let the gun hang loose. 'What are you guys doing here, you and the broad?'

138

'Not a lot at the moment, we're interested in old ghost towns.'

'You're a Limey, yeah? Come all the way from England to look at holes in the ground? Who's Bill?'

'A friend of ours. He's interested in holes in the ground too. What about you?'

'What about me?' He looked to be in his mid to late 20's, a Hippy type.

'What's your interest here; enough to go around pointing guns at people?'

'There's a whole lot of mother-fuckers in there who are dead set on destroying the natural world.' I was getting a picture now. I had heard how militant some of these environmentalists could be.

'And you want to stop that?' He shook his head.

'We can't do much out here in the sticks. Peaceful protest doesn't work here. We can only hinder and hold up their progress.'

'We? There are others here?' He shook his head again.

'Not any more. I had a few old buddies from Nam here for a while but they lit out more'n a month ago, have to do it myself now.'

'Do what exactly?' His teeth showed in a smile.

'A bit o' hinderin' I guess; well you happenin' by has sort of fucked that.' He sat in silence for a long while like he'd retreated into himself. I wondered if I might just stand up and walk out of there, but the gun came up as I eased my feet back under me.

'Easy man. The military taught me how to kill people, I don't want to add you to the tally; ain't got no quarrel with you far's I know, as long as you sit tight.'

'It's just that I'm in the wrong place at the wrong time?' I said. He laughed and let the gun hang loose again.

'Me an' you both man. Tell you what. How's about we turn back the clock. You walk down those stairs and stay put down there for say, 15 minutes, and then rejoin that gal of your'n; give me a chance to hightail it outa here?' I suddenly felt something approaching affection for him.

'That's the best offer I've ......' The place erupted to the sound of a bullhorn.

'We have this place surrounded. Anyone in there come out with your hands in the air.'

He was on his feet in a flash. I instinctively levered myself upright against the window, the burlap fell aside as I did so flooding the room with light; the gun was again levelled at me, and his eyes were wild. I could do nothing but just stand there with my guts tied in knots. I caught sight of a movement above and I raised my eyes without moving my head; the trap was no longer in place. Then everything happened at once.

The bullhorn roared out its demands again as a figure dropped lightly into the space between us. There was a shot and the figure staggered and recovered. My left arm felt touched by a hot iron. The figure resolved into a rear view of Shelman and two more rapid shots echoed in the confined space Footsteps stormed up the stairs and I was once again staring down the barrel of a lethal weapon. I heard Shelman yell something like "area secure!" and the weapon was lowered.

**

'He didn't seem a bad sort really.'

Ganymede had already told me that Jess Bannister had died instantly, and I was accompanying him back to that upper floor room. I had one arm in a sling. It was only a flesh wound but I wouldn't be able to use it properly for a week or two; Banister's bullet had passed through Shelman and hit me. I had visited Shelman in the sickbay; he had taken a nasty shoulder wound, serious but not critical. He had even joked about us being blood brothers.

I learned that he had entered the roof space via the gantry from the derelict building next door. I have never got over the feeling that there was an unnecessary death in that room.

'This is where he was holed up most of the time.' said Ganymede.

We were in the room off the main one; it contained only a bare iron bed frame. 'They cleared everything out. He had enough C4 and dets to do a lot of collateral damage.'

'I suppose you've got to admire their crusader spirit guv.' He gave me a sharp look, but said nothing.

We rejoined Gessler and Reynard in the room below.

'Sorry you had to have an experience like that Dave,' said Gessler, 'but some of those Nam vets were badly affected by what they've seen and been told to do by Uncle Sam. It's no wonder they picked up so readily on the flower power, universal love, and save the world thing.'

When we were alone later I asked Bill Reynard what Gessler was really saying behind that remark. Not so much about my

140

experience but about the admission that there were phoney goings on in that part of the world. He shrugged.

'Every war has a secret war behind it David. They are all very similar to the programmes we are currently engaged in. Every so often, whatever the activity, there are attacks of conscience in people engaged in the covert activities. Our friend Major Gessler gives certain indications that he is not happy about the secretive nature of governments over the Alien/UFO business, or the setting up of these extensive underground bases. Whereas we more or less muddle along and except the reality of other world influences and the technological morsels the Americans offer us as sweeteners. Gessler is, if I'm not mistaken, privy to a far bigger picture.'

'And you think it bothers him?'

'Not perhaps in itself, but I think he may be suffering from a conflict of loyalties.' Our little tete-a-tete was taking place in the canteen and I could see Ganymede approaching with Genna; Reynard changed the subject. 'Here comes a very bright young lady, I hope you appreciate that she might well have saved your life.' He was referring of course to the warning she had delivered. I asked him if my reference to something that might be of interest to him had got the message across.

'It puzzled me for a bit I must admit until I realised that you might be in there with a head case.'

'Subtle, very subtle.' Ganymede was grinning; he had just caught the tail end of our chat.

Over dinner I was informed that Genna and I were being flown back to Denver and that we were to take a break until my arm was healed and fully functioning.

Chapter 22

Denver

We enjoyed a whole week of trying to get to grips with Denver before anyone enquired how my convalescence was going.

Our base, already arranged for us by Ganymede, was a guest house on Race St near Cheesman Park in a leafy suburbia. Our hosts Mr and Mrs Sullivan were both ex-service persons. They offered full board with options. As Genna and I wished to make the most of our stay in Denver we opted for bed, breakfast, and evening meal and we chose to take our lunch breaks anywhere we happened to be during our sightseeing.

We soon learned to appreciate the quality of American food outlets. If there was anything resembling the traditional British greasy spoon establishment we failed to find it. The Americans demanded and received everything in the way of quality and service.

Our hosts had obviously been specially chosen, for it soon became plain that they knew exactly where we were coming from and why we were there. Jack Sullivan was an ex-fighter pilot and his wife Clare had, until becoming a landlady, worked in the intelligence section of the local Air Force Base. It was no longer a surprise to discover that they were both retired majors. We were shown to a double room; they were obviously going to treat us as an item.

'We live alongside ICBM's here David, Sullivan confided in the bar one evening soon after we arrived. They're just over at Lowry Field. When you've had your fill of sightseeing I could take you for a drive over that way.'

'I said I would appreciate that. It is not often you get invited to see weapons that have the potential to put an end to the world.

That's how, on the fourth day of our stay, Genna and I found ourselves in a Buick Special Station Waggon heading out in the direction the local Air Force Base. Ganymede had phoned me, and it was at his request I had spent the latter part of the afternoon for what turned out to be my final physiotherapy session. Next day we were to pack and get ready to fly back to the UK. Consequently it was already late in the afternoon that we finally headed for Lowry. We were headed down a four lane highway with a median strip carrying a line of power towers. We had just topped a hill when Sullivan drew our attention to it.

'What the hell do you make of that David?' We were driving into a sunset and I had difficulty locating what he was on about for a moment, and then I could just make out an oval object silhouetted against the setting sun; it appeared to be hovering over the power lines. Up ahead a number of cars had pulled off the road and people were out of their vehicles looking up at it. Jack Sullivan pulled in behind them and we hopped out.

I heard a gasp from Genna beside me and I didn't need to wonder why. From beneath it revealed itself as a circular craft about 60 feet in diameter. The underneath was revolving in an anti-clockwise direction; there was no discernible sound from it. It occurred to me that she might be remembering something from the Winchester incident; I reached out and gave her hand a reassuring squeeze.

'Never really believed these fucking things were real – sorry Miss Rees ...' Sullivan looked slightly shame-faced. Genna gave him a tight smile.

We must have stood there gawking for ten minutes or more while it hovered above us, and then we did hear sounds as three helicopters approached from the West. They were about half a mile from us when the disc began to move silently away towards the East, just fast enough to keep distance between itself and the helicopters. We watched until the last of the helicopters had disappeared over the hill behind us.

'I think we'll head back David. I've had enough excitement for today.' There was a slight shake in Sullivan's voice as he slipped in behind the wheel. One of my legs started to set up a trembling as I took my seat; had I just seen my very first operational space vehicle from another world? I could only hazard a guess at what the occupants may have looked like. It took several miles before my leg settled down.

**

We left the Sullivan's with mixed feelings. We had enjoyed a brief holiday with very nice people, and had been much impressed by our first real contact with an American city rather than just passing through. Jack and Clare drove us to the airport and we said our goodbyes in the departure lounge.

Clare hugged us both.

'Now you take care of one another, you hear.' After a sober handshake from Sullivan we passed through our gate.

143

It was a British Airways non-stop flight and we landed at Heathrow 9 ½ hours later. Philo Makris met us as we passed through customs and drove us back to my flat.

'I'll see you in the Complex tomorrow David, and you Miss Rees.'

**

'I'm not sorry to be back, are you David? It was good, but I found it a bit scary, especially at that honeycomb mountain place. Denver was nice though, I liked it there. Not sure about the visitors from space though. Do you think you could live in a place like that?'

'I would need to think about that Genn. I liked the openness of it there and the clean feel of it all, and the views; especially of the Rockies. But although on the surface it all looks very laid back, it's a bit like a sleeping volcano. Underneath? Well I'm not sure. I'll stick with England for now; something I'm more familiar with.'

Bill Reynard cornered me next morning as I was making my way to my office. I needed to get back to practising what he liked to call "walking in inner worlds". I tried not to think of a backlog of UFO reports that may have accumulated in my absence.

'David, I think a further regression is in order.'

'Funny you should say that Bill, with the carry on these last few weeks I'd almost forgotten the real reason for my being here.'

We spent about an hour returning to the bedroom and the woods of my infancy. He explained that it still might spark off something. Not that we would be in any position to know what the outcome might be until such time as I came face to face with someone or something on the same wavelength, but it might be as well to nurture the possibility.

'As I see it,' he said, 'although you are that much older now your implant is still in place,' he said. If it is a location device then your friends from those days still have a way to contact you. Basically everything is the same as it was then, even your telepathic ability.'

'You think the implant was placed in its present spot to thwart any attempt to remove it?' I said when we were through.

He appeared to consider that. 'I think that's the most likely explanation, and it's encouraging to think that you could well be contacted again.'

144

'That means I suppose that contact is still possible at any time; or not at all?'

'You seemed to be enjoying the recollection of those times.'

'I think they were remarkable, and I do wish now that, up to a point, I really did have that telepathic capability.'

'You have David, we all have. For some reason it operates below the level of conscious reality.' I realised he was in earnest now. 'I think in your case, since you experienced it in the past you need bring the desire to do so again to the forefront, make it an expectation. Never mind when, just assure yourself during meditation that you can do it again. This is not conventional psychotherapy I'm giving you David. Since I got into this remote viewing stuff I discovered just what the mind can possibly achieve, and I'm not talking brain David. Brain just picks up on the sensory world and passes it to mind and the mind determines how we operate.'

He had lost me about halfway through that diatribe, but I nodded as if I understood; perhaps I did up to a point, if I was only sure what the point was.

I suppose I felt as I made my way back to the flat that if I was to earn my keep I would need to do what Bill suggested and entertain a positive belief that I had the ability to converse telepathically, but who the hell with? Ah! If only we could see around corners.

Genna was on the way out when I arrived.

'Thought I'd better show my face down there David, what are you going to do?' I explained about the session with Reynard. She laughed.

'I'll leave you to your inner world then, but for goodness sake don't get lost.'

I couldn't help wondering if that was possible as I stood at the window and watched her head for the Information Bureau. Was it Reynard or Ganymede who had once said something about all things probable being possible? Having found Genna I decided against getting lost, I certainly wouldn't make that a positive expectation.

I awoke with a start. As often happened when following Reynard's mental exercises I had fallen asleep. It was 1 pm and I was hungry. I had no brief for the afternoon so I made a sandwich and a mug of tea and settled back to listen to the news. It was November the 22nd 1963.

Most of it had already been reported in the national dailies. So following the much publicised visit of John Fitzgerald Kennedy to Texas there were the benefits of the newly opened Deptford Tunnel and the death of Robert Stroud, a controversial character who became known as The Birdman of Alcatraz, all recounted in the expressionless voice that was synonymous with BBC announcers.

It seemed a day for deaths. Aldous Huxley an intellectual authority on just about everything and C.S. Lewis of whom I knew absolutely nothing, both kicked the bucket. No one knew how their deaths were due to be overshadowed, but they were; in a newsflash that reverberated around the world and was to leave an indelible imprint on the memories of people as to where they were when the President of the United States was assassinated in Dallas Texas. It prompted me to head immediately for the Complex.

Grave faces there indicated the speed at which bad news travels. There was a new face there that to me looked less grave than the others. Reynard introduced him. Robert Franciosa looked relatively jubilant.

They had obviously been in conversation which ceased the moment I stepped through the door. Franciosa shook hands, and then turning to Reynard said.

'Well that's it sir, we'll take care of the fort while you're away. Have a good trip.'

'Who is that Bill, and why does he make me feel uneasy?' He took a long, hard look at me before answering.

'You felt it too eh? Franciosa is CIA David, top bracket. There are several others around the place. They are here by courtesy of Special Branch and the MI's in some sort of caretaker role while we are away.'

'Away, we only just got back; away where?'

'One guess David. You anyway, I have to go to London. Depending on how things go there I should be able to catch up with you in the States.'

I nodded. America was exercising a strong magnetic pull over our lives that I was beginning to resent.

'What is it this time?'

'Franciosa says he doesn't have that information. He's lying of course, like his purpose for being here. It's just a feeling David, I'm not even sure it's justified.'

'You think their cred doesn't check out?'

146

'Oh I've done a check on that, no they're for real all right, but the feeling won't go away. Anyway here it is for what it's worth. You've got 12 hours to get your act together and join a flight to New York.'

'It's a rush job then.' I didn't require an answer.

'You are to rendezvous with Ganymede at Heathrow. You are to travel in uniform by the way.'

Genna had resumed her duties in the Complex sick bay. She had opted to move in with me and would move her stuff into the flat while I was away; I hoped I wouldn't be away for too long.

Chapter 23

Bowdie

I felt strangely self-conscious as we boarded the TWA flight to New York; it was only the second time I'd walked abroad as a major. To be met by a smiling stewardess and welcomed as Major Kent was a first. I realised as I was shown to my seat I was certainly getting preferential treatment over Ganymede. He was following behind me and I looked back; he gave the long slow wink, he had dropped behind on purpose.

On this, my second flight to America, plus several internal flights, I was beginning to feel like a seasoned air traveller. The little I'd done in the army had been done mainly in Dakotas and converted WW2 bombers; there was little comparison to be made with the extreme comfort and service I now found on this TWA flight to the US of A. The estimated flight time of 5 hours seemed a vast improvement on the 12 or so hours I had once spent travelling from Cyprus to England in the mid fifties in an old Hastings bomber. That hadn't been accompanied by drinks on request from soon after take-off by charming, fresh-faced, and shapely cabin staff.

In the Hastings it stopped at orange juice and water from our water bottles, and it was oxygen masks when bad weather drove us to twenty thousand feet. No stretch of the imagination then could have foretold that in less than a decade I would be travelling in a style I was quite unused to. But then neither could I have envisaged anything that had, and was continually happening to me since my first steps into the Complex. Ganymede appeared to accept this luxuriant mode of travel as nothing more than his due.

After the initial flight meal I settled down to work my way through the in-flight movies. I chose O' Toole's Lawrence of Arabia over Give us a Peck Gregory setting out to kill a Mockingbird, as the first one. Beside me my guv'nor seemed more interested in the Land of Nod; He slept most of the way, waking finally as we settled down to a slow descent on the land of the free and the home of the brave. I had yet to learn how free, and how brave; or otherwise.

As we approached the queues at the arrivals desks we were intercepted by a Humphrey Bogart lookalike, minus the sneer, in a blue suit tailored to cast doubt on any concealed armoury. He flashed an ID just long enough for me to clock a bald eagle, plus a fair semblance photo of the man before us, and the letters CIA. He addressed Ganymede.

'Good evening sir. My name is Jaques, Robert Jaques. If you and the Major here will follow me,' he gave me a brief nod, 'I have your onward transport waiting.' We fell into step behind him; all formalities for arriving in the US appeared to have been waived, I couldn't help a sneaking feeling of importance.

Outside the terminal a man similar to our escort stood at the open boot of a black limousine. He looked as though smiling was something he barely achieved without tremendous effort. He relieved us of our luggage, closed the boot, and slipped into the driver's seat. Jaques did the honours of showing us into the rear seats before joining stone face. He turned to us as we headed out of the airport.

'Your internal flight leaves for Albuquerque at midnight.' He looked at his watch. 'That'll give you about five hours; time to freshen up and grab some chow, and get some shuteye before take-off.'

Forty minutes later we were doing most of that in a small hotel in Lower Manhattan, with a promise that we would be returned to the airport in good time.

The previous flight without sleep, and a couple of martinis with the hotel meal; I settled for a fillet steak with trimmings, must have knocked me out. I woke decidedly groggy to the sound of voices. Jaques and a very fresh looking Ganymede waited patiently for me to get my bearings and follow them through the door. I should have followed him into slumberland on the outward flight instead of watching movies. I was to regret that even more on arrival at Albuquerque after a further 4 hours flying time, plus the prospect of more to come.

'It's called jet lag David.' He was less than sympathetic. 'It's always advisable to get the head down as much as possible regardless of what the clock says.' Now he tells me.

The shock of the cold desert air at 4 am revived me somewhat. Jaques and stone face hadn't joined us on our internal flight. We were met by a USAF lieutenant and led behind a large hangar to where our further onward transport awaited. I eyed it with misgiving; a helicopter; I would hardly be able to catch up on my sleep in that.

I was thankful my Manhattan meal had already vacated my stomach, so although the unpredictable gyrations that appeared

149

to accompany helicopter flights caused it to move in an offbeat way, I didn't disgrace myself by throwing up. It was still dark when we touched down at what by then I hoped was our final destination. I wasn't prepared for the reception committee as we disembarked. The dawn light revealed a huddle of figures standing before a wooden hut. Two detached themselves and advanced towards us. Although well wrapped against the chill air, they were vaguely familiar. Then there was no mistaking Quan Ling as she greeted me. Makris and Ganymede were already in urgent conversation.

'Hello David Kent, welcome to Bowdie.'

'Hi Quan Ling. So this is where you disappeared to.'

I looked at my surroundings. A sprawl of decaying buildings, of both wood and stone occupied a wide and otherwise desolate valley. Pockets of mainly parched looking scrub somehow managed a half-life in the stony ground. All around rose hills, bare of everything except the remains of a few isolated huts. It was not a place liable to find itself in a holiday brochure.

'What is this Bowdie?'

'It's an old mining town that prospered and died when the gold and the will to look for it petered out David.'

'I've heard of places like that.' I tried to imagine giving up everything and coming here in search of gold; my imagination wasn't up to it. 'So what's our interest here?'

Ganymede and Makris, still in conversation were drifting towards the hut into which the other part of the huddle had already disappeared. Quan Ling and I moved instinctively in the same direction.

'There's been a visitation here,' she said. I stared at her.

'ET's?' I was surprised at the ease in which I now considered beings from elsewhere a reality.

'That's right, and they are still believed to be here somewhere.'

'Here, where?'

'Somewhere underground. The mine-workings here are very extensive.' We were at the hut door when I heard it. I paused at the doorway and looked back at the helicopter we had arrived in, it stood silent its rotors flopped down at rest, so what was I hearing. I looked at Quan Ling. The sound was getting rapidly closer. She pointed to where two odd looking craft were approaching over a hill to the north.

'Here come the cavalry David.'

'What the hell are those?'

'They call them Chinooks, the latest addition to the USAF. They are being used by their special forces; Ranger units for rapid deployment operations.' The air was now vibrating as they came in with their twin rotors thudding.

'What are they doing here?'

'I think if we go inside we will soon find out.' By the time we were inside, the sound of the Chinooks had receded towards the south and only the whisper of their passing remained.

It was surprisingly warm inside the hut which was about the size of an army Nissen hut. But apart from two familiar looking tortoise stoves the resemblance ended there. It appeared to be assembled from materials resurrected from the remains of old mine buildings. It easily accommodated the dozen or so occupants including our foursome. The seating comprised a series of two- tier bunk beds ranged around the walls.

A USAAF colonel was the only uniform present apart from mine. I realised in time that, that made saluting obligatory. He returned it casually in a manner I had come to associate with movie versions of US officers and he welcomed us, introducing himself as Bob Draper. He then waved us towards some vacant bunks before returning to a low tone conversation with two sober-faced young men in lounge suits; I was beginning to instinctively recognise members of American secret services. Directly opposite us lounged four casually dressed men who were regarding us with veiled interest. My own interest quickened as I spotted the equipment stowed beneath the bottom bunks. On one rare occasion during my army service we had once liaised with an SAS assault team. This jaunt into the American wilderness was beginning to take a more ominous turn.

The colonel finished conversing and the two sober faces headed for one of the bunks. Then he moved to a spot where everyone had an unobstructed view of him. Along one side of him sat the two other members of the assembly.

They bore the tanned and weathered look of the outdoors and were both dressed in jeans, tee shirts, and leather boots. At a rough guess they were both in their mid forties. Each nursed a jacket across his knees; the dominant colour in both cases was red. I didn't have long to wonder about that, or why they were here.

151

'For those of you who have just arrived I'll run briefly through the events that have occurred here recently. Afterwards these gentlemen ...' he indicated the two men beside him '... will give you the fuller story. Three nights ago several strange lights were reported in the skies over Sante Fe. Apart from local individuals who reported them at varying times during the night, police patrolmen also reported them, and those reports were forwarded to Kirkland Air Force Base. Kirkland AFB failed to make any radar contact and interceptors directed to the area failed to locate any intruders. The incidents were logged, and in the usual way the files were handed down the line for any further investigation; usually into the hands of UFO researchers.' He smiled. 'That comment is not made in a derogatory sense. Whether or not any of you believe in things from outer space, I would like to say that I will need very little more evidence to become a convert to such a belief.'

I glanced towards the SAS; their faces were impassive. I realised that whether they believed or not they would do whatever was found to be necessary; and we still weren't sure what that was. The colonel continued.

'24 hours ago Kirkland AFB received a report from the local police that someone on a CB radio, or a walkie talkie, was babbling about being engaged in a pitched battle with men from space.' He looked apologetically at the two men beside him. 'Unfortunately because Kirkland didn't take the report seriously there was some delay in getting someone out to the location. When they finally did, several hours had elapsed, and what they found has created the biggest flap ever experienced in this neck of the woods. It is the reason why we are all here at this time. Those noisy aircraft that passed over just now contain 2 Ranger companies that are at this moment combing the area where the call originated. They will be moving this way in their search among buildings and abandoned mines for ... well your guess is as good as mine. In the meantime we sit and wait until they join us, and then we may be invited to join the hunt.' He nodded towards the two men beside him. 'I now hand you over to Martin and Russell Stevens who have been debriefed and are at liberty to tell you in their own words what happened when they and two other friends decided to go deer hunting a few nights back.' The red jackets clicked in; deer didn't wear them. The man nearest Colonel Draper stood up and laid his jacket on the chair behind him.

He had a direct way of talking, crisper than the customary American drawl; or was it nerves? I realised later that what he had to say may have, in some way, contributed to the latter.

'I'm Russ Stevens and this,' he waved a hand towards his companion, 'is my brother Marty. A few nights back, along with a couple of friends we decided to do a spot of deer hunting in a patch of forest just over the hills from here. I say patch because there isn't much of that around these parts.' He was unsmiling, considering the irony of the comment. 'We hunt in the old way, bows and arrows, or crossbows. No guns apart from a handgun in case we encounter a bear or a cougar, although we don't hunt them unless they hunt us.' I did then detect a fleeting grin.

'It is, probably, thanks to our method of hunting that we are here today.' I detected a sudden interest in the proceedings from the four who were obviously no strangers to the silent kill when the need arose. 'We were out there for a couple of hours without making a contact. We usually move in line abreast and keep any wind in our faces, and keep a bit of distance between us. You get a feeling sometimes that there is something up ahead. This happened so we stopped and stayed put, listening for movement. Then we heard something heading towards us in a hurry so we switched on our flashlights. Suddenly the deer were among us and past us before we could raise a bow. Then Billy Nuttall, one of the fellas with us, yelled, "It's a fucking bear!" and there was 'oso' heading straight for us; it didn't make sense. Bears eat meat sure, but usually it's already dead before they get to it; never did hear of one trying to chase a deer. A couple of us drew our handguns as it lumbered towards us, but before anybody could shoot it let out a squeal like a stuck pig and crumpled up on the ground just yards from us. It was then we saw them ...' He paused as if the recollection was disturbing. '... three funny looking guys; skinny, with big heads, you know, a bit like little toddlers, and later when we saw them closer up, as ugly as sin. They were about a hundred yards away.' He was sweating profusely and I wondered how much of it was due to the warmth of the hut.

Billy Nuttall fired his handgun. I don't know if it was at these little guys but next minute Billy collapses, much as the bear had done. We all doused our lights and headed for the ground. Billy's dad dragged him behind a tree and crouched over him, and me and Marty here were doing our best to keep our heads down behind a fallen tree. We were in the Marine Corps at Iwo

Jima and Guadalcanal during War 2, so we had been in tight spots before; it was just a matter of working our way out of this one. We didn't know what state Billy was in, but we figured he and his daddy were out of sight from them weird guys. With our lights out the night was nearly as dark as the inside of a cow's belly, so unless those guys could see in the dark maybe we could get the drop on them; we were no strangers to these woodlands. It was silent as a graveyard now, and just as spooky. It was like both sides were waiting for somebody to make the first move. Our old platoon sergeant was fond of reversing the old adage and saying, when in doubt, go for it! We knew that a hundred yards to our right there was a stone hut, no roof but most of the walls were still standing, it might give us some protection from whatever weapons had brought down the bear and Billy. If we headed for it, it might draw them away from where Billy and his daddy was concealed. There comes a time when you've got to act on a decision, and like the sergeant said, go for it. I gave Billy's daddy a buzz on the W/T and told him what we planned. I asked about Billy. He said he was breathing and there was no sign of any wounds; that sounded promising. I told him we were on our way and signed out. There was reasonable cover all the way and we weren't too bothered about making plenty of noise. We made it with not much more than a puff of breath left between us. We didn't have to wait long for a response. It came almost before we were breathing normally, well as normally as anyone can under the circumstances. First with a buzz from Billy's daddy to say there was movement in our direction, and next the sound of twigs cracking as the critters moved in on us. By now there was a lightening in the sky to the east. Not a lot, but enough to bring the shapes of the trees into sharper focus and other more indefinite shapes moving among them. We loaded our bows and waited. There weren't much else to do. Like with the Japs we wouldn't know what we were up against until they showed their hand. Marty and me had a window opening apiece. The shutters had rotted away long since, and it wasn't ideal for keeping a lookout without being seen, but needs must, as they say. We needed to see what these guys were up to, so rather than duck and dive and create movement we just kept one eye apiece pealed through the openings. It was getting lighter by the minute and I could see there were three of them standing at the edge of the clearing, about 80 to a 100 yards away. They didn't seem in a hurry to do anything other than just stand there looking towards the hut. Not for the first time did I wish I'd brought along a rifle. Our crossbows weren't effective much over 40 yards and our hand guns were for scaring off big predators, neither Marty or me were great shakes at using them with any accuracy.'

There was a disturbance at the door and a young Ranger lieutenant stepped into the hut and looked around in embarrassment. He was about to retreat back through it when the colonel stopped him. He turned to Russell Stevens.

'Sorry Mr Stevens but we'll have to hold it right there, it looks as though we are on the move.' Stevens looked almost relieved as he retrieved his jacket and resumed his seat. The Ranger lieutenant continued across and had a few words with the colonel and then left.

'Well how about that for starters?' Ganymede and Makris had wandered across and joined Quan Ling and me.

'How about, wow! Guv?'

'I've no doubt we'll catch up with the rest of that story later.' Makris was looking to where the SAS were already on the move draped in their hardware and shouldering their bergens. I noticed that they had also donned flak jackets and had flashlight attachments to their weapons; there seemed little they ever left to chance. He turned to Ganymede. 'I'll take David and Quan Ling along then sir.'

'Please Philo. I'll catch up. I'd like a quick word with the hunting johnnies and Colonel Draper.' He moved off in their direction.

Despite a bright sun the air still felt chill after the fug inside the hut. The area looked even more desolate and uninviting then than when we had first touched down. We fell in behind Makris who seemed to know exactly where we were headed.

Chapter 24

The lighting in this subterranean world where men had grubbed, often without success, for the favours of lady luck, was provided by a generator chugging away somewhere above us. We followed Makris along rusted rail tracks, occasionally passing bucket-shaped wagons in similar condition. We finally reached an open area where the tracks ended. It was an immense cavern from where I imagined the gold ore had been blasted out. Areas of quartzite glittered under lights strung across the old mine faces. Several tunnels led off the cavern; they had probably swallowed up the bulk of the rangers and the boys from Hereford who had preceded us. About a dozen rangers were lounging around one tunnel entrance.

Someone with our greater comfort in mind had arranged old oil drums and planks around a propane heater.

'We now await events,' Makris said as we seated ourselves. 'We are only here as observers remember. The Americans are very definite on that, and anything we see, hear, or experience while we are here is not for common knowledge.' More people were emerging from the tunnel we had entered by, Makris looked that way. 'Here's the rest of our party now.' The Stevens brothers followed by Draper and Ganymede joined us on our improvised seating; both Stevens wore back packs and carried crossbows. Draper deposited a grip at his feet and removed a W/T and placed it on the plank beside him. I looked expectantly first at Ganymede and then at him. The colonel gave me a grin.

'I can see you are dying to know what's going on major, indeed I think you all are. So I'll bring you up to speed. Ten minutes ago I received word that the SAS assault team had made contact with an alien body.' I felt Quan Ling tense beside me. 'It was in an advanced state of decomposition.' I caught the look that passed between Russell and his brother. Draper had also turned to look at them and continued. 'It appeared to have a crossbow bolt transfixed in its neck.' An almost imperceptible nod from Marty. 'They are at present examining a steel door that is blocking further ingress. It appears to have neither hinges nor means of opening and even more puzzling to be only recently sited, they are not even sure if it is actually steel.'

'I suppose they could try explosives.' I offered.

'It was suggested but I'm not authorised to sanction that; it'll have to come from higher up.'

'And in the meantime?'

'In the meantime major, I expect they'll sit tight and have a brew up, isn't that what they call it?' Even Makris joined the laughter. 'There is nothing from the Rangers yet. They are covering a different section of the workings, most of which are interconnected by the way, so they might end up the other side of that door.' He sighed. 'Ours as usual is a waiting brief I'm afraid.'

'Perhaps while we're marking time our crossbow warriors could continue with their story.' Ganymede looked at them.

'Not a lot more to add if we leave out that most of the time we were nearly shitting ourselves,' said Russell. 'You've already figured that we got one of them; that was Marty. I couldn't move. I got hit by something when I took a few pots with the hand gun. I got in a couple of hits but it didn't seem to affect them; they just staggered a bit and then kept coming. I guess Marty here would best be telling the rest.' Marty nodded.

'Yeah maybe. Russ didn't seem to do any real damage with the gun and the noise wasn't going to scare them. When I looked at Russ he was stood like a statue; figured there wasn't much coming from there. They was pretty close by then, twenty-five, thirty yards maybe. I figured if god wasn't on our side I wouldn't bother with heaven, I just stood up, let fly a bolt and ducked down again. Then I loaded another bolt and waited. You sort of space out at times like that. Like you was about to be executed; waiting for the blade to fall or the trap to give way I guess. Anyway nothing happened other than a strange sort of twittering like birds settlin' down on a roost. Russ seemed to have come out of his rigor mortis by then and was crouched down like me. Don't know how long we waited, we were too shit-scared to do clock watching … sorry Miss,' he glanced at Quan Ling, 'but I finally thought to take a peek. They weren't out there no more. We waited a while longer just to make sure, and that's when I called the cops. Then we high-tailed it outa there like the devil was after us.'

'And after all that you're here for the follow up?' Quan Ling voiced what we all must have been thinking.

'Well, I guess we can't come to much harm with all you guys around; and the Rangers and they Sassy boys, right Russ?' Russell nodded, but like the rest of us he could hardly have imagined what the outcome of this operation would be.

Draper's W/T gave a metallic buzz; he raised it to his ear.

'Draper!' A pause as he listened, and then. 'Say again.' He was sober-faced as he regarded us over the phone. 'I have no authority for that lieutenant.' He was frowning now as he listened to what we weren't privy to. Then he looked heavenward as if seeking an answer to something, before giving way to some inner frustration. 'Okay blow the damn thing, it's an obstacle in the way of an ongoing operation, I'll deal with the brass; they'll have to get real, just keep me posted.' He signed off. 'Another door,' he said. 'I think we're into funny business.'

'Are you thinking what I'm thinking Colonel?' Ganymede sat with his hands gripping the edge of his seat and idly swinging his legs between the drums below.

'That these ... whatever they are, are holed up in there somewhere behind those doors?'

'I think we have to accept that as a distinct possibility sir.'

'The SAS assault team have come a long way to get in on this act; will you give them the go ahead too?' The quietly spoken question effectively masked Ganymede's possible follow-up; if not why not? But Draper had got the message, and he had already put his head on the block after all. Without answering he pushed buttons and listened for a moment before speaking.

'Green light sergeant Daley, do whatever is necessary.' He signed out and was about to say something when an explosion reverberated through the tunnels. It was followed almost immediately by a further one and a tangible displacement of air in the cavern.

'So what do we do now?' I was addressing Colonel Draper, but I was watching Ganymede out of the corner of my eye; he had risen from his seat. 'You said we are here as observers, when do we start observing?' The W/T buzzed before he could answer. He listened before turning to me.

'I think about now major. Your boys breached the rock alongside the door and are through into a chamber that appears to be recently vacated, it is now secure.'

'We can move now?'

'I guess now might be as good a time as any.'

The pair of cross-bowers were already on their feet and slinging their back packs. Makris and Ganymede withdrew hand guns from their clothing and were checking the magazines. I realised with a jolt that I was unarmed, nobody had mentioned coming armed. Quan Ling was standing beside me, she pressed something into my hand; hard, heavy and metallic. I looked down. It was a 9mm Glock. She followed it with spare magazines.

'Take mine David, you might need it.'

'But what about you?'

'Not my party David. I have a date back in Sante Fe, this is as far as I go on this one; Philo will fill you in, good luck.' I stood watching her retreat back along the rail track and then I turned to follow the others.

'I'm with the colonel on this one David,' Ganymede said. 'We'll follow the remaining rangers in.' He delved into the knapsack he'd brought along and produced a W/T. 'Here you'd better take this, although they are a bit hit and miss underground. Draper's already having problems with his.' He followed it with a flashlight. 'You'll need this too. Now you'd better go, best to stick with the pack on this one.'

Makris indicated that I should join him along with the Stevens brothers and moved off in the direction of the tunnel taken by the SAS assault team.

Chapter 25

I needed the flashlight as soon as we entered the tunnel and it was then I realised that the Stevens Brothers had both donned headlamps. Probably all part of their hunting equipment; I wondered what it was we were actually hunting now. Makris appeared content to share the available light as we made our way forward.

We came upon the body. It was laid close up against the wall of the tunnel. A look confirmed what the SAS had reported earlier. Surprisingly, considering the state of decomposition, it smelt no worse than a bad case of BO and even that had been modified by the acrid stench of cordite that lingered in the air.

We caught up with the assault team about ten minutes later.

**

The SAS trooper recognised us as we approached and lowered his machine gun. He looked past Makris and addressed me. 'Sergeant Daley and the lads are in there sir,' he indicated the opening behind him. The door remained in position but they had blown a hole in the rock alongside it. 'It's a bit of a squeeze but it wasn't a good place to let off too big a charge.'

We wriggled our way into a cavern covering an area roughly the size of a circus big top. The sides rose in a perfect dome to a height of 30 feet. The whole surface reminded me of the tunnels in the Complex; smooth and like opaque glass. We were in something resembling an upturned Pyrex bowl; it was clinically empty. It left me with the uneasy feeling that whatever had occupied it had been spirited away.

'Most odd, David.' Makris voiced the understatement as he studied our surroundings. 'What happens now sergeant? Our brief is to accompany you as observers; you're the boss on this one.'

Daley looked first at Makris and then at me as if trying to decide which of us, despite my uniform, was boss of our party before replying; Makris got the vote.

'Our task is to search and apprehend any suspect bodies that may be holed up in these mines Mr Makris.'

'And you know the nature of what those bodies might turn out to be?'

'Up until we arrived here, no, and that has caused us a problem.'

'In what way?'

'In this sort of environment, if we run into a battle situation, the use of anything other than MG's and small arms is a no go. Explosive devices apart from PE, which we used to get in here, would chuck around metal and rock, and the blast could damage us as much as any contacts we might make.'

'Let's hope the Rangers know that.' I said.

'I'm sure they do sir. If they don't, they won't be long finding out. I can't figure out what this place is for, but it doesn't look like anything you'd associate with hairy-arsed miners. I've got to assume that whoever is responsible for it might prove to be a tough proposition if we are confronted by them.'

'I think you're more than a mite right in that assumption.' Russell Stevens took time out from looking around him in bewilderment.'

'Yeah, like you were saying earlier, and if it's the same lot that you came up against perhaps we should have brought our bows along.' Daley was smiling as he spoke.

'You can sure as hell have mine,' said Marty. The longer I stay here the more I get the creeps.'

'Well gents, we've had a look around and there doesn't seem to be any other way out of here so I guess we move on.' Daley saw us and his squad back into the tunnel. 'Perhaps major you can raise someone and find out what's going on further in.' There was no response to my call. Ganymede had been right about W/T reliability in this underground maze.

The crystal bowl had brought us to a dead end; we made our way back to our starting point. There was still no joy from the W/T as we set off down the tunnel that Ganymede and Draper had taken. It was a single file job, Daley's squad leading in with him ahead of me and Makris bringing up the rear.

A massive explosion suddenly erupted somewhere ahead and we all threw ourselves flat. Invisible hands pulled at my clothing and I felt myself lifted along backward then dropped, still in a prone position, back onto the rock floor. I was fighting to drag air back into my lungs. My head was buzzing like the fit of dizziness that occurs after a prolonged fit of coughing removes all the air from the lungs. And then the silence.

'Fuck that!' It came explosively from one of the SAS up ahead, and then it was followed by the calm voice of Sergeant Daley as he rose to his feet.

'Everyone okay?'

The murmurs of assent seemed to satisfy him. 'My team will move on then sir,' he said looking down at me. Follow at your own pace when you feel ready. At a rough guess, whatever that was, it sounded messy, he added.'

We caught up with the rangers very soon afterwards. They were crouched looking over their sight lights at the scene of carnage.

Something moved under my foot. I looked down and recoiled in horror. I no longer wondered what those men with the plastic bags were looking for after a terrorist bombing.

'Someone's made a cock up here,' Daley sounded grim. Beyond the scattered bodies of the rangers a door similar to the one we had left behind sagged drunkenly inward; it was surprisingly unmarked. He pointed to what looked like several stovepipes lying among the causalities. 'Fucking bazookas, they must have fired them simultaneously. What a fuckin' mess; talk about overkill.'

There were figures moving around beyond the doorway. The cold fingers of fear moved in on me; a soft pearl-like glow seemed to emanate from them. I was watching ghosts.

They looked identical to the one we had found in the tunnel further back.

'They're the ones, said a voice beside me, and I realised that Russell Stevens had moved in beside me. I heard click as he cocked his crossbow.

Three of them emerged from the doorway. They were now sharply outlined by the soft glow behind them; they stood as if summing up what they saw. I reached inside my jacket for the Glock and felt a restraining hand on my arm and Russell Stevens was whispering in my ear.

'Sit tight major they can't see us here.'

A shot echoed around the cavern and one of the figures staggered. The other two raised an arm apiece and there was a cry from the ranger whose nerves had got the better of him. There were more shots and more cries and then silence, and as if by magic all flashlights were extinguished.

'They seem to be learning something these gung ho jerks.' It was brother Marty's voice from my other side. I realised we were in stygian darkness; it was a comforting thought. 'They'll go for the gun flash or movement,' said Russell.

There was the soft whisper of a crossbow bolt being released followed by another on my other side and I realised the Stevens boys were in action. The ET's stood unaffected as the bolts just bounced off them. They were obviously trying to locate the source. On the third flight one of them staggered and went down.

'Bingo!' Hissed Marty. 'Neck shot,' I felt one side of my body go suddenly numb and I couldn't move. I was falling backwards. A strong arm stopped me going the whole way.

'It's okay major, you just took a hit.' It was Russell's voice in my ear as he supported me. 'They're firin' random, guess even them jokers can panic. They're gone now; dragged their buddy back through the doorway,' hissed Marty. 'There don't appear to be no further movement back there.'

It was full a half an hour before my body was functioning properly again, but my mind seemed to have other ideas, like it was darting about unable to settle on anything specific for more than a second at a time. I was only vaguely aware of what was going on around me.

'They are taking a looksee through that door now.' Russell Stevens had stayed with me. I could see Marty was moving through the doorway with several of the Rangers, and then I was looking around the cavern. It was as light as day in there and it was empty; the ET's had vanished.

'I wonder what's in there.' With a jolt I realised Russell was still beside me; I hadn't moved, and then the shock when I realised my eyes were still closed. I opened them; the scene was little changed from just before I'd been hit. It was still dark in our corner. Flashlights were moving once again among the indistinct forms of the wounded and dead Rangers. Beyond the doorway were the bobbing shadows created by the flashlights in there too. I tried to rationalise what had happened to me; something had knocked me out of synch. I switched on my torch; Russell stared at me from the surrounding glow.

'You okay Dave? You look like you just see'd a ghost.'

'I think maybe I just did Russ.'

**

A check revealed fourteen casualties, all Rangers. Perhaps it was wrong for me to feel glad that Ganymede and Colonel Draper were not among them. I decided not to mention my strange experience to Ganymede; I'm sure Reynard could explain it.

'Nothing we can do here,' said Makris, maybe we'll find some answers up ahead.'

We picked our way through the bodies and beyond the door. This time it was no Pyrex bowl, but still a cavern, rough hewn by the sweat of miners in search of Eldorado. Our lights picked up the outlines of several tunnels; all except one were blocked a few yards in. Russell Stevens noted my look.

'It's called back-filling,' he said. 'It saves having to hump it up to the surface.'

Daley and his men led the way into the open one. We progressed about a hundred yards before the tunnel widened into yet another cavern. In the tiny islands of light we could make out the bulk of figures with weapons trained on us. From somewhere in the surrounding gloom came Ganymede's voice; we had arrived at the same place by different ways.

'It's okay, they're ours.' The rangers lowered their weapons, the relief was almost audible. Ganymede and Colonel Draper were soon apprising us of the situation. 'Another of those bloody doors has brought us to a dead end,' said Ganymede. 'The rangers have set up listening devices, and there is evidence that the area behind it is occupied, by what or whom your guess is as good as mine.'

Daley and his men settled down in a spot slightly apart from both us and the rangers. I half expected them to start a brew but they sat silently smoking; waiting. They were used to moving on their own initiative, but the 'killing house' in Hereford where their skills were honed could hardly have prepared them for this cat and mouse game or with the obstacles that were being presented in this scenario.

Makris explained what we had come upon in the section allotted to the other rangers. Draper listened, the only trace of emotion showed in a tightening of his jaw muscles. Then turning to Ganymede, he said. 'I've decided that we might have to approach the situation here differently. I have already lost men, and we still don't know exactly what we are up against. I feel we should withdraw and evacuate the casualties, and get back to the drawing board on strategy. These guys seem to have established some sort of Fort Knox here.' He moved away in the direction of the rangers.

In the dim light I could see the SAS had gone into a huddle, they were obviously discussing the situation. They seemed to reach a decision, Sergeant Daley moved across to us and spoke directly to Ganymede; he had obviously worked out that it was neither Makris nor me that headed our team.

'We are pulling out sir, if that's okay. This looks like too big a nut to crack with small arms.' He didn't need to comment on the disastrous use of heavier weapons the rangers had employed. Ganymede agreed.

'I think you're right sergeant. Whoever is holed up here hasn't yet shown their hand weapon-wise apart from some kind of stun gun, which appears to be a very sophisticated and effective piece of technology. And this kind of battleground favours them rather than us. We may have to leave them and come back another day. This is of course a Yank operation, so the ball is in their court to come up with something.'

When Daley and his men had moved off we sat and waited for Draper to return. Ganymede informed him of the decision regarding the SAS assault team.

'I agree sir. This is a far from satisfactory way of handling a situation like this, but we didn't know that when we set out. I think we are now the wiser, and the sooner we get our asses out of here I for one will be a lot happier.'

Chapter 26

There was a helicopter already ticking over when we emerged from the mine workings. Two Chinooks were waiting to load the body bags and the remaining rangers for their evacuation. The SAS assault team had retired to the hut to await the arrival of their own transport. It was then that I learned I would be leaving without Ganymede.

'I'm going back to the UK with the assault team David.'

'We seem to have lost Makris guv, I don't see him around.'

'Philo is going along with Colonel Draper to Albuquerque. I want you to rendezvous with Bill and Quan Ling when you get to Sante Fe.' He handed me a slip of paper with an address on it.

**

I took a taxi to that address. My name opened doors. I checked in my grip which contained little more than toiletries and a change of underwear, and I was shown out to the pool area. Quan Ling waved me over to where she was seated at a poolside table. The young man who had delivered me hovered,

'You wish for a drink senor?'

I ordered a small beer; Quan Ling was already nursing something long and cool. She was wearing a plain white dress that ended just above the knee. As always she looked cool and elegant. I felt very much out of place in uniform. I took one of the vacant chairs.

'Hello David. It didn't go well at Bowdie then?'

'The speed of bad news always amazes me Quan Ling. Disaster just about describes it.' I said. She nodded agreement.

'Bill Reynard will be down in a minute or two, he'll want to know exactly what happened there; he's just finishing packing.'

'Packing?'

'Toothbrush, pack of cards,' she laughed. 'Clean shirt and socks. We are out of here in a few hours.'

I looked around me. Everything oozed comfort for the weary traveller.

'You mean I'm not to enjoy a day or two of this.'

'I'm afraid not David, there is no rest for the wicked.'

'Where to now then?' My beer arrived. I took a swallow.

'Nevada again, you've been there once, haven't you?' I remembered my journey into Reynard's head, and I laughed.

'Twice actually, once in my dreams.' She looked puzzled. I didn't have time to explain as she was looking past me.

'Here's Bill now.' She rose up. 'I need to get changed into something more suitable, I'll leave you two to chew the fat.' She moved off, still clutching her drink. Reynard took her vacated chair.' He was grinning.

'Well David that was some fiasco from the little I've heard so far.'

I gave him a blow by blow of how it had been from my perspective.

'It sounds a tricky one. The incumbents are well established and could have been there for years already.'

'And for a few more years to come, unless they can be bombed out of there.'

Two hours later we were boarding a military flight for the arid wastes of Nevada.

**

The first person I saw as we entered the hangar was Arthur C; we had been driven out there as soon as we arrived. I hadn't seen him for ages and the crushing handshake took me off guard; how dearly I wished to return it.

'Hi Davy, long time no see. I didn't know you still wore the monkey suit.' It was hard to believe how much I was coming to resent having to wear my major's uniform just to impress.

He led us to a building that took up a good third of one end of the hangar. An armed guard stood aside as we approached. We stood before a window and Arthur C pointed.

'How about that then?'

I peered in and was joined by Reynard and Quan Ling.

It was seated in a large armchair, but after a brief study I realised that the occupant was toddler-size, doll-like. Small featured except for the eyes, they were disproportionately large, black ovoids. It was staring straight at me, I turned slightly away.

'It's okay Dave, it's a two-way mirror; it can't see you.' said Arthur C.'

'It?' queried Quan Ling. 'What exactly is *it*?'

'That's a good question. The nearest thing we can come up with at the moment is that we just don't know,' he chuckled at his own joke. It seems prepared to cooperate but it doesn't seem to have any language capability; we can't communicate with it.'

'Where did it come from?' Reynard turned to Arthur C.

'It was found camped out at a crash site about two weeks ago, there were two others but they were badly out of it.'

167

'Like this one?' Arthur C nodded. 'Almost identical, they could have been triplets.'

'I see, and no way of communicating.' Reynard gave me a meaningful glance, well meaningful for him, but lost on me.

'Not a dickybird, as you people say.'

'So what do you intend to do?'

'We haven't got much choice other than to run as many different languages past it as we can dig up in the hope of getting a response. My opinion is that it's a waste of time, but we don't have another choice unless someone's into ET lingo.'

'Supposing I said that might be a possibility, General.' Arthur C gave Reynard his full attention.

'You mean you can come up with someone like that?'

'Well sort of.' Reynard was looking at me again, and this time I got the message.

'Well you just tell me what you need to bring that about Bill and you've got carte blanche.'

'Just time General, just time.'

**

'Did you notice anything about that ... dolly David?' We were in the quarters allocated for our stay at the base. It was obvious how Reynard was going to refer in future to whatever it was sitting in that room.

'Such as?' Was the best I could manage.

'The mouth David, its mouth was barely a feature, a rudimentary blob.'

I had noticed of course, but I didn't grasp the significance then, but now Bill Reynard was almost spelling it out.

'You think it only communicates telepathically?'

'Go to the top of the class Major Kent.'

'And you think ... no don't tell me ...'

'We can only give it a try David.'

And that's how I came to be sitting opposite the little doll-like being from god knows where.

I was otherwise alone, but I knew that beyond the large mirror behind me were assembled some of America's top brass anxious to see if Reynard's baby was capable of delivering the goods. I'm afraid for a while at least that baby was incapable of delivering anything; I was suffering from what I can only imagine was stage fright.

The dolly sat relaxed regarding me with those large expressionless eyes. It was clothed completely in a form-fitting silver grey uniform up to its neck. On the upper sleeves were coloured symbols that could possibly indicate badges of rank. There was nothing frightening about it. In fact even as I sat returning its unblinking stare I felt a mild euphoria creeping over me. It wasn't dissimilar to the feelings I got in the early stage of my regression sessions. Reynard had advised me of the possibility and told me not to fight it; just go with it. I closed my eyes.

An image formed in my mind, much like the ones I experienced in meditation when I travelled in the inner world, but this was a much sharper series of images. Like the rapid frame changes of a TV advertisement. A bejewelled night sky. A giant bell-shaped craft in a brilliant blue sky. And the dolly itself seated at a console among others of a similar kind. The images repeated themselves several times before resolving into something resembling an asteroid travelling in space. I opened my eyes; it was as if a spell was broken. I was met with the same expressionless stare, but the doll's posture was no longer relaxed; it was sat up, alert.

I realised that the images were an attempt to convey something to me, but I was at a loss as to how I was supposed to respond. My mind went back to those childhood encounters I had been regressed to. There didn't appear to have been a problem communicating then. Even as I was thinking more images began to flash into my mind, they reminded me instantly of my first days at school. There was my teacher at the blackboard chalking up the very first words I was to learn, I realised the Doll was into my mind, reading my thoughts. Were these images meant to convey that we needed a common language in order to communicate properly; interpreting images could be rather a slow process and not very reliable. Was I to understand that language as we understood it was an unfamiliar concept to this dolly? As if in reply the teacher image receded to an insignificant dot to be replaced by strange arid landscapes alternating with the rural scenes of my childhood. I realised something similar to those times in my bedroom and in the woodland was occurring. The rapid exchanges of images seemed to blend into a form of knowing that required no conscious interpretation. The realisation that I was actually communicating telepathically with a being from out of this world shocked me into consciously being back in the room where there was just me and the doll, and somewhere behind me a group of people wanting answers.

'It's all impressions Bill.' I said later after he had rescued me from immediate interrogation by the brass. 'Some of it is quite graphic and at other times I am actually experiencing what it is thinking, like when I made that mind trip of yours to America.'

'So, where does it come from?' I could see that he was quite excited and rightly so. His belief that telepathic ability could be awakened in me was apparently justified.

'If I say, from somewhere in the asteroids, would that make any sense?'

'It's difficult to believe that they could support life as we know it.'

'That's just it Bill, are we dealing here with life as we know it?'

'I suppose that is something we hope to discover …' 'It most certainly is, and more besides.' A voice suddenly bellowed in our ears

The man who burst into the room unannounced wore the insignia of a three star General. A short man of medium build, he had to look upward to address Reynard; it wasn't something that appeared to bother him, unlike a lot of short arses I had come across.

'Who the hell are you?' Reynard had whirled around at the interruption. 'I was promised time to get what we glean from these interviews documented.'

'I'm sure you will be given every opportunity to do that, but perhaps you need to understand the situation here Mr Reynard. We want to know at the earliest if these guys represent any kind of a threat to national security, and if you have any information regarding that, we want to know, pronto.' He smiled suddenly and thrust out his hand. 'Montgomery Patton, base commander. I'm here at the behest of my masters to monitor this project.' Reynard accepted his demonstration of goodwill and I did likewise.

'We are being hounded by the politicians,' Patton said. ' I'm sure you're familiar with that scenario, they sit on their asses and insist on getting every last cent's worth out of the defence budget.' Reynard agreed on that score. Patton turned to me. 'That's really some gift I hear that you've got there Major Kent.' There was no doubt he had been well briefed. 'It could make you quite a security risk around here and places like the Pentagon.'

170

Reynard explained the unlikelihood of anyone being on my wavelength. Patton gave no indication as to whether he accepted that judgement or not.

**

I sensed nothing in the way of hostility from this doll-like creature. It seemed content to communicate with me, although I realised that it was suspicious of the motives of all the figures of authority it had come into contact with so far.

I got a strong feeling of an aura of femininity emanating from it on the second morning. I felt later this was not really the case and that its sexual orientation was neither one way nor the other, however I did not want to think or continue to refer to an obviously feeling person as an *it*. I needed a name and for some odd reason Aime came to mind; it seemed appropriate. There was an immediate feeling of approval from the doll.

It is of course difficult for anyone not experiencing a communication in non-language to understand that it actually works. Even I am at a loss to explain how the transference of thoughts can be interpreted instantaneously to convey the necessary information. That was however the case, and to simplify things I feel I need impart what I gained from interviews with Amie in ordinary terms.

Everywhere I went now I was escorted by at least two military policemen, and I was permitted to talk to no one except Bill Reynard. Everything including my interview notes was forwarded to the authorities through him.

The importance of my role in being perhaps the only person on Earth able to communicate with Aime was not lost on me. But whenever I entered her room there was an immediate feeling of empathy between us and I was never to lose sight of the fact that I owed her more consideration than I was prepared to give to my superiors.

In a sense I felt protective towards this being who was beginning to appear as not wholly biological, but was nevertheless a person; a personality in its own right. She apparently needed neither sleep or food, nor anything biologically necessary for survival. Every morning I found her exactly as I had left her the day before, dwarfed by the easy chair and resembling body-wise an emaciated 5 or 6 year old, but always I had the feeling that she was pleased to see me.

I was given lists of questions each session, all geared to discover how much of a threat people like Amie posed. The

171

military mind could countenance no other purpose for alien intrusion.

Over the course of several days I was able to establish that she was an engineer, and the pilot of the craft that had crashed. There were things that she was not prepared reveal, the location of her home planet for instance. The earlier reference to the asteroid featured only as a forward base in our solar system.

I got that she felt unsafe answering questions formulated by the military personnel and that no amount of reassurance regarding her safety would induce her to reveal little more than her name, rank, and number directly to them.

I discussed this with Bill Reynard who was of the opinion that she was acting under orders from a higher command, and that we, including the military, would have to be content with whatever crumbs of information she was prepared to make available.

The brass were beginning to get impatient with what they considered a lack of progress. Monty Patton was apologetic at having to convey their displeasure, but agreed there was no alternative but to keep plodding away. To remove me would be counter-productive. The only suggestion he could offer was to have a word with one of the bright young linguists on the base as it had been suggested that in order to get a free flow of information Amie and I needed a common language. I was as anxious as anyone to know what Amie was all about, but not for reasons other than natural curiosity when confronted by someone from another world, perhaps another dimension, and one exhibiting obvious signs of friendship.

I think the big surprise when I suggested that a common language in our exchanges might be advantageous, was that Amie was just as anxious to learn about our world as we were of hers.

The linguist, Charlie Noble suggested I start with a kindergarten primer in which simple words related to simple illustrations. He argued that whole nations learned their communication skills from that simple beginning; the results proved amazing. I read to Amie at first and left progressive primers for her to study overnight.

As she did not require sleep her appetite for knowledge was voracious and I very soon found that encyclopaedias' were replacing single volumes. Her command of English went up in leaps and bounds, and in a few weeks rather than the months

172

anticipated by Noble she could have taken her place in the highest halls of learning in the land. Her academic acuity would have left an Oxford don for dead. Much to the chagrin of the brass she still refused to answer questions of a militarist nature.

It became increasingly obvious that she was only ever going to impart knowledge that could be beneficial to the human race.

I was given an insight into conflicts that had and were still taking place between opposing factions on a galactic scale. It seemed that dominance and control were not solely to be attributed to despots and dictators on Earth. Amie's only previous contact with Earth had been some 6,000 years ago in the Himalayan and Indian sub continent region. She was then part of mission in search of a missing expedition sent to relieve one of their bases in that area; there was no trace found of either the base or the expedition. At that time she informed me there was a nuclear war going on; a family dispute over the division of territories.

'How familiar that sounds,' said Bill Reynard when we were in private discussion in our own quarters prior to putting anything on paper for the brass. 'That could relate to the wars spoken of in the Mahabharata.' He saw that I had no idea what he was referring to. 'It's an Indian Epic about warring godlike creatures. The antagonists appear to have been familiar with flying machines and weaponry that we've only begun to develop in the last few decades.'

'She did mention that it was at that time she was conversant with Sanskrit, the one and only Earth language she has ever been familiar with.'

'She has been around for some time then?'

It was now time to drop my bombshell. I had been nursing it for several days wondering what effect it would have on the powers that be.

'How does a few million years grab you Bill?'

He looked at me for what seemed an age, he was obviously searching for an adequate reply; it wasn't often that he was at a loss for words. When they did come they were oddly no surprise.

'Makes sense strangely enough David. She's a robot of some sort, way beyond our comprehension at this time, she's far in advance of anything we can concoct with a digitally operated mechanical toy. How can I put this? She, that is, the essence of her being, inhabits what amounts to be some sort of semi-biological machine. Don't ask me to explain that because I can't.

173

I think she would have to spell it out for us to even get an inkling as to what kind of creation it is.'

There was a knock at the door and Montgomery Patton's head appeared around it; he advanced on me. There was no preamble.

'People back there think you might be holding out on them major.' His smile didn't quite take all the edge off his voice.

'I can't imagine why they should think that,' said Reynard. 'Major Kent is trying to conduct interviews under circumstances quite without precedent. The very least they can do is wait and see what comes out of it; unless they feel they have something else that will fill the bill here.'

Bill's staunch defence seemed to take Patton on the back foot. He frowned and dropped into a chair opposite us.

''You know this alien creature has got us by the balls on this one Mr Reynard and we are very much in yours and the major's hands here. For myself I'm okay to go along with you guys but this whole alien business is causing a lot of concern in very high places.'

'And your masters are cracking the whip?'

He looked at both of us in turn. 'Shall we say they are more than a little nervous. I have my own way of dealing with political flak, but most of the people that I'm working with out there are almost as alien to me as this Amie person.' He looked directly at me. 'I don't want you to feel that I personally am pushing you for results major, you look like an honest broker.' He raised a significant eyebrow. 'If there is such a thing?'

'What do you make of that Bill?' I said when he'd gone.

'I guess even a three star General has to watch his back at times David.'

Chapter 27

Amie's appetite for anything in the English language was voracious, plus the fact that her memory was, without doubt, photographic. We were soon conducting the sessions in English and there was no further need for me to interpret the images and feelings she projected but they still, despite her expressionless exterior, gave an animated completeness to her conversation. The result from the other side, relayed through Monty Patton, was a series of specific questions which Amie steadfastly refused to answer.

Then one morning as I sat down I was aware of a subtle change in our relationship; she wanted to give me a very clear picture of what she was and perhaps what we, humanity itself, was and how we related to her and her kind.

She began. 'Everything you have provided me with over these past weeks in the way of books and data I have sent to my asteroid base for translation and it has been returned in my own language. This now enables me to give you information concerning your Earth in an historical sense of which you have no true knowledge.'

'Does that mean that you are now prepared to answer the questions that are constantly being asked?' The answer of course was no, but that she would give information of value to the human race.

'First of all you need to understand what you are, an Immortal Spiritual Being, for simplicity, an ISBE.' The words, delivered in the usual emotionless manner nevertheless impacted strongly. I had certainly never thought of myself as an immortal spirit; I had considered that to be a lot of religious flannel. I must confess that I hadn't given much thought to any alternative possibilities. I was if anything, an agnostic, sitting on the fence with my bum mainly in the atheist camp. I wondered what else she would reveal.

'If that is confusing for you, rest assured it is not only true, but all persons will continue to be ISBE's whether they believe it or not.'

'Does that mean that you are also an Immortal Spiritual Being?'

'Of course.' She sat staring at me with those strange expressionless eyes but I was beginning to sense a feeling of a warm personality within that doll-like exterior. I wondered how I was going to pass on this sort of information to people who could only regard an alien being as a potential threat. She was obviously aware of my thoughts. 'I doubt that anyone beyond the glass wall,' she was referring to the two-way mirror behind me, 'is ready to accept what I have told you. I will therefore volunteer information that you can pass on which will not be of harm to my race, but if taken seriously will be of benefit to all of humanity. One other thing you need to understand is that like me you are not your body, although it is a necessary part of your existence on your Earth plane.

This body you see before you is necessary for the functions I need to perform. I am a pilot and engineer of a space vehicle for instance, but I can, and do, exist outside of it. Oh! Don't be surprised, you also exist both inside and outside of your body but not in quite the same way as I do. You do it in dreams, daydreams, and at times when your mind takes you to places other than where you are physically. My body is a technological fabrication, manufactured, if you like, to perform all the functions necessary for a pilot and engineer of a space craft. Like your body, mine too is controlled by my thoughts, like you I am its life force. The bodies of my crew were also designed for their specific tasks aboard a space vehicle. I see you have a problem with that, but that in part is because of the way you have been conditioned over the last few thousand years on your planet.'

Your body is a biological necessity for your existence on the Earth plane, and like mine is only necessary for as long as you need it. Mine, like yours is simply a tool that enables me to operate in an environment of choice and accomplish the tasks it is best suited for. I can dispense with mine when I have no further use for it.'

'You mean you can leave it at any time, leave here?'

'At any time.'

When Ganymede first told me that I would encounter things to blow my mind, did he really mean when I came up against the likes of Amie? Or was he simply talking about the covert advances in technology? I wondered too what Reynard would have to say when I relayed this information to him. But my mind was already working on this, and I could only suspect that Amie was giving it some help.

'So when you are left alone at night apart from the TV monitors, you, the real you can be elsewhere at will? Where do you actually go?'

'I return to base and consult with my superiors.' A thought struck me.

'Your crew members, does that mean ...?'

'Their bodies were rendered useless by the impact, they left instantly. Their bodies were more biological than mine due to the variations in physical requirement.' I was aware that despite her reluctance to be questioned by my superiors it wasn't extended to my questions. The realisation that some sort of rapport was building between us created a kindred spirit feeling; in me anyway. She obviously had no problem anticipating my questions, she often answered before my mind could utter them.

'My purpose for being here in this part of your planet is because my superiors are concerned about the escalation of nuclear explosions taking place in this area. We were monitoring levels of radiation to determine harm to the environment. Unfortunately our craft was struck by an electrical discharge, but I don't need to explain thunderstorms to you. Each of our bodies, although synthesised, has its own unique frequency, its own identity. This in turn is tuned into the nervous system of the craft which enables the craft to be operated through our thought processes, thus doing away with complicated control systems.'

'Am I dreaming this?'

'No you are not. When the atmospheric discharge struck, it short circuited the crew's energy connection with the craft which resulted in the crash. I am from a civilisation that is millions of your years old and one that controls one quarter of the physical universe. We are the Dominion. Our aims are to discover and claim new territories much like your own terrestrial explorers. The similarity ends there though, we do not subject anyone to tyrannical or oppressive rule, and neither do we exploit their resources for our own gain. Our main purpose is to eliminate every last vestige of an empirical system that for billions of years has dominated, corrupted and enslaved two thirds of the physical universe. It is the Old Order. One that enslaves people, corrupts their minds, bewilders them with laws that are impossible to keep, and restricts their ability to think for themselves.' I had to admit. It certainly sounded all too familiar.

I realised I was fast losing my role as an interviewer, Amie was my tutor and what she was teaching was straight out of gobsmacksville. I did my best after lengthy sessions with her to record all that she had passed down to me, but the brass still persisted in demanding answers to specific questions posed by

177

them. She steadfastly refused and continued to release only the information of her choice. There were no favourable responses from the brass, they likewise steadfastly refused to see Amie as anything other than a potential threat.

There was apparently no limit to her capabilities or to the resources of the Expeditionary Force of which she was a member. As a citizen of a civilisation that had been evolving for millions of years, travel between galaxies and even dimensions offered no barriers. The Expeditionary Force had arrived relatively recently in the Milky Way Galaxy; less than 10,000 years ago. In answer to my thoughts as to why they hadn't made themselves known to Earth populations or made a base here, I got the following.

'Earth is an unstable planet. Its poles shift radically every 20,000 years or so. Its land masses float on a molten core and collisions between continental plates cause destructive earthquakes and volcanic action. Last but not least important is the instability and unpredictability of Earth humanity itself.'

All her information regarding Earth and its history is relayed to her from her Communications Officer on the asteroid base.

It was Reynard who put me wise to the danger signals behind the scenes on the Nevada base.

'They are tearing their hair out over the alien's intractability. They have jumped to the conclusion that her refusal to answer their questions is because the Dominion has a secret agenda that puts Earth security and defence systems at risk.'

In view of what I knew of her, and the matter of fact way she had acted throughout, I told him that couldn't be true, and that sort of thinking was more in the realm of immature school kids. Nevertheless he advised me to warn Amie.

'I think she is already aware of danger from that quarter.'

'From what you've told me I don't doubt it David, but you never know what these people might do to get their own way.'

'You are not really happy with the way they operate are you Bill?'

'We have been in the UFO and ET arena for the past sixteen years David, and we've seen the good and the not so good. I say the not so good, because part of that might have been because we made a horse's arse of a job of it. Here we have an alien being that happened to drop in on us by accident. If what she says is true that she can leave any time, then she is not in her sense a prisoner, so why does she stay?'

178

'I think she wants to put us right about all the things we are getting wrong, to mention nuclear testing and environmental damage for starters.' Reynard laughed.

'Well the people here don't think like that, they suffer from what we call paranoia. They know, by what you've handed them, although most of them are hard-pressed to believe it, that Amie could take off in the same way as her crew members did and just leave the 'dolly' behind. But they think that she remains here in order to suss out their innermost secrets and pass them back to her superiors.' He didn't need to explain paranoia to me.

'How does Patton see this, do you think?'

'I think he wants to appear as a Mr Nice Guy and he probably means to be, but I think he is a loyal member of the Paranoia Society and will always come down on their side.'

I found it easy to accept Reynard's assessment. As Ganymede had once said, he was out of the top drawer as far as psychiatrists went.

It was to happen soon, and sooner than expected. I was halfway through a morning session when I was summoned to the base commander's office. As usual when I moved about the base outside of the interview room or my quarters I was escorted by two heavily armed military policemen. As there were four this time I took that to be an exercise in intimidation. Reynard was not invited along and it was some time before I would see him again.

The office was large by any standard and contained a conference table and chairs beside the usual office paraphernalia. The bodies present, apart from the base commander Monty Patton, included ex Army Air force Secretary Symington and several generals I recognised from newsreels and magazines including Nathan Twining, Lauris Norstad, and Jimmy Doolittle. All were in civilian dress and I wasn't up to speed on what their service commitments were since Lyndon Johnson had taken over on the death of John Kennedy. Three other nameless characters appeared to be intelligence agents.

It was apparent from the start that they were going to beat the same drum; why wouldn't Amie answer the questions they wished to put to her? What were the intentions of whatever civilisation she came from? And even more importantly perhaps, how the craft she arrived in was constructed and how it could operate without any known conventional controls.

In answer to their requests, I could only repeat what she had told me. I addressed my answers to Symington who was chairing the meeting.

'With all due respect sir, the alien being refuses to accept any questions formulated either by persons present here or from similar authorities.'

'Why do you think that is major, do you have an opinion on that?'

'I cannot offer one sir. I can however repeat her own words when I ask her to at least consider your questions.'

'And they are?' I could see how my audience were focussed for my reply. I was reminded of lions stalking game on the Serengeti.

'She distrusts the motives of what she calls this administration and the way in which she feels the requested information would be misused. She is also under obligation to give only information that could be of benefit to humanity as a whole.'

'Obligation to whom?'

'I assume she is referring to her superiors; her own people. She is of her own admission a serving officer in the Expeditionary Force.' There were nods that could be of understanding. These people knew the importance of giving and obeying orders.

'How can we be sure major that you are relaying the products of these interviews correctly?' It was Twining who had taken up the questioning. He saw immediately from my reaction that it might be interpreted as a question of my integrity, so he hastened to add. 'This telepathy business, it's not an exact science, is it?'

'I can't answer that sir. But I've been given to understand that it's a gift rather than a science, or more correctly a latent ability, one that has atrophied through lack of use among humans. He nodded and smiled.

'Very well put major, but in order to put our minds at rest over that issue, we,' and he included with a hand gesture all those present, 'have a suggestion. We want you to try once more to get the alien to answer the questions we wish to put to her. Should that request still be ignored we would like you to take these …' He reached into a brief case and placed a sheaf of papers on the table before me. '… and get her to read through them. They are the typescripts of the interviews you have conducted so far. We would like her to sign to the effect that they are a true representation of the information she has given you.' He looked toward Symington. 'I think we can conclude the meeting at this point Stuart.' Symington nodded and then turned to me.

'We will of course be closely monitoring these exchanges between you and the alien, major, and we will require you to give a verbal account of progress.'

I could have told him there and then that there would be none, but if they wanted to spend a fruitless period behind the two-way, all joy to them. As for this having been a meeting, I hadn't been slow to notice that no minutes were recorded; it had been simply a way of telling me to get my finger out.

Back in the interview room I found her relaxed as usual and regarding me with her usual lack of expression. It seemed a shame that their technology hadn't allowed for some visible form of emotion or body language. I knew that she was already scanning my mind even as I sat down. I presented the documents to her but she made no move to accept them, insisting that if my commander did not trust the reports that I had passed on, then how could he trust the signature of a spacecraft officer and engineer?'

I could understand the logic of that, and I folded the papers and slipped them into my jacket pocket. I was about to give a verbal response to those monitoring the proceedings when that action was made unnecessary. The door behind me burst open and armed MP's rushed into the room. Two grabbed Amie and held her down, immobilising her in the chair. As I went to stand two others pinioned me and thrust me back in my seat. One other stood to one side of Amie holding a rifle to her head. A man in a white coat pushing a trolley had followed them in and wheeled it behind Amie's chair. What followed happened in seconds. He slipped a metal band down onto her head and turned back to the trolley; it contained a machine similar to the one Genna had once used to implant my ID, only this one had a more sinister purpose. White coat yelled "Clear!" and the MP's released her and moved away.

Amie's body stiffened and shuddered. White coat turned a knob on the machine and her body relaxed and sank back in the chair. He turned the knob again and repeated the operation.

I sat transfixed, unable to move under the pressure of the MP's and wondering what the hell was going on. Amie, slumped in her chair, was now being examined by another white coat who had entered the room. He made a signal to someone behind me and a gurney was wheeled in. Amie was lifted onto it and strapped down. I was then escorted out of the room and back to my quarters. I was locked in and a guard posted at the door.

An hour later there was a knock at the door and General Twining entered. It was obviously thought to be time for an explanation for what had occurred. He was mildly apologetic. He asked me to accompany him to another section of the base, explaining on the way.

'The alien has been immobilised because we believe that she and whatever civilisation she is from is potentially a military threat to the USA. It was a course of action to prevent her departing and returning to her base as she said she could do during the interviews. We considered it a grave risk if she reported back what she has observed during her stay here, so we think our action is justified. While he was talking we entered a small room in the base hospital. The two white coats involved recently were connecting Amie up to monitoring equipment. She lay unmoving I couldn't tell whether she was alive or dead.

My visits to the sick bay back at the Complex had familiarised me with EEG and 'vital signs' equipment but I couldn't understand what use it could be here, Amie didn't have a biological body. Not for the first time did I consider that the actions that had recently occurred on this base had been taken at the expense of common sense.

White coat No I, I don't recall his name although I do believe he was introduced to me at some point, explained that he had administered mild electric shocks in order to subdue Amie long enough for the military authorities to come to a decision about her.

'Will you try to communicate telepathically with her?'

'I already have,' I said. I was as anxious as anyone to find out what had or was happening to her. 'There is no response. Quite frankly I think you have done exactly the opposite of what you intended.' I couldn't keep the rancour out of my voice.

'Well we will keep her under observation here and we may call on you later to try again to establish communication.'

I couldn't see much point but I agreed. To me that dolly lying apparently lifeless had come to be a real person to me.

I was escorted back to my quarters and locked in under guard. I wondered where on earth Bill Reynard had got to while all this was going on. Nobody seemed prepared to enlighten me.

Next morning I was taken back to the interview room. Amie's chair was gone and the room returned to what I assumed was

182

normal function. Soon after I was told to sit down and wait the white coat entered with a civilian carrying a hard, black suitcase. The civilian was introduced; I don't recall his name because what followed left me highly indignant; I was told I was to undergo a lie-detector test.

The white coat tried to convince me that it was for my own protection and that because all the interviews with the alien had been telepathically conducted and she hadn't authenticated them, everything depended on my word alone. I realised that if I was to get out of this jungle I had no option but to submit to the humiliation of the test.

Questions revolved around whether I had faithfully recorded the information passed to me. Had I fabricated anything with the intention to deceive? Did I believe what the alien had told me? The net result, after an hour long session in which the polygraph charts were also analysed, was a clean bill of health. I gave the interview room and its occupants a two-fingered salute as I was marched back to my quarters.

I was asked several times over the next few days to attempt communication with Amie, but each time proved negative. Seeing her lying there inert convinced me that she was no longer operating her body.

After a week I was told that my services were no longer required. I received a written order which officially discharged me from any further involvement with the base and the alien, plus an Oath of Secrecy document for my signature. The gist of that document being that any disclosures I should make regarding my experience on the base would constitute an act of treason against the USA. I had no sooner signed than I was relieved of it. A few minutes after the courier departed a beaming Reynard walked through the door, held a finger to his lips, and beckoned me to follow him.

'You never know what's bugged in a place like this,' he said as we wandered away from the building. 'Sorry I wasn't around to hold your hand David but you were quarantined while you were doing your stuff with the dolly bird. How did it go by the way?'

I gave him a brief summary of the events up to and including the debacle in the interview room and Amie's departure. 'The transcripts of the interviews are with the brass here but I'll do my best to document everything I remember once we're shot of this godforsaken place.'

'Well the good news is, that will be in about 16 hours. We are booked on a mid morning flight out of Albuquerque. There was no bad news as I re-entered my quarters, and there was no longer a guard on the door. I found it difficult to settle. I lay awake for a long time going over the events of the past weeks. It was in that borderline area between sleep and waking that I heard her voice. I sat up in bed and found the bedside light switch half expecting to see her; I realised that wasn't possible, her body was already somewhere within the security system and beyond the reach of the outside world. But she, in essence, was here with me.

'Hello David,' she said. Her thoughts were friendly; it was her. I asked how she was. She said she had suffered no damage. She had left her body before the shocks had been delivered and had since returned to her base.

I asked if I would ever see or be in contact again and she assured me that as ISBE's it was inevitable for us to be in contact whenever we both desired or needed to be. I woke feeling refreshed and relieved of the burden I had carried since those last moments in the interview room.

.

Chapter 28

Albuquerque

We hitched a ride to Albuquerque on a C54 Skymaster, arriving in good time for our connecting flight to New York. Any plans I had to follow Ganymede's earlier advice and get some sleep on long flights was temporarily forgotten when I caught sight of Genna in the airport lounge. She was sitting with him. It would always be a source of wonder to me how quickly that man could get around the world. She rose and came across the moment she saw me. I looked sideways at Reynard.

'You never said.' I accused.

He grinned. 'You never asked. She's your reward for being a good boy; you've done everything we expected of you.' Before I could acknowledge the compliment my lips were full of Genna. He discreetly moved away. It was several moments before we came up for air and made our way to a quiet spot away from the others. Reynard had taken Genna's vacated seat and was sat conversing with Ganymede.

We had hardly had time to exchange much in the way of news when we observed Makris coming through the doorway; he headed straight for the duo. The low tone conversation was brief and one-sided, coming mainly from him. He left as quickly as he had arrived with only a token nod of recognition in our direction. His face gave away nothing. Ganymede waved us over.

'Change of plans I'm afraid, David.' Beside him Reynard looked apologetic; I couldn't help a feeling of unease. 'You and I will not be taking this flight, we are wanted elsewhere.' It seemed my unease was justified. I looked again at Reynard without being quite sure why.

'Something to do with the Honeycomb,'

He said. 'No. I have to get back to the Complex there's been a problem there, some casualties, I'll need to take Miss Rees with me.'

'What happened?'

'The report is sketchy, but it might have to be closed down, I'll know more when I get there. Makris is recovering your baggage and will accompany you to Honeycomb.' Even as he spoke the New York flight was being called. I walked with Genna to the departure gate; our reunion had been short-lived.

**

Another stomach-churning take off reinforced my conviction that helicopters were a long way from my favourite mode of transport. The 'Huey', I was informed by Ganymede, was such a reliable machine that it was being used extensively in Vietnam. A single period of turbulence shattered any reassurance that knowledge might have induced. As usual he immediately settled for shuteye, but the motion of a helicopter in flight kept me slightly on edge. I needed a distraction. I reached for a newspaper protruding from the pocket of the seat in front of me. It was a week old. I failed to find the US bombing of targets in Laos by mercenaries interesting, or the fact that a Liverpool group called the Beatles had half of America's teenage girls piddling themselves with delight. Perhaps if there had been more detail I might have spent more time on the fact that Liz Taylor had found her new dick of the month. The only thing of mild interest, perhaps because I had a loose association with what happened there, was the report of several minor earthquakes in south west New Mexico. As it was barely a couple of lines I stuffed the paper back and settled for a study of the uninspiring scene passing below.

Gessler and his shadow met us on touchdown and ferried us once again to the 'Montana Hilton' where we found Arthur C and Quan Ling awaiting us. I suffered a further finger-crushing from the General, mitigated somewhat by a light welcome kiss on the cheek from Quan Ling before she moved off to talk with Makris, whose face which, usually as reserved as a professional mourner's at a funeral, was transformed into smiling animation. No points for guessing, I thought as I followed the others through the foyer to the cafeteria. We headed for a table with seating for four. Shelman moved to a separate one.

Arthur C soon put us in the picture as to why we were there, certainly why I was.

'We have a landed UFO about a mile from here, and an unusual situation. It's one of the smaller craft; a scout ship we believe.' He was looking directly at me as he spoke. 'As far as we can make out it doesn't appear to be damaged or even to have crashed.' He continued to stare at me; I felt he wanted a response.

'That certainly does sound unusual sir. Landed, you say, not crashed?' It was weak but the best I could do.

186

'Oh it gets even more bloody unusual Davy, we know it's occupied by at least two crew members, they appear occasionally in the dome.'

'So what's happening so far?' Ganymede beat me to the question. It was answered by Gessler on a nod from the General.

'Very little I'm afraid sir. We can only get to within yards of it; they appear to have some sort of force field in place. We are euchred.'

'I see,' said Ganymede. 'What do the top brass suggest?' Arthur C and the Gessler looked at each other.

'We are keeping this one to ourselves for the moment, and that is why we've sent for you Davy my boy.' Arthur C grinned. 'I heard you did the business with the alien at the AFB in Nevada and we figured it might be worth a try here.'

'Thank you for your vote of confidence sir.' I said. 'I'll do whatever I can, but there are conditions.'

'Conditions?' Arthur C's face clouded.

'It's regarding telepathic communication sir.' Ganymede interrupted, and gave a brief word on the wavelength issue.'

Arthur C nodded and his grin returned.

'Fair enough. I guess we can only give it a try. Those guys are obviously not keen on coming out of that thing, and we sure as hell can't get in to them.' He turned to me. 'I guess your kinda our Hobson's choice Davy.' He chuckled and looked at his watch. 'You guys get some chow and then we'll trot over there in one hour's time, okay?' He rose and headed for the door followed by Gessler and Shelman.

I looked at Ganymede after they'd gone. Once again that uncanny knack he had came through.

'You're wondering why the top brass haven't been tipped off on this one.'

'It had crossed my mind guv.'

'Bill Reynard was right about Gessler being on overload.'

I must have looked puzzled, but then I was trying to recall what Reynard had said about the major. It was something about keeping the lid on the burden of things he had seen and had knowledge of during his service on secret bases.

'Is it a burden guv? I mean all this secrecy; keeping things out of the public domain, this building of virtual cities underground? Collaborating with these big gray guys? Is there something going on that even we are not aware of?' It was that last thought that

187

gave me the answer, and Ganymede was watching me like a hawk.

'I think we'd better order up some grub David. I have things to say and I do it better without an empty feeling inside.'

Ganymede had always had that ability to come up with the unexpected; things that boggled the mind, mine anyway. This time was no exception.

'Make no mistake David, what I'm going to tell you could put us all in the cooler or worse. It all goes back to Roswell. Gessler was a lieutenant at that time in charge of a clean-up squad, sworn to secrecy on pain of death on what really happened there. It is from the big cover-up at that time that the CIA originated, and has been evolving ever since. One high spot of CIA operations is believed to have been the assassination of James Forrestal US Secretary to the Navy. Dogged by what was going on behind the scenes he blew a valve and had a nervous breakdown. His alleged suicide from the 16 floor of a hospital left a bad taste in the mouths of a lot of people. He was not the first to fall out of favour over his insistence that the public should know what really happened at Roswell and other places in New Mexico in the late forties, and from what happened to Jack Kennedy, Lee Oswald and Jack Ruby recently, he was not the last.'

'The link being UFO's and alien beings.'

'They all represented a threat to the establishment with the knowledge of what they knew, or suspected, and their intention to disclose it.'

'Are we vulnerable? I mean we've seen a lot of what's going on.'

'Anyone in the know from top generals to the lowest in the ranks is a potential accident waiting to happen.'

I was wondering why he was telling me all this. Was there something in the wind that I wasn't aware of? I didn't have to wait long for the blow.

'Bill Reynard told me before he left that Gessler wants to blow the whistle on what he knows.'

'Bloody hell that could put us all in the shit.'

'Not necessarily, it depends how it's done. The point is David ...' He hesitated for a second or two ... 'Both Bill and I agree that something needs doing to inform the greater public.'

'I thought that was out, in view of the panic it would create.' I was having some difficulty with what I was hearing.

'That could happen of course, but that needs to be set against a wider picture of black ops agendas; the underground cities, and what the robot dolly warned of a planned depopulation. Think of the panic and misery if that was put into operation.'

'That hardly bears thinking about of course, but does that mean dumping the whole works onto the public?'

His head shake was emphatic. 'No! First and foremost the UFO and alien issue needs to be transparent; no further cover-ups and disinformation.'

I wanted to get this clear. As a team member I could be part of whatever it got involved in, and the consequences.

'Are you saying that we are going to join Gessler in his whistle blowing?

'No David, what Gessler does is his problem, but if he goes ahead it may well put us in jeopardy. 'At the moment we are trying to get him to wait, as there might be other ways of getting the same or a similar result; openly blowing the whistle is asking for nasty accidents.

'Okay. So the public, after the disclosure of the truth regarding the nature of our neighbours, what then? Are they to be told why big underground cities are being built, and how to accept depopulation?'

'That is an issue already being worked on David. I can't disclose what measures are already being taken; you'll just have to trust me on that.'

'I'm learning to put a lot of trust in just about everything guv. Do I have a role to play in any of this?'

'Not directly.' He grinned. 'I'm sorry if you are beginning to feel just ornamental, but you've fulfilled the function you were originally co-opted for admirably.'

I laughed. 'What are you saying; I'm now a spare part?'

'Not at all, it's just that once our plans are formulated and operational we'll all have little to do but sit back and watch results.'

'Can I be frank guv?'

He looked perplexed. 'Of course, go ahead.'

'Don't get me wrong because I would still like to contribute to the team effort in putting an end to all the official bullshit and whatever underhand crap is intended for the people of this world but, I'd prefer to do it less upfront.'

He seemed to spend a moment digesting that, and then he said. 'Are you saying that you'd like to keep clear of the field work?'

'Something like that … no exactly that. If I'm completely honest as far from it as I can possibly get.'

'I see.' He studied me for a moment. It happens you know. It's a bit like battle fatigue. Sometimes it can be worked through, at others …' he gave a resigned gesture. 'One of the problems with being in covert operations and being privy to top secret information is how to get out of it without spending the rest of your life looking over your shoulder. If it's any consolation David most of us want out at some time or other, its just a matter of when and how without causing waves.'

'What about Arthur C, you said something about top generals also being vulnerable. How would he react if you were to do a runner for instance?'

'You let me worry about that David. None of this is going to happen overnight, but things are already beginning to smell a bit off. Bill has been doing his remote viewing act at the Complex and it looks as though there's a move afoot to decommission it. That Franciosa guy and his sidekicks are not really there as caretakers.' His words set off alarm bells in my head.

'But Reynard and Genna are on their way back there, are they in some sort of danger?' He shook his head.

'They have no intention of going there David. Oh don't worry, Bill will take extra good care of your Genna, but it could be a while before you meet up again. Meanwhile we need to carry on in the normal way, and pay our space buddies a visit.'

'One more question guv. What about Philo Makris and Quan Ling, and for that matter, Shelman?'

'Shelman is Gessler's problem. Makris and Quan Ling are of a mind and preparing to disappear when the time comes. Now let's get on with our job and hopefully prove you're not a spare part.'

Chapter 29

I sensed something as we left the Landrover and began walking towards the domed disc. We passed through the loose perimeter set up around the craft. Gessler and Shelman stayed with their vehicle. The impressions came in with a rush.

'They're Amie's people,' I said, barely able to contain my excitement.

'Are you sure about that?' I nodded and sat down on a handy chunk of rock worn smooth by wind and weather. Ganymede remained standing.

'Well one of them at least.' I closed my eyes. 'I'm getting impressions.'

'I think that's what they were hoping for here.'

'It'll not be like it was at the AFB with Amie guv. She had time to learn our language, I think this one is telling me that they have fixed a malfunction on their ship and will soon be on their way.'

'What are they doing here?'

'I get like – exploration ... no ... reconnaissance ... they are seeking something.'

'Any idea what exactly?'

'Something about an installation – a base of some sort.'

'That's what we are building here. Why would they be interested in that?'

'That's not it. I'm getting the idea that it's a base that's already here.'

'Well we do have facilities here.' Ganymede turned to face me. 'The Montana Hilton?'

'No, it's not that. I'm getting something similar to what Amie was on about; she referred to it as the Old Order.

'I read through your notes, something about there still being remnants of an old order that needed mopping up, wasn't it?'

I held up my hand for a moment then let it drop.

'Sorry guv, I'm not getting anything.'

Even as I spoke the craft was rising and drifting silently away. Within a few seconds it had disappeared. It was as if it just switched off like a cine film. We looked at one another, and I could see that even the imperturbable Ganymede appeared startled. He was however the first to speak.

'How about that David? No wonder some people think they are only imagining seeing these things.

'And that's it Dave?' said Arthur C as we sat around the messroom table later.

'I'm afraid so sir. The actual contact lasted only minutes before they were up and away.'

'Okay. I'll leave it with you to put in a written report. You say your impression was that they were somehow linked with this Amie person; you think they were these robot types?'

'That was my impression sir.'

'Okay,' He turned to Gessler. 'Not a lot to go on major, but it might be as well to keep our eyes and ears open. The deputation of interested parties will be leaving later today. I think it was a good idea of yours to keep them occupied underground while this ET business was going on, don't want any of them pulling out or withdrawing the funding. I think that concludes our little meeting unless anyone here wishes to contribute further,' he paused and looked around; there was no response. 'Okay lets all get our noses into the feed bucket.'

After lunch I sat talking with Quan Ling and Makris. Ganymede had drifted off with the General. I had no idea where Gessler and Shelman were when it happened.

'Think there are a lot of people that are very unhappy about what is going on here.' Quan Ling said. I looked at her, puzzled. I was not sure if she was addressing me or what she was even on about, but then she looked directly at me. 'I'm talking about these underground bases David.' She looked at Makris as if uncertain whether or not to continue. He nodded and placed a hand over hers; her gaze returned to me. 'The ones we've seen recently are more like underground cities capable of supporting thousands of people.' She looked again at Makris.

'We think there is preparation being made for something,' he said. 'As Quan Ling says, it's as if there is an intention for great numbers to live underground. '

I wondered if there was a simple explanation for that. The secret bases I had seen were already quite extensive and multi-levelled. The Complex was minute in comparison. Quan Ling and Makris were obviously genuinely concerned, and I had known Quan Ling at least long enough to know she wasn't prone to exaggeration.

'Is anyone else aware and wondering about this?' I was thinking once more of Reynard's remarks concerning Gessler, and I wondered just how much the good major knew that we were being kept in the dark over.

'I believe that the amount of interest and the money being poured into this project by various governments in the 1st World is causing a bit of head-scratching,' said Quan Ling.

'I think I'll have a quiet word with Ganymede, I said, without knowing quite what sort of quiet word. He usually kept things pretty close to his chest and I realised I might be out of order asking questions that he might not want to, or be able to answer. Despite everything, I was still an underling in this outfit.

The continuous rumbling of distant machinery stopped. 'Tea-break.' Makris grinned.

A slight tremor ran through the ground beneath our feet. We looked at one another. Makris' grin faded as the tremor increased in intensity and a shudder went through the whole cavern. The lighting dimmed momentarily and came on full again, and then everything was still and silent. The alarm klaxon sent the adrenaline surging through me and we were all on our feet and moving fast.

Arthur C and Ganymede joined us in the outer cavern minutes later; they were both out of breath as if they'd been running. The General looked shaken. He beckoned to Quan Ling as he clambered into a Landrover and she joined him. They headed out into the open. Ganymede indicated for Makris and me to follow him back into the mountain. The sound of approaching sirens heralded the arrival of a rapid response team.

'The Old Man will organise the search and rescue teams, things have gone apeshit in here,' Ganymede muttered as we followed him into the main tunnel. The response team including a party of Rangers passed us as we entered the main working area. Gessler took us to one side. He hardly needed to tell us what had happened; it was all too evident. The team operating the boring machine were being treated by two duty medics; one looked to be in a bad way. Three lay unattended; no longer in need of it. The machine itself dominated the scene however. It lay partially destroyed and slewed on its side exposing much of the hole which appeared to have broken through into open space. Beyond the opening was a luminescent glow similar to the one I had seen at Bowdie. I hardly needed it spelled out; we had found the alien base that the Dominion was seeking, but it looked as though they had beaten us to it.

Gessler continued to bring us up to date, as under Arthur C's direction the Rangers deployed and a section of the response team donned protective gear and approached the opening.

'We are getting radiation readings from inside the hole and we still don't know what caused the explosion,' he said. But I was getting something as the ground once more trembled and there was the sound of distant explosions; the robot pictures in my head were messaging me. I grabbed Ganymede's arm.

'We've got to get out of here guv, they're going to blow the whole place up.'

He looked at me for a moment as if weighing the odds as to whether what I was saying was true or if I was off my trolley. He realised I was still onboard and the wounded and dead were being stretchered out. And then they came. I watched fascinated as they came through the opening; there was two of them, one walking upright the other crawling on all fours. The upright one was tall and reminded me of Jarl; one arm was extended aggressively in my direction. I felt the hit and realised I could no longer move; I was paralysed. The one on the ground had raised himself up and was extending an arm in the direction of the Rangers whose fire was having little effect. Within seconds all six crumpled and dropped to the ground. A single gunshot sounded beside me and the one on his feet clutched at his throat. I was aware of Makris moving in front of me and there was another shot. When he moved away I could see through clouded vision that both aliens were down and still. I must have passed out, the next thing I remember was being jolted along on a stretcher. I was fully recovered by the time we reached the open air and were driven down to the old mine buildings. I wondered how much danger Makris had put himself in by shielding me, and whether the power of those alien weapons differentiated between an armed and an unarmed threat.

The casualties were already accommodated and awaiting evacuation in the building where I had been confronted by Bannister. There were a disconcerting number of body bags, I wondered if there were aliens among them.

The sound of explosions was still coming from the mountain itself. Ganymede came over and hunkered down beside me.

'It sounds as though Amie's people are doing a proper job, guv.' He nodded, gazing thoughtfully into the distance.

'Are you getting anything from them?'

'Nothing now. They are probably on their way home.'

I looked around for Makris. He was deep in conversation with Quan Ling but he must have felt my eyes on him. He looked across and I mouthed my thanks; he gave me a single 'thumbs up' and turned back to Quan Ling. An hour later the Chinooks flew in and the casualties were evacuated; the two love-birds left with them.

It was a week after the explosions ceased that the contamination team entered; they recorded extremely high levels of radioactivity throughout the mountain.

'I think that's put paid to any joint base here,' said Arthur C, can't say I'm unhappy about that.'

'I don't think the Old Man is the only one having thoughts like that,' Ganymede said as we flew out later.

'Like maybe, Gessler?' I said. He lowered his voice although we were seated well to the rear.

'I'll get to Gessler in a while; in the meantime I'll do my best to bring you up to date. Makris and Quan Ling are opting out. They plan to quietly disappear.' I think he got the reaction he was looking for; surprise on my part, but he hadn't finished. 'I had a message from Bill Reynard; the Complex has been destroyed. He says it's the work of Franciosa and his boys.'

'Look Guv, you're beginning to dumbfound me; they're CIA, part of what all this is about.' He shook his head.

'According to what he picked up by remote view, they actually came with the blessing of the Pentagon.'

'You mean top brass is against these secret projects?'

'I didn't say that. I think it means that there is a faction within the 'home of the brave' that doesn't agree with the real purpose of some of these top secret projects.'

'And what is that purpose, Guv?' I was hanging on his words now, with a feeling of deep unease, as if I intuitively knew what was coming next.

'Of that I can't be absolutely sure, but how about the main purpose to which bunkers and suchlike underground retreats are put?'

'To make sure people in key positions ... like governments can still run things in the event of some big catastrophe.' I was thinking of Churchill and Hitler.

'Exactly David, so in these days of a nuclear stalemate and Russia backing down over the Cuban thing, where could any expected threat come from?'

'How about, just in case guv? Both sides have enough nukes armed and ready to blow the world apart. It would only take one trigger happy nut case.'

'I would think the safety measures are pretty well in place to prevent that. No David. I don't think it's nut cases we need to be keeping an eye on, it's a cold, calculating bunch of ruthless bastards that want to take complete control of this planet and everything on it.'

'You mean these ET bods?'

He burst out laughing.

'David! I would have thought by now, given what we've seen of their advanced technology, they could probably take over without a shot being fired if that was their aim.'

I couldn't argue with that of course. But something else had been niggling away at me. 'These ET's that are holed up in these underground bases guv?'

'What about them?'

'I was wondering what their agenda might be. As far as I can make out they leave us alone unless we try to interfere with them; whose side are they on?'

He sighed. 'If only we knew? What you say is true. You think if they were left alone they would cease to be a problem?'

'Something like that.'

He was shaking his head. 'If it were only that simple David. We know of those that are collaborating with certain elements in the military. We don't know how many, or the extent of that collaboration. Those that we are trying to ferret out of their well established bases could well belong to what your dolly bird refers to as the 'old order'. She does say that their influence still holds sway in this part of the galaxy.'

'You think those bases might be outposts or garrisons of the old order?'

'We have noticed that some of their bases are often situated in the vicinity of these underground cities that are springing up.' It was beginning to sound decidedly sinister to me. He appeared to be saying that there was a link between the alien bases and the cities being built under the apparent auspices of our governments.

'What is the real reason behind these underground cities and bases guv? I've been persuaded to remain with this team which seems to be taking sides in a battle of giants; I want to know what I'm fighting against.' He regarded me quietly as if mentally rehearsing what to say. Nevertheless, in view of what I had learned about this crazy world since I had thrown in my lot with him I was still hardly prepared for what came.

196

'From what Major Gessler tells us, the bottom line of the business we have been pursuing up to now has been aiding and abetting a possible global disaster.' I had never seen him looking or sounding so serious. 'I want you to listen carefully to what I have to say.' As if I wasn't already doing that.

'Somewhere at the top of the tree there is an extremely powerful body of ancient, moneyed aristocrats, topped up with industrial giants and governments that have been infiltrated by their minions. This conglomerate goes under the title of the Illuminati. Their influence extends throughout the world. Their minions have infiltrated every strata of society; they are, for want of a better word, puppeteers; they manipulate key figures in world governments. They orchestrate wars, economic crises', shortages and gluts. They control the media, and that means they can, and for the most part do, influence the way we think. In the course of history they have turned us into a race of dissatisfied people; greedy, grasping, coveting, mercenary. A people David, that consider clawing their way up over the backs of others, subjugating, oppressing, even killing to gain their ends is normal and justified. Most, because they accept it as the norm, are blind to it, or like ostriches, bury their heads in the sand; that's life they say.' He paused, inviting comment.

'I understand most of what you're saying guv, even given some thought to it myself, but how do you fight that sort of thing. How can you put that sort of system into reverse?'

'That's a hard one David. But in a way we need follow that guy Bannister's example; with a bit of hindering. If we take the example of an unwelcome, well equipped enemy occupying a country, which is much like the situation we find ourselves in, we do what the little guys always do against the big guys.'

'Guerrilla warfare?'

'You're not just a pretty face are you? Guerrilla tactics; we deprive him of the means to carry out his business. We destroy his bases, his supply lines and wherever possible those who carry out his dirty work. In addition to that we use his own weapons, like propaganda and infiltration into key positions, against him.'

'A big job guv,'

'And a long haul. We'll be long gone, and so will those who come after us, but we'll have made a start; we'll have made our contribution. According to Gessler we may be facing people who are prepared to carry out a selective depopulation of this world.'

'How would they achieve that,' but even as I said it my thoughts were already anticipating the answers.

'Neutron bombs, orchestrated wars, viruses, even old-fashioned death camps,' he said simply.

**

A long time ago, or so it seems, I was recruited into a strange world, a world that has become even stranger with the passage of time. What I was hearing now was making sense of things that had often puzzled me. I was often annoyed by unnecessary complications in what in essence were simple things in life. Bureaucracy ruled, and usually by people with nothing better to do than pass silly rules in order to justify their existence and maintain their position at the top of the heap. Would that same bureaucracy condone, even legislate for selective depopulation? It was not only possible but highly probable, and that even *selective* might degenerate into indiscriminate acts of genocide. The possibility that the Hitlers and Stalins in past centuries may have been influenced by this Illuminati mob loomed large.

Ganymede's revelations triggered something else, in the more immediate present, which was bothering me.

'This business at the Complex, is Genna Rees okay?' He seemed glad of the respite; he even allowed himself a smile.

'She is in safe keeping David, and Bill will see to it that she remains so until you catch up with her.'

'It'll be pretty dangerous stuff taking on these people guv.'

'Fraught, I guess.' He was looking up towards the front of the cabin.

'Okay, what is this that you are going to propose?'

'Perhaps you should hear it from the horse's mouth.' It was then I saw Arthur C rise from his seat and head towards us followed by Gessler and the ever present Shelman. The General and Gessler sat in the vacant seats facing us, Shelman relaxed into a seat across the aisle, like an off duty predator.

'Dave boy,' Arthur C sat like a portly Indian chief oozing benevolence towards his assembled braves. 'I'd like to say at the outset that we consider that you've been a valuable asset to the team. You may not think so, but thanks to you and what we've learned through you about the Dominion, we've been doing a lot of investigating, and consequently have been forced to rethink our role in the secret ops scene.

What we've just experienced back there at Honeycomb has sort of reinforced our belief that there is an agenda in certain

198

quarters to collaborate with these secret alien sites. We even suspect that the decision to commission a base at Honeycomb was made in the knowledge of an alien base being there. I don't think that breakthrough into it was anticipated. We don't know for sure what that agenda is moving towards, but we now know that there are at least a dozen top secret bases that are actually shared by ET's and the US military. I also know that in Adams County Pennsylvania they've turned a whole mountain into what amounts to an underground Pentagon. Now you don't need a high IQ to figure that one out. I'm not suggesting that that is shared by aliens, but we suspect that given the whole spectrum of black ops like The Montauk Project and the Camp Hero mind manipulation experiments, it wouldn't be surprising to find that ET technology is involved, even controlled by these Old Order guys your telepathic buddies speak of.

In the distant past, according to our legends, we had a long association with beings that came from the skies. They were friendly beings who taught us much about how we should conduct our lives and live in harmony with the natural world. Much of those teachings I regret to say have been slaughtered on the altar of materialism which like a cancer has crept insidiously into the gut of affluent society. Very few of us are immune to it. We reach out for bigger, better and prestigious trinkets that we are told, and invariably become convinced, are what makes us one up on the guy next door. We deny that of course and say it just makes us feel good about ourselves.'

It was a bit difficult for me to grasp that these words were actually coming from a US General, but I was obviously committed to hearing him out.

'The point is Dave, while we have our suspicions about the motives of ET's that are openly collaborating with the military, people like Jarl for instance. On the basis of your communications with Amie and the ones at Honeycomb we are apt to consider that the Dominion is favourably disposed towards us. Would you say that was true?'

'All I can say sir is that the relationship with Amie was a friendly one. But the Dominion, you may recall, has spent the last hundred thousand years or so ruthlessly destroying Old Order bases and supplanting their territories throughout the Galaxy.'

'You were given an assurance though that they were replacing a despotic regime, and that I'm afraid is what there is a lot too much of on this planet, both openly and covertly. We would like your support in changing that state of affairs.'

It sounded a very tall order, and I said so. He returned with a serious nod of confirmation.

'The point is Dave we may always be a long way from achieving that on our own, we may need outside help. You may recall the series of earthquake shocks in New Mexico a week or two ago?' I did.

'Three, spread over April. They were pretty low on the Richter Scale; about 3 if I remember sir.'

'They weren't earthquakes Dave my boy.' He was beaming now. 'We nuked an underground city and I'm hoping for more of the same.'

So that was what Ganymede had meant by hindering. I looked at the others in turn; even Shelman permitted himself the rare grin.

'No not us personally,' he hastened to add. 'All we did was a bit of ground work. Your old shipmate located them. It was specialists nominated by friends in the Pentagon that did the business.'

'So where do I come in?'

'We may need those special abilities of yours Dave my boy, and with Makris and Quan Ling opting out; we're also a bit thin on the ground. Also according to information I've received from the inspection team at Honeycomb everything has been put to rest. Bill Reynard will continue to cooperate with us on the remote viewing but wishes to remain in the background, unseen. Our part in this is to retain our present image and continue much as before, with one major difference.' He fielded the query before I uttered it. 'As we no longer have a base in the UK instead of travelling from there to here on assignments we will be here on the spot.'

'You mean actually live here – in the States?'

'You catch on quick Dave, that's what we are asking of you.' He laughed. 'Trips to the UK will be exclusively for R&R. So what do you say, will you continue on the team?'

'Do I still keep the flat in the UK?'

'Unless you find something better, of course.' 'Then I'll accept on one condition.' His face sobered visibly.

'And what's that?'

'I don't want Genna Rees mixed up in any of this.' His smile returned and he reached out unexpectedly and crushed my hand. 'You have my word Dave.'

Chapter 30

1964

Nothing much happened for the latter part of '63 and well into '64. With the Complex gone we had a slightly nomadic existence among a variety of bases. We were still the poor relations in this mad world of black operations and ultra secrecy.

The decision not to involve Genna posed a problem until we received a letter from Clare Sullivan inviting us to visit and maybe stay over for a day or two. The outcome couldn't have been more fortuitous. With a few words in the right ears Genna was seconded to the AFB at Lowry. Arthur C was keeping his promise. It meant there would be periods when we didn't see much of each other, but she would no longer be involved in our ongoing operations; which were to see, hear, and pass on to our faceless allies anything of advantage to our new cause.

Election time and the American three-ring-circus came and went in a welter of razzamatazz. Lyndon B Johnson moved from caretaker president after JFK's assassination to become the elected 36th President of the USA. The Beatles were still taking the country, if not the world, by storm, all but eclipsing the Ranger moon shot, and the news that Liz Taylor had definitely added another notch to her bedpost . All the while the space race was gaining momentum and the public were fed a good measure of released information; if nothing else it sold newspapers and upped viewing statistics.

Underground nuclear tests however reached new levels and only because the Christmas Island tests in 1962 could hardly be kept secret did the media have a field day. But even then the public were never aware until much later that the members of the armed forces who participated in those tests were little more than guinea pigs.

Our call came late in May. For me that meant cutting short a weekend with Genna and flying south to a meet with Gessler and Ganymede. Reynard, I was told would be along later. I decided in view of any instruction to the contrary to leave my uniform behind. I had come to doubt that it gave me any authority whatsoever in the cavalcade of American brass I was encountering.

I landed at Alamogordo Airport and was met in arrivals by Ganymede. A chauffeured car took us to a hotel not far from

202

Holloman AFB; I think it was the Hampton Inn. I dumped my bag in a single ensuite room booked for me and joined the others at a restaurant table. Gessler nodded and Arthur C half-rose, thought better of it, smiled, and subsided into his seat again; for once I was spared the crushing handshake. I looked around; there was no sign of Shelman but a burly figure was approaching the table. He sat he sat down and Arthur C introduced him as Arnold Koba. He had a cast of features similar to Arthur C who referred to him as a distant relative. Koba was invited to recount his earlier story of a UFO sighting he had recently experienced; I supposed it was for my benefit.

He had been fishing late in the evening at one of the many lakes in the area when all around him was suddenly bathed in light. At first he thought it was the moon coming from behind clouds. Then he became aware of his shadow passing from the left to the right of him. He looked around and up.

'There it was, an illuminated orb passing across the sky towards the Sacramento Ranges. There was no sound except for a light breeze rustling the lakeside reeds. There were no distinct features because of the glow, and I realised that I might be seeing a UFO,' he said. 'There was one sighted jn the area about a month or so ago by a Lonnie Zamora, a serving police officer. A very reliable man by all accounts. Anyway the craziest thing happened even as I watched; it suddenly changed shape, like a flattened oval, and shot off at tremendous speed.'

'What do you make of that Dave?' said Arthur C. I wasn't sure what he wanted from me so I looked at Gessler.

'We think it was definitely a space craft, certainly not of this world, as for the shape changing, a banking manoeuvre would explain that, and the flattened oval as it resumed an even keel.'

'That sounds about right,' said Ganymede.' I agreed.

'How does it match up with the Zamora report?'

'It doesn't,' said Gessler, 'apart from that also being oval in shape.'

'I don't suppose the Zamora sighting could have been one of those lunar landing modules on test?' I said.

Arthur C shook his head. 'We've checked that out Dave. Both with White Sands Missile Range and Holloman AFB, and there were no tests in progress, and they had nothing in their possession that even remotely resembled what Zamora described.'

Reynard returned to the fold next day and it was decided he try and get an insight into what was going on in the area apart from the joint US and UK Base in the nearby Sacramento Mountains. From the local maps we drew up reference lines converging on the Zamora site and along the flight line of both the Zamora and Arnold Koba craft. With that done we had a list of coordinates for Bill Reynard to work with.

I joined up with Koba that afternoon and we drove down to Bonito Lake. I could almost picture him as a portly figure in buckskin and beads and a feather or two in a headband, but a strong Texan drawl shattered the image and the baseball cap dispelled it completely. But he was a mine of information about the area and I was treated to the legendary visitations to his tribe of the men from the skies. I recalled Arthur C's words from what seemed a long time ago now. "It's all very old hat to my people Dave. They always knew that there were others out there".

By that evening Reynard still hadn't come up with anything, which wasn't surprising considering the area that he had to cover. By ten I was off to bed. I read a few pages of Ian Fleming's new novel 'You Only Live Twice'. Not that I was a fan but because in a way he was, or had been, in the same line of business as we were. I found it difficult to concentrate and I must have been dozing off when I heard her voice in my head.

'Hello David.' I came wide awake; it was Amie, she came straight to the point.

'Your friend is having problems in locating an Old Order base?'

'That's true; none of the coordinates have worked so far.'

'Not surprising, it has been established for over six thousand years and is well protected. We have only just located it ourselves but we have no ships in your quadrant at this time.'

'We were hoping to deal with it ourselves,' I said. 'We thought it was an undesirable base set up by our own governments.'

'That is a separate issue; both are a potential threat to your planet. Your governments have plans, embryonic at this stage, to depopulate your Earth, but of course you know this. They are being encouraged in this, sublimely, by the Old Order. The end aim is absolute control by the Old Order. Even your governments would become puppets on an enslaved planet.'

She then gave me a set of figures. 'You will have better luck with these. They are the coordinates for the underground city.

Your Major Gessler will know what to do with them. We will take care of the Old Order base in our own way, in our own time.' Then she was gone.

I rang Bill Reynard despite the hour, which was past midnight. By one 'o clock we were all in powwow. Arthur C was over the moon at what had come through and Gessler was already setting the wheels in motion.

'You realise of course that all this will take time, some weeks at least maybe a month,' he said. 'There will be a lot of innocent people working in there and we'd like to get them out if possible.'

'And if that isn't possible?' said Ganymede, but he already knew the answer. Gessler shrugged.

'We can only try. In the meantime I think we'd be well advised to put some distance between this place and ourselves. We don't want anyone to even suspect our involvement in what is going to happen here.'

'It was Arthur C who suggested we do another set of friendly observations back at Area 51. He himself was off to a conference at the Pentagon; a meeting of like minds,' he said with a wink. Reynard also had business elsewhere and left at noon next day. We packed up and vacated a few hours later.

But, as they say, there is no rest for the wicked, and as Ganymede and I sat down for our first meal back at the Area 51 base a rather tense looking Gessler followed by Shelman approached our table. Gessler sat down heavily opposite us and Shelman as usual hovered a short distance away. Gessler nodded to me and looked at Ganymede.

'I'm afraid the news is bad sir. General White has been involved in a helicopter crash. It is still not clear what caused it but an investigation is underway. The General was the sole survivor, but I'm afraid he had a fatal heart attack in the hospital where he was being treated for his injuries.'

Ganymede sat silently for several moments as if taking in what had been said. I wondered how deep a bond, if any, existed between him and his natural father. I sat there dumb. I still found it difficult to grasp the suddenness with which people could leave this world; yesterday he had been his ebullient self. At last he spoke. 'These people at the Pentagon he was meeting, where do we place them?'

'Friendly sir.'

'Do you think someone is wise to us who isn't?'

205

'That's always a possibility.'

Ganymede appeared to consider that. 'The heart attack, is that confirmed?'

Gessler removed a folded paper from his breast pocket. 'We received this teletype a short while hour ago, it's the autopsy report.'

Ganymede opened it up, read it through, and glanced up. 'His injuries were pretty severe but not life threatening. I suppose though, bad enough to bring on a heart attack?'

Gessler nodded. 'I would seem that way, but there's more to it than that; the accident itself.'

I could see that Ganymede's mind was already leaping ahead and taking me with it. His next words confirmed it. 'It wasn't an accident?'

Gessler shook his head. 'The investigating team found loosened joints in the oil lines, enough to seize up the motor within minutes of takeoff.'

'Do you think we might be in danger?'

'I think that is also a possibility; a strong one sir.'

'You're the one with a finger on the pulse here major. What do you really think?'

'I think it would be wise if you and Major Kent moved on sir.'

'Can we do that without attracting attention?'

**

That is how we found ourselves after dark entering a windowless building in its own compound. Shelman stood guard when we entered. Gessler shut the door firmly and switched on the lights. He had described the function of the place earlier but I was still trying to grapple with the concept of travelling great distances instantly. Mentally I knew from experiments I'd conducted with Reynard it was possible to do that mentally, but to enter a portal physically and emerge elsewhere in physical form, how could that be achieved?

Ganymede didn't appear to have any problems with it; in fact he looked positively self-assured. Gessler showed us into what he called the transporter suite which contained little more than cubicles. Ganymede indicated I should enter one and he would take another. I was more than a little apprehensive, but Ganymede's actions were encouraging. Once inside the cubicle I passed through into a screened area. I had been given a coordinate which I was told to concentrate on. There was a whirring sound as if something somewhere had been switched on. Within a few seconds my body began to tingle. This went on for a minute or two then stopped. I went to move and found myself falling to one side. I dropped to my hands and knees and crawled out of the cubicle. I looked around but the room was different and there was no sign of Ganymede. It was occupied by two men in uniform, one approached and helped me to my feet, or more correctly, foot, for it was then that I discovered to my horror, my left one was missing.

'Welcome to Australia,' said the other one coming forward and supporting me on the other side. 'It looks like you've left something behind Major Kent.' I looked down again hardly believing the obvious, only vaguely aware that there was no pain; no sign of any bleeding.'

They helped me to a waiting vehicle. Once I was sitting down I tried to review my situation. I realised only then that Ganymede wasn't with me; the absence of my foot had completely cleared my mind of everything else. Only one of the Australian officers, they were both captains in the Royal Australian Air Force, was accompanying me in the vehicle and I turned to him.

'I went into that bloody contraption with a friend,' I said with unexpected savagery, 'why isn't he here?'

He looked at me puzzled before answering.

'You're the only one that came through major and I was instructed to deliver you to someone at the Alice.'

'The, Alice?'

'Sorry, Alice Springs. You have heard of it?'

I had of course; I'd read the book by Neville Shute. This disastrous turn of events was making me angry and with the loss of my foot not a little terrified. I desperately needed to regain some measure of control of my feelings.

'You know who I am, who are you?'

He grinned. 'No names no pack drill major. I'm just a friend, a friend who knows other friends of yours in the US of A.'

'Who is this someone waiting for me in the Alice?'

'Haven't a clue, I was only told, a particularly friendly friend of yours.'

I realised there wasn't going to be anything added to that and anyway my foot was my major concern; I really didn't give a fuck about anything else. I brooded and dozed for most of the journey which seemed to go on forever; in fact it was well over two hours before we drew up outside a rambling bungalow in what I discovered later was in the south of the town.

My left foot, or rather, where my left foot no longer was, was tingling. I reached down out of habit to rub it and the shock of its absence hit home. I groaned and the captain turned in concern.

'Are you all right Major?' I assured him I was okay and he helped me out. The driver took my other side and I half hopped towards the front door. Halfway there and it opened, and I felt a stinging at the root of my nose and my eyes filling with tears; I was so choked I couldn't say her name. All that had happened in the last few days and especially the last few miserable hours came to the surface.

It was a good ten minutes after the RAAF had departed that I was able, through my own drying tears, to console a tearful Genna and do my best to tell her what had happened. She had only arrived in Australia from Denver the day before and was still suffering jetlag.

'And you say that Ganymede never came out of that thing either?' I shook my head wearily. She was knelt down before me.

'I think I'd better see what's happened.' She raised the shorn off trouser leg. She looked up in amazement. 'It's like it was guillotined David, and sealed. It's not like any amputation I've ever seen,' she said in an awed voice. 'And you say there is no pain?' I shook my head.

'It just feels so bloody odd, and I don't know what to do about it. It doesn't seem like I need hospital treatment, and how would I explain to anyone how it happened, they'd think I was stark staring mad.' She rose up suddenly.

'We need some advice on this David. Perhaps I'll give someone a call later, but first I'll fix you something to eat, I expect you're hungry.'

'Thirsty mainly Genn, a cold beer if there's such a thing.'

'There is my darling,' and she leaned down and kissed me before leaving to get it.'

I relaxed back into the comfort of the settee, and a feeling of joy dispelled the early gloom; she was indeed a very friendly friend, but what was she doing in Australia; what was I doing here, Ganymede hadn't been very forthcoming.

She returned with the beer and one for herself. She went off to make her call and when she returned she filled me in on the events since Reynard had turned up at Lowry AFB and told her that the team were getting out.

'So he must have known about Arthur C almost as soon as we did?' I said.

'It would seem so.'

'And he's here now, in Australia?'

'That's who I rang just now.'

'When can we meet up?'

'Good question. His advice is that we move on from here and lose ourselves. There are no identity cards in this country. As soon as we get settled and have an address we will each receive a driving licence, which is all we'll ever need in the way of an ID.'

'And this?' I pointed to my lack of a left foot.

'Before we leave here you'll be fitted with a prosthesis.'

'An artificial foot. Bloody hell that man thinks of everything. When do I get to see him?' I was beginning to feel a bit better about life or maybe it was the beer, and then I realised that Genna was shaking her head.

'I'm afraid that's not to be David. Bill thinks it's better if we go our separate ways, at least for a while.'

'I suppose he knows about Ganymede.'

'He never said, but I suppose so.'

I was reluctant to leave it there. We had come a long way together, and now it seemed as if a shutter had come down between us. That Genna had landed on my side of it was a great consolation. Thoughts however, instead of moving smoothly were rattling through my head like the tramcars of my youth.

'So how do we live, are we redundant; paid off, job seeking?'

Genna smiled. 'I was coming to that. Our civil service pay continues because we are still to be listed as active. It will be paid monthly into accounts already opened for us at the ANZ Bank in Melbourne Victoria.'

'You say *we,* not *you* and *I.* It sounds as though we are being treated as an item.'

'Bill's nobody's fool.' She laughed, and leaned across and planted a kiss on my lips. 'Is there anything else you'd like to know Daffyd?'

'Does active mean we can still be called to account?'

'I got a definite *no* on that from Bill.'

'In that case, as long as you continue with the tender, loving care Miss Rees, I have no further questions – oh except one.' She looked at me expectantly. 'Will I be able to dance when this prosthesis thing is fitted?'

'I don't see why not, they've come a long way from the peg leg.'

'That'll be interesting because I never could before.'

The attempt to lighten the moment failed miserably and we were both once again reduced to tears.

Chapter 31

Melbourne January 1980

I looked up from the keyboard; I still wasn't competent enough to type without looking at the keys. For a moment the dull thump against the flyscreen door puzzled me, then I looked at my watch; it was a few minutes after 8 am. I got up from the workstation and walked across to the picture window; the paper-boy's bike was just disappearing out of sight beyond my immediate neighbour. I turned and looked out across the road, the morning sun was already laying the shadow of the gums across the road, and onto our lawn; it promised to be a fine early autumn day. I heard Genna as she padded down the passage and opened the front door. The screen door squeaked in protest as she pushed it clear and retrieved the paper. I sat down at the computer again. I swivelled the chair as she entered the room with it and handed it to me.

'I'll make a coffee David, breakfast in an hour, okay?'

'Yeah fine Genn.' I smiled up at her, my mate, my nurse, my beloved Genna. The last few years had left their mark, but beneath the now worldly, slightly, careworn face I still saw much of the young girl who had implanted my ID all those years ago soon after Ganymede had introduced me to the Complex. She moved too with that fluid motion that would put boardwalk mannequins firmly in the shade; they walked like they had a pine cone stuck up their arse. Genna glided.

I placed the newspaper aside. I would read it or not depending how the mood took me. My work out there in the field of covert operations had taught me, among other things, to take much of what was released to the general public with a big pinch of salt.

I turned back to where the labour of recording past experience still lay unfinished. My left foot was tingling again, almost, but not quite, like pins and needles. It was an annoying feeling, because it was still charging around somewhere in the great 'out there'.

I stared at the screen; did I really want to go through with it? A little surge of anger and frustration began to well up within me and impulsively I reached out and highlighted the two paragraphs that I had added that morning before hitting the delete key. Would anyone be interested enough to ever read, or even believe any of it? I turned the computer off and went back to the window just as the lid of the post box at the end of the drive clanged shut. I watched as the postie retreated and then I went to retrieve the mail; there was just one for Genna, it looked official.

I met her in the hallway and exchanged it for the coffee. I waited as she opened it and read the contents. She was smiling as she looked up at me.

'I'm all clear David.'

The past week had been a bit stressful. Genna had got through the change without recourse to HRT only to discover a lump in her breast. We had been holding our breath as we waited for the results of her tests. How do you rate the relief at finding it to be a benign cyst? The sword of Damocles no longer hung over us. We could get back to enjoying the sweet life. We hugged and spilt coffee. 'That's okay darling, I'll sort it,' she said, giving a jubilant skip as she headed for the kitchen. I was left with a problem of my own.

**

I stood looking at a clear blue patch of sky. Ganymede, the man who I had come to rate as a good and respected friend, was out there somewhere, lost to this world, and along with my foot, doomed to travel in time and space forever. Thoughts of him had been clamouring in my mind recently, almost as if he was trying to contact me. I was tempted to mention it to Genna, but when the lump in her breast had surfaced I figured she had enough to contend with.

Over the years he had gradually receded into the past, coming to mind only occasionally; usually if his name came up in conversation. Now, it seemed as if he wanted to be heard.

Aime had said we were all ISBE's, so regardless of his physical state that would mean he still existed. It was that which had prompted me to try to get hold of Reynard to see if telepathic contact was possible. A letter I had sent to his last known address had been returned; not known here.

There was no word either from Kevin Bell. Kevin was a journalist friend I had become acquainted with a few months previously. At the time he was investigating what he described as some dodgy goings on in the Federal Elections. It was felt that the dismissal of Gough Whitlam's government in 1975 had left a lingering bad taste in the mouths of many Australians.

We got talking over a few beers at one of those functions that men's wives sometimes dragged them along to. Kevin was

212

unaccompanied and didn't appear to be the type to be dragged anywhere. I can't remember quite how we got around to it, but we found we had a mutual interest; extraterrestrials. Kevin turned out to be an investigative journalist and he had the scars to prove it; mainly a nose that had been broken at least more than once. He promised to make a few inquiries on my behalf regarding Bill Reynard. His approach to the cases he covered, according to his contemporaries, was akin to that of a terrier down a foxhole. I recalled that meeting.

'Shark, was it?' his eyes flicked down then up and looked straight into mine as soon as we had settled ourselves, along with a couple of schooners, at a vacant table.

It took me a moment to realise what he was on about. I didn't think my limp was all that pronounced. I had a good prosthesis, and most of the time I could almost ignore the loss of that foot, at others it would drive me up the wall. Genna had suggested that it was jogging around out there in space trying to get back to where it belonged

'Oh that.' I gave a laugh. 'You wouldn't believe it.'

'Try me.' He took a swallow of beer without taking his eyes off me.

I studied him for a moment. In the fifteen years or so since it had happened it had hardly ever been a topic of conversation, most people avoided discussing another's disabilities with them, Kevin was obviously an exception.

'I suppose you could call it an accident.'

'Oh, right.' His interest seemed to wane and he took in more beer. Accidents were probably pretty much run-of-the-mill to him. I was urged to unsettle his complacency.

'Yeah, I sort of lost it in a stargate.'

He lowered his glass carefully to the table; I now had his full attention. It was a full 10 seconds before he spoke.

'You know about those things?'

I nodded, wondering now how far I intended to go with this. Wrapped up in my head was a hell of a lot of classified material. Some nasty little accidents tended to happen to people who went public, or even talked openly about what went on behind the scenes. Kevin's initial reaction indicated that he was aware of stargates anyway. I was encouraged to carry it further.

'This is strictly off the record?'

I could sense the wagging of his terrier tail as he picked up his glass, drained it, and stood up.

'Yeah, too right mate.' He reached for mine. 'I'll shout another of these, don't go away.' He returned, set the glasses down, and looked expectant.

I told him what had happened after entering that room in Area 51. He stared thoughtfully at me when I had finished, took a long swallow of his beer, and laughed. 'Pull the other bloody one, mate. So between Nevada USA and Pine Gap South Australia you lost a good friend and one of your feet.' He was shaking with suppressed laughter, I could feel my anger rising.

'You think it's some sort of wind-up; a joke?' I tried to get up but my leg suddenly went into spasm, I sat there and just let it agonise.

Kevin lifted both hands in surrender, and he was shaking his head.

'Sorry David, that's my wicked sense of humour, but that's the reaction you'd get from the general public.'

'You said this was off the record.'

'It is mate.' He looked at me straight, deadly serious now. 'Look, I've been kicking this stargate thing around for a couple of years now. I've heard rumours that it's probably the answer to space travel; a matter of minutes to the moon or Mars and back, but you're the first person I've come across with any firsthand experience of it. I'm really chuffed, mate.'

I felt considerably mollified, and the pain in my leg had eased off.

'You believe me then?'

His nod was emphatic. 'I don't suppose there's any chance of you getting back into Pine Gap?'

'I've sworn off Kevin, too many crazy things going on in those places. I was just glad to get out of that life in one piece.'

'But that's it mate, you didn't.' He couldn't contain a chuckle. 'Would you go in if you thought you could catch up with your foot again?'

'Now it's your turn to talk out of your arse, it's been a long time gone.'

'I've heard that people can still feel lost limbs.'

'I know, it's a problem sometimes. My wife says it's because my foot wants to get back on the end of my leg.'

'What do you think?'

'I think it's simply a matter of the brain still trying to send messages to it.'

214

'But you don't know that. It's possible that in this case, taking into consideration how it happened, that it might just be the other way around.'

He had a point of course; it hadn't been a physical amputation; more of an energy severance; my foot had lost the body it was attached to.

'Kevin, it's been fifteen years. I've learned to live with it. No, I wouldn't want to go back in there even if there was a chance. And chance it would be; I wouldn't even have a clue what the coordinates would have been before Ganymede and I went into that room. Even if I did it would be like travelling through time and space looking for a disembodied foot. There could be hundreds, thousands of bits and bobs out there, all in energy format; even whole bodies.' I shuddered at the thought. No guarantee that I wouldn't end up like him either.'

'Yeah okay, I get your point.' He looked thoughtful for a moment and then continued. 'You say you spent something like three years or more swanning around secret establishments and you had high enough clearances to come and go much as you please, how do you do that?'

It was then, or I thought so for a very long time afterwards, that I made a mistake. I told him of the ID implant. It was also then that he came up with a plan.

I mentioned it to Genna as we drove home.

Chapter 32

'What do you think Genn, is it feasible?'

Kevin and I sat watching her expression as she considered what we had proposed.

'I don't see a problem as far as removal and re-implanting the ID. That might be arranged through Bill Reynard.' She looked at Kevin. 'He was our old boss way back before we realised what the real agenda was behind all this black ops business. He got out before we did and went to ground ...' I was listening to this in amazement. It sounded as though, where I had drawn a blank, she could still get hold of Bill Reynard, just like that; I had to hear this out. 'The big problem as I see it apart from the fact that you will be taking on David's identity and someone might tumble you is that we won't know whether or not it will work until you are actually in there.'

'All the more reason to go one step at a time Genna. Let's get the implant thing out of the way first and not go negative on things we haven't come across yet. As a newspaper man I have a stake in this, remember, and as a member of the human race I don't feel I can stand by and let a bunch of maniacs fuck it up.'

It was occurring to me that Kevin knew a lot more about things than he was prepared to let on. I almost wished that I could have gone in with him; but only almost. I turned to Genna.

'Didn't know that you were still in contact with Bill, Genn,' I said. I tried not to sound miffed or accusing. 'I've been trying to get hold of him over the Ganymede thing but it appeared he'd moved on.'

'I haven't been until quite recently David. I ran into him in the hospital in Melbourne when I was having those tests; He's working there in psychiatry. He more or less swore me to secrecy. If I'd known ...' she tailed off, frowning with concern.

'Not to worry, you were not to know I wanted to discuss something with him.'

**

I hadn't seen Bill Reynard since he and Genna had left for the Complex, more than fifteen years before. He'd spent some of it putting on a bit of a paunch and some grey, thinning hair. His face though still looked slightly cherubic, with hardly a wrinkle in sight. I told him I wasn't even aware that Genna had been in touch with him, or even knew his whereabouts.

'I wanted out of the whole business,' he told me, when along with Genna and Kevin we met up with him in Melbourne suburbia to discuss the ID switch, 'I did manage to keep my head down for a few years. I thought Australia would be a good place to disappear. But I was approached by an old friend who I hadn't seen since my university days; he had obviously been keeping tabs on me. He convinced me that my dream of retirement would be a waste of valuable resources. To cut a long story, he persuaded me to join his team. I decided to keep some distance as I knew that you and Genna wanted no further part in this kind of work. Even I'm very much part time; only on call when my particular talents are required.' He permitted himself a grin at 'talents'.

'Well you certainly kept a low profile as far as I was concerned,' I chided. 'We are friends, and I'm sure continued contact wouldn't have been any threat to your association with this very old friend of yours.'

He looked a little shame-faced as he nodded in agreement. 'Yeah. Sorry about that David, but I was still doing some remote viewing on Area 51 and I discovered there were people who were trying to locate me. The last thing I wanted was somebody picking up on my coordinates and sticky-beaking in my backyard.'

'Well, your cover's blown now mate.' Kevin chuckled as he said it. 'But no one will hear it from me.'

Reynard said. 'I hope you know the risk you'll be taking going into the Gap. It's been tried several times.'

'Through the back door, I know, and never seen or heard of again, but I'll be going in the front way with a proper ID.'

'That's something we still need to put to the test.' Taking a bunch of keys from his pocket Reynard indicated for us to follow him.

He led us to a section of wall in the hallway and pressed a button on a zapper on the key ring. The section slid to one side revealing a steel door fitted with a deadlock. He inserted a key from the ring and turned to us with a grin as he opened the door.

'It's amazing how a simple old lock can fool these guys brought up on digital gizmos.' I knew just what he was getting at; even the ET weapons in the Stevens' forest and Bowdie had been no match for hunters out on a crossbow shoot. We descended into a basement area which was set up like a laboratory. He pointed to an apparatus that looked vaguely familiar; it looked like an upgrade of the one Genna had used to implant my ID back in the Complex. She eyed it a little uncertainly.

'It's donkey's years since I used one of these things.'

Reynard put an arm around her shoulders and smiled down at her. 'Not to worry my dear. It's not my forte either, but I'm sure that between us we'll sort it out. The difference between the older models and this one is that this one has a retrieval facility. The implant procedure is exactly as before once the chip is sterilised.' He looked first at me and then across at Kevin. 'None of this will cause either of you any discomfort.' He waved his arm in the air. 'I had mine removed over ten years ago; didn't want a hit man turning up on my doorstep.'

He proved to be correct. Apart from a slight tingling after its removal all I felt was relief in knowing that I could once again move freely anywhere in the world without fear that I was being tracked.

'I don't suppose it's about time I had mine removed?' Genna looked expectantly at Reynard. 'Did they ever report back on the one I had removed after my abduction? He eyed her curiously before responding.

'The ET location one? Funny you should say that. I keep very little in the way of souvenirs.' He walked to a wall cabinet and returned with a small phial. He held it up against the light for our inspection. There was little to see apart from what appeared to be a seed-like object less than half a millimetre in size suspended in gel.

'And that's it?' she said, 'They could target me any time they wished?'

'It would appear so, and whether they ever did we can only speculate … unless …' he paused … 'unless it was planted during your abduction,' he shrugged and walked across and replaced it in the cabinet.

'Without leaving any external sign?' I said. 'We were given the impression at the time that it was longstanding.'

'With these beings we are always left with a puzzle David. Attempts to analyse that device went on for years with net result. In the end they handed it to me with the suggestion that I might have better luck contacting the other side.' He gave a wry grin and changed the subject. 'Regarding your Complex ID Genna, it occurs to me that we still might be able to make use of it at some future date.' It was then I decided to step in, I didn't like what was being implied here.

'Hey, hang on Bill, don't even think of it. Genna is not going back into that system ever again.'

Reynard raised his hands in a gesture of surrender.

'Okay okay, it was just a thought David. It might have been handy for Kevin to have a bit of backup in there.'

It was then that Kevin chipped in. 'Hey, wait on you guys, this is my lurk, and I don't want anyone, even Mrs Kent here, charming though her company is, sticking their neck out on my account.'

'I quite understand Kevin,' Reynard waved us towards the basement steps. 'Let's leave everything where it is at the moment and just work out how to get Kevin in there first.'

And then I remembered something; I couldn't wait to speak to Reynard once we had exited the basement and we were settled in his lounge room with a celebratory drink apiece.

'Bill? About Ganymede?' He looked at me slightly puzzled. 'He was obviously ID'd at the Complex, yes?' He nodded still looking puzzled.

'We all were David, why?'

'Well do you think it's possible that wherever he is he might still be tracked by it?'

Reynard looked thoughtful and stared at me for a moment before setting down his glass and shaking his head.

I can't see how David. Those portals just reduce you to a basic energy field. The implant would get the same treatment; its coding would be unreadable.'

'Do we know that for sure?'

He appeared to consider that.

'All we know for sure is that unless you make it through the shift you know longer exist as a physical being. Ganymede, like your foot, never made the journey, there's no need to suppose that his ID would or could.'

'It might be worth a try though.'

Kevin, who had been following the exchange between us, said. 'Where do we get hold of one of these tracking devices?'

'Only in high security at places like Area 51 and Pine Gap I'm afraid.' 'They have computer systems there capable of knowing when a mouse farts in Whitehall.'

'Well then, all going well I might at least be able to give tracking your friend Ganymede a try.'

219

Chapter 33

We gathered again a week later at Reynard's minus the intrepid Kevin. We were hoping for some news of him; there was none. It was four days since he had left the outback township of Alice Springs in the Northern Territory for the final leg to the Gap.

'I'm afraid it's a case of no news is not good news, he should have managed to get in touch by now.' Bill had sent out for an Indian and was placing the containers on the table; we helped ourselves to the choices we had made. 'I'll give it another twelve hours then I'll give the remote a whirl.'

Genna and I bedded down to a restless night and we awoke unrefreshed to the smell of breakfast underway. It was a cheerful face that Reynard turned to us from the stove.

'The news is as good as we could have hoped for. As yet he's not made contact with me, but he appears to be able to move around the Gap without being challenged.' He loaded our plates and set them before us. 'Get stuck in and we'll work on a way to make contact.'

'Do we really need to Bill? Anything going to him from the outside could seriously compromise him. It's not like the old 'dead drop' routine. With all the surveillance gear and guards they've got we wouldn't get within a couple of miles of the place.'

'You're right of course David. He said he'll give the tracking a try if he can, but like he said, he's in there to get information about what's going on and to let the world know about it.'

'We could have supplied him with more than enough,' said Genna

'He's that rare phenomenon, a good newspaperman, he'd still feel the need to check the facts, and even supply documentary evidence, and we left all that sort of stuff behind when we decided to opt out.'

Genna and I decided to go back to Adelaide and await events there. Reynard promised to keep us posted.

Two days later the mail arrived halfway through a breakfast that I'd played with between odd mouthfuls and finally pushed away. Genna rose at the sound of the mailbox cover being dropped back in place.

'Not hungry darling?'

I shrugged. 'Sorry, maybe later.'

220

'I'll see what's come.' Minutes later she handed me a white envelope. I stared for a moment at the typewritten name and address in the window; it had a Melbourne post mark. It looked official, but then so did all mail with a window. I thumbed open the envelope; it was from Reynard. I read it through twice, the second time more slowly; I wanted to make sure I'd got it right. Then I reached for that morning's Advertiser and thumbed through it.

It was just about the size of two postage stamps in the bottom right hand corner of one of the pages. It reported a fatal car crash on the Stuart Highway north of Port Augusta South Australia. The driver was identified by papers in his possession by officers of the State Highway Patrol as one Kevin Francis Bell a journalist employed by the Melbourne Age. The police reported that there was no other vehicle involved. I showed the letter and the report to Genna; that made two of us stunned by the news.

'They certainly know how to tie things up neat and tidy, I wonder how they got onto him?'

'I don't think we are ever likely to know Genn.' But I was wrong, the phone rang. She answered it and handed it to me.

'It's Bill Reynard.' When he'd finished what he had to say I thanked him and handed the phone back to Genna; she replaced it and said, "Well?"

'Kevin did make contact. He left a message on Bill's answerphone, it seems that Ganymede's ID implant is still active; which means that he's still around somewhere, but only he knows where, and what shape or form he's in.'

Genna shuddered. 'That sounds a bit gruesome David. Do you think that's how they caught up with Kevin; they were monitoring his every move.'

'I think that's quite possible love. To make his sacrifice worthwhile we'll have to try and find out why that ID is still active. Reynard wants a meet ASAP; perhaps we can get a flight this afternoon. Apparently he's called on that friend who occupies a position in high places.'

**

A bronzed, grey-haired stick of a man was Major General Clarence Harris, and sprightly for a man I judged to be well into his 60's. He almost bounded out of the chair in which he was sitting when we entered the room. Reynard introduced him as an old friend who had just popped down from Darwin to brief us,

221

among other things, of events that had just taken place in New Mexico.

His "Good day" was a fuller version of the typical Australian greeting and it was delivered with a cultured intonation, I felt obliged to respond in like manner.

'Bill here has been singing your praises David and if it's any consolation I already have people working on tracking down your friend Ganymede's ID.'

'Thank you sir.'

'Clarrie will do fine David. We are all friends here working for the greater good. You are, I know, as disenchanted by the way this world is being run as we are.' I nodded agreement as Reynard guided us towards the dining room.

'It's cold cuts I'm afraid.' He pointed to the buffet assortment. 'I've given my cook the evening off so we won't be disturbed. Just grab a plate and help yourselves, and my drinks cabinet is at your disposal.'

Genna and I had missed lunch to catch our flight; I for one needed no urging. Since settling in the big brown land I had also developed a passion for craytail.

'Local lad drops me off a few occasionally.' Reynard smiled at my unspoken query. 'They are undersized, but the more delicate flavour is worth bending the rules for.'

His friend Harris agreed, he already had some of the delicacy added to his plate.

'If that common market ever gets going up in Europe there's a rumour that the fishermen up there will be throwing any excess to their quotas back in the sea, even the dead ones,' he said as he sat down.

'That sounds just stupid waste, it surely can't be justified?' Genna looked a trifle dumbfounded.

'It's unfortunately what tends to happen when bureaucracy takes over from common sense my dear, we can only hope in that case the latter will prevail.'

We ate in silence for a while. I wondered just what Harris was about to reveal about a recent event in New Mexico. It was a good twelve years since Reynard, Genna, and I had been in that area. He finished a mouthful and sipped his wine before continuing.

'You may recall the incident at Socorro where a policeman named Zamora reported a UFO?'

222

'I remember, there was also a report by a local Indian, wasn't there?'

'That's right. Well as a result of remote viewing we discovered there was also an American base nearby that was harbouring a number those big gray guys; they might actually have been in control there. We decided to place it under surveillance just to see what was going on there. We fear that the two agents we sent in may have been compromised. Unfortunate of course, because they weren't able to get any information out, it meant that we lost that round to our opponents, more or less confirming that grays are at least exercising a measure of control there. We are still assessing the situation remotely and efforts to dislodge them will be made.' He studied our faces for reaction before continuing.

'In the meantime we have to reconcile ourselves to the fact that we have these superior technological forces right on our doorstep?'

'Not on the doorstep Bill, but actually co-habiting with us.'

'Of course, a sobering thought, Clarrie.'

'I'll give you a less sobering one.' Harris was beaming. 'There is a very odd twist to all this. There are those among my associates who feel that the alien base was not necessarily a threat to us; humanity as a whole.'

'Doing battle with us could hardly be called friendly.'

'No, but if we think about it Bill, our bases have long been infiltrated by elements on this Earth who do not have the best interests of humanity at heart. They are into mind control, the cloning of a soulless army of robots to exercise complete control over minds and bodies; they seek to enslave humanity in the guise of protecting it from alien invasion. We, you and I Bill, and Genna and David here are part of a force that is building up to oppose them. Make no mistake, the major threat is from within the corridors of power itself, and if it's any consolation it is also in those corridors that we also have allies who know what the hidden agendas are. Even as I speak now they are making plans to defeat any attempt at global enslavement by an elite.'

'So you are saying some aliens established here may be possible allies at a future date?'

'I'm saying that it's a possibility. In my opinion, which is a personal one, albeit formed after years of experience in my dealings with black ops, ET's and unidentified intrusions into our space. If our space visitors ever intended to take us over they could have done so countless thousands of years ago with impunity. I'm sure many of us have come to that conclusion, but we never have been and never will be, except for accidents or malfunctions on their part, or an occasional lucky break on our part, a match for their technology.'

Reynard chewed thoughtfully on the remaining mouthfuls of his meal before pushing his plate away and reaching for his drink. He nodded in Harris' direction.

'Well Clarrie I hope we are the wiser for what you've had to say.' Genna and I murmured agreement. 'I'd like to raise a glass to a successful outcome of our future endeavours and the sincere hope that our contribution will be beneficial to humanity.' Harris joined in the toast.

Chapter 34

Harris and Reynard spent the rest of that evening sharing reminisces with us. Neither I nor Genna were ever sure as to exactly what had happened at the Complex.

'I'm afraid that I was to blame there,' Harris confessed. 'The British government were getting a bit shirty about it and up till then of course we didn't know about the hidden agendas on the American side and we wanted to be closer to where the action was. With the help of what I call good CIA – oh they're not all hunter killers -- we arranged a little firework party and moved the whole outfit across the pond to where you were all re-directed.'

'I take it that by friendly CIA you mean Robert Franciosa and his boys?'

I looked across at Reynard who shrugged.

'Nobody asked or questioned it at the time David. Makris, Quan Ling, and Ganymede preceded you there. Ganymede said he'd explain it all to you, I assumed he did.'

'Nope, not a dickybird Bill. Genna and I liked the American lifestyle so we didn't feel the need to press for explanations. Mind you, a lot of what went on in the bases we didn't consider too choice, but then we were pretty well brain-washed into believing we were doing the right thing.'

'Too right David, I think we can all lay claim to that. It was soon after that, if you remember that Bill here disappeared from the scene altogether. I persuaded him he'd be far more useful if he joined my team.'

'And Quan Ling and Makris, neither of them stayed around for long? We seem to have lost her somewhere along the way, Makris too. There is work going on for some big bangs in the future, but that'll keep; maybe later, eh?'

A phone rang. Harris apologised and checked his mobile before rising and moving to the end of the room; it was some minutes before he returned to the table and sat down. He looked at me; he appeared to have a problem with something.

'That is decidedly odd David. Can you do me a favour and cast your mind back over the last time you saw Ganymede?'

'No problem, it was when we were preparing to exit that Dreamland place.

'I've never actually witnessed what goes on in those portals David, what's the procedure?' I looked at Genna. I was being asked to relive an experience I would rather forget. She smiled and nodded encouragement.

I took myself back to when Ganymede and I were passed into the transporter suite.

'Where to start?'

Harris grinned and produced a notebook and pencil.

'Step by step from the beginning if you can David.'

'We had been through a form of induction. As you know we've picked up a lot from the ET's, so meditation is an integral part of travelling through inner space. I don't know how relevant that is to being beamed to a different location.' Harris looked toward Reynard who nodded.

'So it requires, in part anyway, a desire to be elsewhere?'

'That's right; it's a sort of projection of consciousness to a desired location.'

'It has parallels with remote viewing Clarrie except that in that case our bodies stay put.' Reynard chipped in. Teleportation as far as I understand it involves the generation, at least in part, of high frequency electro-magnetism

'Thanks for that Bill.' Harris scribbled something on his pad. 'Okay David, keep going. You are in the transporter suite, what happens next?'

'As instructed we each enter a cubicle, there were about six of these and although by now I was anxious to leave the base I was a little apprehensive at being separated. Ganymede was encouraging; he'd been through portals before, assured me it was a piece of cake.'

'Right so you each enter a cubicle, then what?'

'I passed into a screened area and some form of force field was activated. We meditate on what I imagine to be a destination coordinate and bingo, we are on our way.'

'And you emerge in Pine Gap minus a foot and Ganymede, but are soon reunited with Genna.' He smiled across at her and pushed his notebook to one side. 'So the last time you saw Ganymede was immediately prior to entering your respective cubicles?' I nodded; I seem to sense what was coming next. Harris regarded us, elbows on the table, and resting his chin on his clasped hands. 'That phone call was to inform me that your friend Ganymede's ID is both active and moving around out there in Northern California right now. From that I can only assume that he is also active and on the move, and that he never

226

had any intention of accompanying you on your trip through the portal all those years ago.'

It was suddenly all falling into place, the enigmatic Wenban-Smith; the man who had disappeared without trace into the Balkans after WW2 had gone back into the sensitive area of America's black operations and left us to mourn his passing.

'A rum bugger and no mistake.' Reynard summed it up. He raised his glass. 'To Ganymede, may his shadow never grow shorter.'

Harris got to his feet and replaced his notebook in his pocket.

'I think that's it for now then.' He stifled a yawn. 'I'm afraid the travelling and the weight of years has taken its toll, so I'd like to hit the sack. My people still have to locate your wiley friend in the flesh and perhaps then we can arrange a meet. If he still wants to keep his head down then we will have to allow him that.'

We waited until he left the room. Major General Clarrie Harris was a man I couldn't help but like.

'It looks as if we are never going to put this business behind us.' Reynard refilled his glass and offered to top up ours. I raised two fingers. Genna declined.

'Most people can retire from the workforce and leave it behind,' she said, 'but not us.'

'So many ghosts,' said Reynard thoughtfully. They keep popping up to haunt us. Even though I opted out a while before you two I still felt a need to keep a finger on the pulse of what was going on behind the façade of democracy.'

'Genna and I decided enough was enough. We didn't think we had anything further to contribute, and apart from Ganymede occasionally making us aware of the gap he'd left in our lives we have enjoyed keeping that world at a safe distance.'

'This has plunged us all right back in it, even if only in a superficial way. I'm sure we are all looking for confirmation of Ganymede's continued existence.'

'I think that goes without saying Bill.' Genna laughed. 'Although if we do meet up again I'll certainly be giving him a piece of my mind, and I know David will give him more than a piece of his.'

Chapter 35

When we came down to breakfast Reynard informed us that Harris left his apologies at having to take off early but his presence was required back in Darwin.

'He's had an invite from the Yanks to take some of his team over. As you are now aware there are those who are opposed to the agenda being operated from behind the scenes over there, and some sort of counter offensive is being planned. Clarrie has suggested that you two might like to go along.'

My immediate reaction was no, thank you very much.

'Bill. I made up my mind a long time ago that I never wanted to set foot there again.'

'I realise that David, and I can understand; I felt the same way, but things have changed. Those nut cases who want to establish their New World Order can't be allowed to have it all their own way. Harris as you know has spent much of his career in and around intelligence agencies and operations mounted in secret by major world governments including his own. The fracas that recently occurred in New Mexico brought some interesting things to light, mainly that several high ranking military personnel were unhappy with the situation there and were prepared to do something about it.'

'You make it sound that on the strength of that you'd be prepared to stick your neck out and go in there again, I'm not convinced that would be a good idea Bill. Bloody hell mate, I'm coming up 50. What are you hoping for, a geriatric guerrilla war?'

'Okay if that's how it sounds David, but a lot of those opposing the current regime, and those that have gathered behind Harris are much of an age. Ganymede is even a few years older, but according to Harris, he received word this morning that he is not only alive and well, but he is a participant in planning further minor earthquakes out there in northern California.'

'Nuking underground bases etc?'

'That's right, and I feel that if he can stick his neck out the least I can do is see if I can offer some support to the same cause.'

It occurred to me that since the death of Arthur C, Ganymede had decided to continue the fight. Maybe the effect of the General's death had gone deeper than a surface display of grief.

I could see that Reynard was determined to rope me in and that he had thrown any decision I might make back onto my conscience. We continued our breakfast in silence. I tried to catch Genna's eye but she was either deeply engrossed in her own thoughts or deliberately ignoring my repeated glances in her direction.

Damn you Foxy Bill, I thought, you know what my answer will be; you're a bloody psychiatrist and a psychologist to boot.

**

'I persuaded Genna to stay and keep the home fires burning,' I said as Reynard and I boarded an internal flight to Sydney, I figured that if we were to encounter any problems stateside I'd much rather she was safe there.

Our onward flight to Los Angeles was already booking in when we got there. It took me a moment or two to realise that the man accompanying Harris was Philo Makris. I had last seen him over ten years ago, around the time that the Complex had been explosively decommissioned. Despite the now iron-grey hair and a slight belly he had aged remarkably well, and he moved with that same easy grace as he came forward with a smile to shake my hand. He struck me as being an unusually friendly Philo Makris.

'Hello David, it's good to see you again.'

'You too Philo, it's been a long time.' He looked around me, half expectant.

'No Genna?'

'Not this trip. Is Quan Ling with you?' He shook his head and grinned. I could hardly believe this was the same Makris I had spent those earlier years with.

'In my country mamma stays at home with the kids David.'

'You mean ...'

'That's right, family man now, twin boys, eight years old.'

'Nice going Philo,' I said and reached out and we shook hands again. Then on a sober note he said. 'Heard about the foot David, bad business.'

'I've learned to live with it.' I assured him.

'A believe a lot has happened since we parted company, and most of it very unpleasant.' His eyes narrowed. 'I'm afraid things are still very much up in the air.'

I felt someone move in beside me and Harris spoke in my ear.

'I think you'll find Philo here will bring you up to speed during the flight David, there are a few things I thought it better not to mention earlier when Genna was present.'

Makris took the seat next to me.

'Thought I had managed to give all this business the elbow,' he said, as we took off. 'Quan Ling and I decided get out of the mainstream and grow some grapes and a few kids.'

'Grapes?'

'That's right.' He laughed. 'I come from a family of vintners, and my parents wanted to retire, so we took up where they left off; a readymade job.'

'Where is all this going Philo? Harris said there were things I needed to know. Is this another Bowdie?'

'It could be, there is evidence of a base there somewhere, but there are also other complications. According to word that reached Harris, Ganymede, Major Gessler, and Sergeant Shelman have gone missing in the Warner Mountains.'

It wasn't the kind of news I needed. If this was anything like Bowdie we could end up having to just walk away again. I tried not to imagine having to leave our people to their fate.

'How the hell are we going mount this operation, these people hold all the cards?'

'I think there is a move afoot to open some sort of negotiations.'

'And if that fails?' Philo's stare was significant, and answer enough.

In Los Angeles we managed to get a feed and a night's sleep before taking to the air again. There were no direct flights to our destination, so we hopped first to Sacramento and then to Klamath Falls, and finally an army transport ferried us to Alturas. It was a town I was never to see. Minutes after landing the four of us boarded a Unimog and we were heading out into the foothills of the Warner Mountains.

Initially we travelled a good road on wide expanses of plain dotted with numerous small lakes. The Unimog's off road tyres on the asphalt road drummed like a jet engine. I closed my eyes. I could easily imagine myself back in flight; It wasn't to last. I opened them again as we bucked and heeled for a while like a ship in a stormy sea; we had turned off road and were heading into the ranges.

'Happens like that,' said Harris, 'fantastic suspension these things, it keeps four wheels on the ground no matter what the body is doing.'

The track, while rough, was not uncomfortable even at around 45 mph. Two hours after the turnoff we drove into a yard occupied by a fair-sized clapboard dwelling with several outhouses. The main building appeared to be in remarkably good condition.

Despite a full sun, the altitude and the onset of autumn combined to put quite a chill in the air. We offloaded our gear and went inside to be greeted by the warmth of a log fire and several people seated in comfort around the room, which in contrast to the outside appearance of the place reeked of sumptuous affluence.

'It's a wilderness retreat owned by a prosperous rancher.' Harris supplied. He only uses it for a few weeks in the summer. It is hoped that we will be long gone before he knows we've even been here.'

'You think this one will be resolved,' I said.

'One way or another,' he said and moved forward to introduce those already there.

Memory plays tricks with names and faces. Major Gordon Tahoma is the one outstanding. Not because of any particular contribution he made, but he was unmistakably Native American. Unlike Arthur C, with his raven black hair, short though it was, and deeply tanned skin he did look capable of bringing down a buffalo from the back of a galloping pony. He looked to be about my age, maybe a year or two younger, and his ribbon line up included those of a Korean veteran. Some of my service mates had been foolish enough to join 'Bunker' Ridgeway and had come back with the same campaign ribbons.

Brennan Maguire, one of the civilians, reminded me of a much younger version of the demented boffin back at my Bletchley Park interview. Maguire I learned later was a nuclear physicist, and like Reynard had remote viewing experience.

The third man, also a civilian, was an oriental with an unpronounceable name, and he held some sort of position within the Japanese aircraft industry.

'Just call me Gerry,' he said, in flawless movie American. Of the others I can put neither faces nor names. They were not introduced, and they remained only briefly. We ended up seven of us luxuriating in warmth and comfort and speculating on what was to come.

Maguire and Reynard drifted off to a separate room, leaving Harris, Makris and me with the others.

'Bill's off to do his RV thing,' Harris said. 'He has a set of coordinates but they are only approximate. If they can lock in, Mr Maguire might be able to describe whatever technology these people have, and its possible use.'

'We believe the base is to be a little less than 2 miles from here,' said Major Tahoma.' Sightings of strange aerial craft in this area have been going on for many decades, back to WW1 in fact. It is only in the last ten years or so that people have had nerve enough to report their experiences to the authorities. Even then many have been held up to ridicule.'

'Now, due to the 1954 rash of sightings throughout the world, investigations in this area produced enough evidence to support the belief that there might be some sort of alien base here,' said Harris.

'Is that why Gessler, Ganymede, and others were up here when they went missing?'

'I'm afraid so David.' Harris turned to Tahoma. '5 days ago Gordon?' Tahoma nodded.

'They were in a helicopter. We have searched this whole region and have failed to locate any wreckage.' Bloody helicopters, I thought.

'The alternative theory is that they could have been abducted, major?' I said.

Tahoma shrugged. 'It's a possibility. Probably the best one we can hope for under the circumstances David.'

'Even though it does complicate the whole issue?'

Tahoma nodded. 'It seems to be the name of the game nowadays.'

Reynard and Maguire emerged from the other room. Reynard was shaking his head. Maguire returned to his former seat.

'No joy I'm afraid. None of the coordinates we tried proved positive.'

'We can't make any moves until we can pinpoint an objective.' Tahoma spread his hands in a gesture of resignation. 'I've got nearly 200 men and their equipment here. Not enough to search several square miles of rough country, and they need to feel justified in being dragged into this.' He looked around. 'Any suggestions?'

'I have an idea.' Reynard beckoned to me. 'David and I might be able to come up with something.'

I followed him into the other room and he shut the door behind us; it deadened the buzz of conversation at our departure.'

It appeared to be a study, furnished with taste. We sat in chairs identical to the ones in the main room.

'Amie? Are you able to contact her?'

'I'm not sure Bill. The impression I got in the last communication was that I could, if it became necessary.'

'I think it has become necessary. Just relax and I'll see if I can kick-start you.'

I raised my hand.

'No need. I'm already getting something.' I closed my eyes; it was easier to focus. Her voice, warm and friendly echoed in my head.

'Hello David.'

'Hi. How did ...'

'We are quite close, and we are aware of your problem. The base you seek is quite near to you but not in the direction you have been looking. It is of the Old Order and we are here to destroy it. We need you to vacate the area, we do not wish to harm terrestrial beings.'

'We suspect that there ...' She interrupted me, reading my thoughts.

'There are people of your kind within the base and we recognise your concern, but the Dominion calls for the complete annihilation of all Old Order bases in this system.'

I explained what was going on to Reynard regarding Ganymede and the others and what the Dominion intended. He made a face.

'They've at least got to give us a chance to get our people out, surely.'

'Amie has always been quite clear on Dominion policy Bill. Compassion and sentiment are not considered of very high priority when they are dealing with the Old Order. Even we who are making such a fuck up of our world are of only minor importance to them. They have no wish to interfere in our domestic affairs unless, en masse, we request it.'

'We need time David, to at least try to get our people out.'

'She understands that, she's giving me coordinates for you; not only for the base but where Ganymede and the others are located.'

Reynard reached out and grabbed pencil and paper from the nearby desk.

'Give Maguire a shout David we may need to do this together.'

'We've been given 24 hours and then we've got to get the hell out of here.' I said as I rose to do as he asked.

Chapter 36

There was something eerily familiar about the old mine workings as we moved into the main drive. Major Tahoma had deployed the bulk of his force and his heavy weapons above ground, some covering the entrance of the main drive. He came underground with us accompanied by a dozen men in full battle order including head lighting and armed only with machine guns; he had already been briefed on the Bowdie affair, bazookas and the like were conspicuously absent.

Both Reynard and Maguire moved forward slightly ahead of us, concentrating on their viewing. Makris had armed himself with a 9mm handgun. I had probably the least effective weapon of all; a twelve bore shot gun I had liberated from the rancher's limited armoury. We followed closely behind the major. The Japanese aircraft man had opted out, and Harris was organising air transport for our evacuation for whatever the future held.

We must have travelled best part of a mile before entering a really open space. There were tunnel openings to the east and west. Tahoma split his force and Makris and I prepared to tag along with him, Bill and Maguire lingered in the centre of the cavern looking upward, I walked back and joined them. Far above us a tiny circle of light; it was obviously an air shaft.

'Probably dug by the miners,' Said Bill and we moved off to catch up with the others. We found them standing in bewilderment before the tunnel openings.

There were no doors like at Bowdie, they were using something far more effective; a force field. I looked at Makris, he was shaking his head. It was at that moment that I heard a gun being cocked. I whirled around and saw them, just as the warnings leapt into my mind.

'Hold your fire!' I yelled. Behind me I heard Tahoma gasp, 'What the fuck ...?' Fortunately Reynard came to the rescue.

'It's okay; I think they are on our side.'

I just stared in amazement at the robot dolls. There were about twenty of them, similar to Amie, but unlike her they appeared to be wearing body armour and were carrying some kind of weaponry. Several carried what closely resembled the radar speed guns that were being widely distributed among the world's traffic police. Their function, soon to be demonstrated, was way beyond the prelude to a speeding fine though. With Tahoma's men guarding the entrance they must have descended the air shaft. It was then that Amie herself came through.

'The directive from our base is that we honour the bravery of people that would put their lives at risk to save their own kind David. The company you see are all free thinking ISBE's. As I explained to you before, our bodies are created for specific use, their bodies are synthesized to operate as warriors. They are under orders to aid you in your objective, and they are briefed to move freely to achieve that.'

I explained that to Major Tahoma who stared at me as if I was completely around the bend.

'It's okay major, David has the ability to communicate telepathically with these people,' said Reynard as Amie's robot army filed past us and with their 'speed guns' neutralised the force fields. Tahoma and his men, battle tested as they obviously were, watched in awe as the little men split and took one of the tunnels apiece.

We followed in our own divided parties; Makris and I with Tahoma, and Reynard and Maguire with the other party. I must admit to a feeling of elation as we tailed along behind what Tahoma and his men must have regarded as toy soldiers; they were soon to be proved more than worthy in battle.

'It's incredible to think that everyone of those little guys is a real live thinking person, Philo.'

Beside me Makris grunted, then said, 'I'm only just beginning to get my head around that, David.'

'I can't get over the feeling that I will wake up and find that everything that's happened since I left the army is all some diabolical dream Philo.'

'If that happened there would be no Genna or Quan Ling; best to stay dreaming eh?' He made an odd sort of sense.

Faint rumblings were coming back to us from up ahead, and Tahoma's men came to a halt.

'Our troops are engaging the foe.' It was Amie in my head. 'I am charged with monitoring progress David, there is little for you to do. Your friends are in isolation under guard, but in your words, we have cracked tougher nuts.'

I passed the information to Tahoma. He put his men on standby and contacted the other team. It seemed strange that the only feedback from this ET battle was a series of subdued rumblings like a muffled thunderstorm. The rumbling ceased and we sat in silence for about twenty minutes.

'Now what?' muttered Tahoma. 'Anything from your contact?' I shook my head and the shadows danced in my head light.

There were sounds coming from within the tunnel and a simultaneous cocking of weapons. We stood tensed and then a tiny figure emerged out of the gloom. He came on ignoring the levelled weapons and behind him I caught sight of Ganymede, soon to be followed by Gessler, and Shelman.

They looked dishevelled and tired. Shelman seemed to have fared better than most; his training under adverse conditions obviously stood him in good stead.

'It is over David. It is time for you all to leave.' Amie seemed to come in on cue. The ET turned on his heel and retreated back down the tunnel.

'Where is he off to?' said Ganymede. His only concession to the ploy at the area 51 transporter room was an apologetic look and a conspiratory wink.

'He will rejoin his comrades,' Amie came back to me. I passed that information to him.

'But they're all dead. That one is the only survivor.'

'They're ISBE's guv. They just hop out of those bodies and nip off back to base.' He looked at me for a long moment, realised I wasn't joking, then grinned. Let's get out of here before we get out of ours, we have been living on water for the last four days.'

**

Back on the surface we watched as the Chinooks moved in and lifted artillery pieces and the bulk of Tahoma's force. I looked up into the sky; it was clear blue and cloudless. I shivered in the chill air; or was it a reaction to what had happened here? There was no sign of any Dominion craft; I felt disappointed.

Safely aboard I had time to study the others. Gessler smiled weakly when he caught me looking at him. He raised a thumb, and then he closed his eyes. Ganymede and Shelman were sat farther back in subdued conversation with Makris; the inquest after the game, I thought. A bloody, deadly game.

I settled back in my seat. The steady thud, thud of the Chinook's twin motors was oddly comforting; perhaps helicopters were not so bad after all.

237

Chapter 37

Home

We dropped Makris off at Alturas airfield. I can only assume that he returned to his beloved family and continued to farm grapes.

We flew on to Sacramento where Major Tahoma was based, Gessler, and Shelman also disembarked there. Gessler approached me on the tarmac. Shelman stopped a little way off.

'Is this where it ends for you David?'

'I would hope so major, but does this sort of thing ever really end?'

'I think this is only the beginning.' He held out his hand. 'Good luck David Kent.' I shook it, it was firm and dry. I believe someone once said it was a sign of honesty. He turned away and walked off without looking back. Shelman stood looking at me for a moment, and then he gave me a casual salute before turning to follow the man I'm sure he would have stopped a bullet for.

There were footsteps behind me and Harris and Reynard joined me to watch the retreating pair get into a large black limousine with dark windows. It sped towards the airport exit.

'I think it's time we headed for home, don't you David?' said Reynard.

'I think I need food and some booze first Bill.'

'Too bloody right,' said Harris. But first I need to find a shower; I need to leave the dirt where I found it.'

Reynard and I could find no argument with that.

'I wonder where Ganymede has got to.' I realised I hadn't seen him since we had disembarked.

'I don't think we'll ever know for sure what he gets up to, or where he is at any given time,' said Harris.

As we left the terminal by taxi he pointed across the airfield to where a silver jetliner stood. Even at that distance the kangaroo on the tail plane was unmistakable. 'There y'go, our carriage awaits,' he said.

**

Even having taken Ganymede's previous advice and slept for much of the flight, it had been a long haul and it was a full 24 hours before I recovered sufficiently to appreciate being back at home with Genna.

I lingered over breakfast; it seemed ages since I was last able to relax. Genna dropped the Advertiser and the Melbourne Age onto the empty chair beside me and went to sort out the toast. I glanced down at the Advertiser, it was dated 18th November; I had only been away three weeks, it felt like three months.

I finished my breakfast before clearing a space and picking up the Age. Over the years it had displayed a guarded interest in UFO sightings since the mid 60's when a class of pupils at Westall High School in Melbourne saw what is recorded historically, and no doubt hysterically, as Australia's Roswell. It was some minutes before I found what I was looking for; a column set aside in the world events section. I skipped over the inevitable media inquest on the John Lennon shooting, and even the actor Ronald Reagan's preparations for a race for the White House paled into insignificance as I read the report of unusual earth tremors in north-eastern California. Measuring less than 3 on the Richter scale, the epicentre, in an area of the Warner Range with no past history of earthquakes, is a range of mountains formed by ancient lava flows. A spokesman for the Australian Earthquake Engineering Society is quoted as saying that it could have been caused by the collapse of old mine workings. The area had been extensively mined for gold in the 1850's. I stared at the report for some minutes. Perhaps for the moment it was best that some odd happenings could appear to be explained in a logical way; who would believe an alternative?

I received a phone call later in the day. I recognised Ganymede's voice; he was brief.

'Picnic a great success, but would advise you stick to the family barbeque in future.' That was it; I was left with the dialling tone. I replaced the receiver.

Genna came and stood behind me, she rested her hands lightly on my shoulders.'

'Was that Bill Reynard?'

'No, Bill is going back into obscurity that was Ganymede; I think that was a goodbye.'

About the Author

Born in Southampton in 1930 He has enjoyed a varied working life. From being a 14 year old welder's mate in the last few months of WW2, he went on to become an Able seaman in the Merchant Navy. From there he foolishly committed himself to two years National Service. Demobbed in 1952 he felt the need to take life seriously so there followed marriage and the raising of a family. Married and divorced twice he now lives with his partner in Brighton. Only in retirement from the workforce did he realise his lifelong ambition to write.